D0887771

TROUBLESOME BLUE

F
Arrowood

1-7-20

15.95

TROUBLESOME BLUE

Mary Cotton Public Library
915 Virginia St
Sabetha, KS 66534
785.284.3160

By
Larry Arrowood

Woodsong Publishing
Seymour, Indiana

Troublesome Blue

Copyright © 2013 by Larry M. Arrowood

All rights reserved. No part of this book may be used or reproduced by any means, graphic, electronic, or mechanical, including photocopying, recording, taping or by any information storage retrieval system without the written permission of the publisher except in the case of brief quotations embodied in critical articles and reviews.

This is a work of fiction. All of the characters, names, incidents, organizations, and dialogue in this novel are either the products of the author's imagination or are used fictitiously.

Woodsong books may be ordered through the publisher, Woodsong Publishing at: www.woodsongpublishing.com.
Woodsong books may also be ordered through various retailers.

ISBN: 978-0-9892291-1-1

Woodsong Publishing
Seymour, IN 47274

Cover design by Move My Church Media
www.movemychurch.com

Printed in the United States of America

Dedicated to my Grandchildren

Aaron Matthew
Zion Monroe Allen
Lucia Rosé
Audrey Michele
Mimi Love

CHAPTER ONE

~

Her daddy was to blame. She wouldn't be on this train, taking this journey, unaware of what lay ahead, if it hadn't been for him. She'd still be home in Cincinnati, enrolled in graduate school, enjoying her friends. But here she was, on this train, traveling away from all she'd ever known. Alone.

She loved it.

A book lay on the seat beside her: *The Little Shepherd From Kingdom Come.* She picked it up, opened the cover and ran her fingers across the calligraphy inscription:

> To my darling daughter,
> "May you play the game of life warily, for your opponent is full of subtlety, and take thought over your every move, for your soul is at stake."
> Your loving father,
> Charles Ray York
> August 1956

The book was one of her many going away gifts. She recognized the paraphrased quote from Murray's, *A History of Chess*. Saturday evenings she and daddy sat in the parlor entangled in their board war as her mother enjoyed crocheting doilies.

"I'll never understand how you two can enjoy that game. It seems so boring." Mother's words echoed in her mind above the rumble of the passenger train. Nancy smiled.

At her daddy's insistence, she'd read Murray's book, a translation from an ancient manuscript on chess. She read the book for two reasons: to please daddy and to try and figure out a strategy to beat him. She'd never accomplished the latter.

Her daddy tutored her about every aspect of winning in life: chess, checkers, rook and tennis. He encouraged her to be competitive, to play to win or not play at all. The first time she ever beat him in tennis he congratulated her. "That-a-girl. Now, never let me win again." He never did.

Through the window of the train houses, cars and people flashed by. Occasionally someone waved. It was like watching a silent film. An hour into the trip darkness settled over the land. The lights in the passenger car flicked on. Nancy closed her eyes.

She had boarded the evening train at the Union Station in Cincinnati. The worst part of the trip was saying good-bye to her parents. Her mother had incessantly wiped tears as her daddy rattled off last minute reminders.

"You'll change trains in Lexington. Don't forget to pick up your luggage for the second leg of the journey. Call us as soon as you arrive." Her daddy was naturally concerned, but she could tell he was very proud of her.

Her mother was more apprehensive. "Do you have your tickets, dear? Charles, check her tickets and make sure they're all there, especially the return ticket for Christmas." Her mother's weepy voice made her cry.

Her daddy balanced the departure with more matter-of-fact conversation. "I'll wire the grant money when it arrives, sweetheart."

"Care for coffee, miss?" The attendant startled her.

"No, but thank you."

She stared out the window into the blackness.

Her daddy was the master of gentle persuasion. He wanted her to achieve. He pushed her to excel. He coached her to be a winner.

But why?

Maybe Daddy pushed me because he didn't have a son? No, he's proud of my femininity, always complimenting my girlish activities. Did he challenge me because he's worried for my future? Mother seems so dependent. Or because he believes in me?

A porter approached through the doorway of the parlor car.

"Need anything, ma'am?"

"No, thank you."

He continued to the next car, leaving her to her thoughts. She laid the book aside and tilted her head against the headrest. Her body swayed gently to the rhythm of the train.

"Next stop, Copeland." The attendant had returned.

She glanced at her watch: six o'clock. I must have fallen asleep. She yawned and stretched her arms skyward. Through the window, dawn illuminated the multi-colored trees blanketing a towering hillside. The scene had changed drastically from the green pasturelands of Lexington. The train snaked through a narrow passageway of trees that flanked the tracks on either side, their limbs ablaze with a canopy of yellow, orange and brown. A worn, narrow path ran alongside the tracks.

Nancy pressed her face against the window, trying to see what lay ahead. The engine disappeared into a sharp curve. She jumped at the sudden blasts of the whistle. The train abruptly braked, shifting her in the seat. She grabbed the armrest, and her book tumbled onto the floor. Her heartbeat accelerated.

Steam hissed as the train slowed.

Nancy retrieved the book and studied the inscription on the inside of the opened cover. Just who might my opponent be? She tried to imagine the faces of those who awaited her, but she could only envision those she'd left behind. "I haven't an enemy in the world, Daddy."

CHAPTER TWO

~

Wesley Taggart had lived a long and hard life, all before his thirtieth birthday. Sitting astride his stallion, he scanned the expansive valley. Wistful thoughts ate at his mind like termites in soft wood. The splendor of the Kentucky Plateau stretching before him should have evoked inspiration, but it didn't. He no longer visited this site in the highlands to be inspired, for to him, it was the loneliest spot on earth. Lately, he wasn't sure why he came.

He stared at the headstone marking the grave onto which weeds encroached. The site amplified a dull emptiness in his heart. A plastic wreath hid the part of the inscription showing the date of death, but Wesley didn't need to read the date, for November 11, 1954, was forever etched in his memory.

"Two years seems like an eternity, Nancy. Lots of things have happened since you left. The children are doing okay, just like I promised you."

The black's ears perked, and he shook his head violently, rustling the bridle. Wesley patted the horse's shoulder. "Easy, boy."

He pulled a piece of paper from his hip pocket and slowly unfolded it, studying its contents.

"It seems Hiram Callahan is being considered for early parole, dear. That doesn't seem quite fair. I'm struggling with that. I wasn't naturally blessed with your forgiving nature."

The black whinnied.

"Just talking to myself, boy."

He wadded the paper and clinched it in his hand.

"Still, I feel sorry for the Callahan children. Since Hiram's incarceration, they've been passed from pillar to post. Every child

4

deserves a daddy. Every child deserves a mother, too. Hiram was to blame for your children being motherless. Maybe Hiram even contributed to the early death of his own wife. None of this makes any sense."

Wesley gazed skyward and breathed deep and long, then exhaled quickly. The movement spooked the stallion.

"Sorry, boy."

He unclenched his fist and allowed the crumpled paper to fall from his hand. He'd been offered the opportunity to speak against the parole. He wanted to tell his side of the story and express why Callahan should remain in prison; still, he wanted to put the whole ordeal behind him. He chose silence, but a silent voice didn't translate into a quiet soul.

Did I do the right thing? What will Callahan's release do to my family, especially little Gary? How long do I blame Callahan? How much blame do I deserve? Was he to blame for choosing this habitat? Are the struggles and sorrows I've faced the past two years providential, or have I taken a wrong turn somewhere?

Wesley shifted in his saddle and pulled his collar around his neck. He suddenly felt cool in the morning air.

Fall brought pleasant weather to the Cumberland Plateau, but Wesley hardly noticed the multi-colored array of leaves high on the mountains. He focused his activities more on preparing for the approaching winter and the hardships it brought to this formidable land. He hoped busyness would help him deal with the past. Meaningful friends told him life would get better. It hadn't. He fought back against a depression that invaded his soul, especially during the lonely evenings. A hard day's work helped, and hard work was a natural for him. He was proud of his financial accomplishments, having built his family a beautiful home along the Kentucky North Fork. In fact, his was the most beautiful home within a twenty-mile radius, but that paled in light of this scene before him. His house seemed but an empty shell since Nancy's passing.

Two buzzards waltzed on the winds of first light, celebrating another dawn. Despite Wesley's inner turmoil, a calm lingered in the morning mist that rose from the river. It was a calm he'd relished in years past. Such calm had drawn him back to these forlorn mountains while other families had left their Kentucky home places, making their exit to distant cities up north, like Detroit and Flint, to find work. He felt fortunate to have his own business in this place, when most of the men who remained here had to commute long distances to find work, often staying for weeks at a time before returning home. Would the past calm he so much appreciated about his life in the plateau ever return to his soul?

The lone whistle of the passenger train broke the silence. A covey of quail spooked the black. Wesley reined him in the direction of the train. Black smoke billowed from the engine and formed a myriad of images as the locomotive chugged along the L&N tracks that hugged the union of the ever-winding mountainside and the North Fork of the Kentucky River.

"Giddyup, boy." Wesley nudged the horse's sides with his heels and the black lunged. He held the reigns loosely as the stallion galloped freely down the hillside, clearing the railroad crosswalk a safe distance in front of the train. Wesley tightened the reigns, and the black slowed. He let him canter in the direction of the approaching train.

The stallion lurched as blasts from the whistle spooked him. Wesley gripped the reins as the Tennessee Walker pranced nervously on the cinder trail running alongside the tracks. The Janney couplings clanked multiple times as the train decelerated for the Copeland Station.

"Whoa, fella." Wesley pulled slightly on the reigns, and the horse stopped. He waved at the engineer with one hand and patted the neck of the apprehensive black with the other. The engineer waved back, a friendly wave.

Through the passenger window Wesley glimpsed the lone face of a young woman peering out. Something about her arrested his thoughts. Who was she? Where was she traveling?

The train passed and Wesley again loosed the reigns. The black settled into a cantered gait. Wesley tried to turn his attention to the workday ahead. His mind kept wandering back to the face of the young woman on the train.

CHAPTER THREE

~

Piercing screams penetrated the rough-hewn dovetail logs of his small cabin, shattering the tranquility of the morning twilight. Thomas Fugate spun on his heels and frantically raced the worn path from the gate of his unpainted picket fence to the front steps of his ramshackle home. He wanted to be inside, but Granny Combs forbade it. At the steps he hesitated, then turned and started back to the gate again. He pressed his hands against his ears, trying to drown out the pitiful screams of his wife, to no avail.

For better or worse, that was how it began. Thomas Fugate ached for better. Hope dimmed with each passing year; unrealized goals faded with time, as elusive as the morning mist of Troublesome Creek.

Emma Lee had awakened him around midnight with strong birthing pains. He had loaded the children into the wagon and rushed them to a neighbor's house. Then he fetched Granny Combs. It was too far and too costly for the services of Doc Lewis, but the midwifery of Granny Combs had done all right for his two other children. She was of no kin to anyone in the community, but everybody still called her Granny. After demands for him to stoke the kitchen stove and fill some pans with water, she'd taken over the house. He took up residence in the front yard, anxiously pacing back and forth from the porch to the fence, twenty and one half steps each way.

The daily toils of marriage had quickly erased the beauty of his teenage bride, and it hurt him deeply to see the pained expression that crept onto her countenance. He was desperate to make life better for her. Life seemed bent on opposing him.

He paused at the gate, glancing skyward. The eastern horizon blazed blood red, momentarily chasing away the darkness of his gloomy emotions. A sinister thought quickly prevented such repose. Is the blood red sky a warning? Is Emma okay?

A screech from a bobcat high on the mountainside mimicked the screams from within the cabin. Thomas froze mid-stride and listened. Has the cat tripped a trap? No. That wasn't a wail of pain. It was more a cry of territory dominance. The cry from the mountainside subsided. Thomas resumed his pacing.

At the gate he stopped and listened. Silence. Then a baby wailed. His pulse quickened.

How much longer do I have to wait? I've got to know.

Emma had grown anxious the past month, uncharacteristically wanting him by her side. He'd missed work all week long. He needed to get back to work, for they desperately needed the money. He had failed to get word to his boss, but he hoped he'd understand. Mr. Taggart had always been a reasonable man, and he surely knows what it's like waiting on a young'un to come.

The cabin door opened, and Granny Combs stepped onto the porch, wiping her brow with the back of her hand. She tossed a bloodied apron across the banister and slowly descended the steps. He waited, anxiety choking his breath.

She didn't speak.

"Well?" he barked.

"It's a strong girl."

"Not that. You know what I mean."

She lowered her head but didn't answer.

"This ain't fair," he yelled skyward and shook his fists into the air. "God, this ain't fair!"

He turned abruptly and ran disconcertedly down the path that paralleled Troublesome Creek.

CHAPTER FOUR

~

Warden Delmar Simmons rattled the door to Hiram Callahan's prison cell with his nightstick. Two guards flanked the warden. Hiram lay in the lower bunk, shirtless. He didn't bother to respond.

"Rise and shine, Calli."

"You like messin' with me, don't you, warden?"

"That'll be Warden Simmons to you, Callahan," one of the guards yelled.

"Mail call, Calli," the warden said.

"Go away, warden. I ain't done nothin' wrong. I got nothin' to say to you, and I certainly ain't expectin' no mail."

"You want me to go away and take these parole papers with me?"

Hiram Callahan lurched upright in bed. His head grazed the top bunk as he tossed his blanket onto the concrete floor. He swung his feet onto the cold concrete.

"What's that?"

"You heard me."

Hiram pulled on a pair of socks and slowly stood, tugging on his belt-less khaki trousers that were too short to hide the dingy white socks.

"Surprised, Calli? Well, so am I. Kentucky State Parole Board grantin' you an early release. You're leaving our cozy Castle on the Cumberland as soon as the court processes the papers. I guess they need you to play mommy to those kids of yours. State's probably tired of feedin' them. I'm tired of feedin' you, too, Calli."

Hiram lunged forward, grasping the bars with his huge, calloused hands. The warden jumped backwards, assuming a defensive stance with his stick. The guards stepped in front of the warden, calling out threats. Hiram laughed. At six-six and two hundred sixty pounds he was well aware of his imposing figure. He grinned at the warden as he scratched his scraggly beard.

"You're a mite jumpy, ain't you, warden." Hiram looked down into the warden's face. "You best not be foolin' with me."

Standing a safe distance from the bars, the warden extended an envelope to Callahan, who snatched it from his hand and stuck it in his hip pocket without bothering to open it.

"When do I get outta here?" He wouldn't admit to the warden he couldn't read.

"Soon, I hope. Be glad to clean out the stench of this cell. I swear you hillbillies are the filthiest people I've ever met."

Callahan clutched the bars with both hands but didn't answer.

"Be seeing you, Calli."

The warden continued down the hallway, tapping cell doors with his nightstick as he passed. Callahan continued to clutch the bars until the warden and his minions were out of sight.

The castle-like building overlooking the Cumberland River had been Callahan's home for over a year. It was Kentucky's only maximum-security prison. He enjoyed his three meals a day and stayed out of trouble while working in the garment plant. It was his second tour of service, for which the warden had no tolerance. He hated the warden, and the warden reciprocated at every opportunity. "Woman killer" was the warden's favorite accusation. If the warden could have his way Hiram knew he'd be housed in what they called the Six Cell House, awaiting the chair. The warden had told him that personally. Instead, he was being released early. Surely the warden wouldn't stoop to such a mean tease as this. Is this a setup with a gang waiting on the outside? He didn't put it past the warden having a scheme up his sleeve.

Callahan wiped perspiration from his brow with the back of his hand and dried his hand on his pant leg. His pacing began. Other prisoners stirred, swearing at the warden for the early wakeup. Breakfast wasn't for another hour, and though Hiram's stomach growled, food was not on his mind today. He opened the envelope and stared at the words.

"You all right, Callie?" The inmate in the next cell pressed his face to the front bars.

"Yea, Jonas. You read?"

"Some."

"Mind taking a look at this?" He handed the letter through the bars and waited as Jonas studied it.

"The warden ain't funnin', Callahan. It says you're gettin' out."

Hiram retrieved the letter. He held it to his heart. A grin broke out. "Early parole, boys. Now what about that?" Callahan yelled to no one in particular.

A cheer arose from the cellblock.

Callahan stepped to the back of his cell and stared at a torn photo taped to the wall. He leaned forward and pressed his brow against the picture. "I miss you, babies. Who's been caring for you? I'm so sorry, but your daddy'll be home shortly." He paused. "I bet Wesley Taggart won't be expectin' me so soon."

CHAPTER FIVE

~

Gary Taggart anticipated entering the second grade. He passed first grade without speaking a single word. Mr. Deaton had coaxed him to speak, but seemed to understand his silence. He had even complimented Gary's ability to write his thoughts on paper. He'd passed the lazy days of summer watching the older boys play marbles in front of the general store, owned and operated by Mr. Deaton's wife. The older boys' teasing embarrassed him, but try as he might, he couldn't speak his thoughts. He knew what he wanted to say, but the words wouldn't come out, so it was easier watching than participating. Occasionally he ventured into the woods and once muscled the courage to explore the mountain up near Coffin Rock, but he didn't go all the way to the rock: caution outweighed curiosity. This morning he passed the time sharpening his pencils and sorting his crayons by color.

His inability to speak was also a crutch. He used it sometimes to avoid getting into trouble. Since he couldn't talk, adults such as Nanny Sue and his daddy didn't ask him a lot of questions. So they didn't know about some of his adventures, especially into the surrounding hills.

Daddy had told him a new teacher was coming to take Mr. Deaton's place. He was glad Mr. Deaton quit teaching, for his switch scared him half to death. Mr. Deaton used it mostly on the older boys, and mostly for fighting, but sometimes for sassing. Daddy also told him the new teacher was a young woman and not an old maid. Maybe she wouldn't be mean like Mr. Deaton.

Gary was excited about the news of the new teacher, but he was troubled by the latest news he overheard his daddy and Nanny

Sue talking about just last night. He'd slipped out onto the front porch where the air was cooler, and as he sat on the front steps, counting lightning bugs, he couldn't help but overhear them. The parlor window to the porch was open, and though they spoke in hushed tones, the still night amplified their voices. They were talking about Hiram Callahan maybe being paroled any day. Gary wasn't sure about the word, but he thought he knew what it meant.

Gary doodled on a notepad with a black crayon. An image of a man slowly emerged. He suddenly scratched a bold "x" across the page and frantically colored over the drawing. He turned the page over and picked through his crayon box until he found the colors he looked for. He drew a smiley sun, surrounded by sky that blended into a green mountain. Halfway up the mountain he drew a building. On the front door, with a red crayon, he scribbled a word: school.

The distant whistle of the morning passenger train interrupted his work. He tossed the pad aside and leaped to his feet. Descending the porch two steps at a time, he sprinted toward the tracks that ran in front of his house. From that vantage point he observed the passenger train as it rumbled into the depot a quarter mile away.

Maybe the new teacher will be on the train. He smiled. His smile suddenly faded when he realized Hiram Callahan could also be on the train.

CHAPTER SIX

~

"Watch your step, ma'am," a smiling porter held out his hand and offered assistance as she descended the three metal steps of the passenger car.

"Thank you, sir."

"My pleasure, miss. You have a lovely day now."

Nancy shielded her eyes with her hand as she stepped into the morning sunlight. She quickly retrieved sunglasses from her purse. The world around her immediately turned to amber. She scanned her surroundings. A single, dilapidated building functioned as a general store, post office and train station. Only three people were in sight: an adult sitting on the porch of the building and two boys playing some kind of game. Was it marbles? She read it was a popular sport among hill folks. There were no roads and no cars. She glanced back at the porter.

"Are you sure this is Copeland, Kentucky?"

"Yes, ma'am. You okay, miss?"

"Oh, I'm fine. Thanks."

The porter patted her on the shoulder. "We come through here every day, morning and evening. You decide to leave, you can get a ticket right over there in the general store."

A sharp whistle blast from the train startled her.

"Gotta go, miss. Be seeing you 'round. God go with you." He trotted toward the rear of the train where a worker tossed mailbags unto the ground.

Having purposefully pulled her dark brown hair into a loose knot for the trip, she ran her fingers through the disheveled strands. I must be a mess. Mother would be fussing if she could see me.

14

"You left this, miss," an attendant called out to her as he rushed toward her with a Mabley and Carew hatbox she'd forgotten in the overhead bin.

"Oh, my. Thank you, sir. I'm a bit scatter-brained."

The attendant handed her the box and quickly boarded the train.

"How I'll miss shopping at the Mabley and Carew Department Store." She stepped lightly away from the train and glanced again at the single building where the lone figure sitting on the front porch had not moved.

The porter walked in her direction as the wheels of the train first slipped and then griped the steel tracks. He ascended two steps and clung to the handrail as the train lurched forward. She stared after him. He waved to her and gave her a thumbs up.

She smiled and mouthed a "Thank you."

The two lads stared at her. She brushed her hand across the wrinkles of her light blue suit and smiled, remembering the special day shopping with her mother and daddy for this new adventure. They'd found the suit at the department store in downtown Cincinnati. The Mabley and Carew Department Store was founded by two businessmen, Mabley and Carew, who, the story went, while stranded in Cincinnati in the late 1800s, took advantage of their misfortune. They walked around the downtown area, and seeing a "For Rent" sign, decided to make an investment. Their venture proved successful, and eventually the clothing store moved into the newest and tallest building in Cincinnati, Carew Tower, likewise named after one of the late owners. She and her parents had ended the shopping trip by taking the elevator to the forty-ninth floor of the Carew Tower, where they strolled around the observation deck, looking at the sprawling river towns on the Kentucky side of the Ohio. The Linking River emptied into the Ohio and separated Newport and Covington, which were connected by two bridges and both cities had connecting bridges to Cincinnati. In the distance they could see Indiana. What a contrast to the single, drab building standing before her now, sitting along a small river partially obscured by trees and overgrowth.

In her wildest dreams, she couldn't have imagined such a place as this existed. She was here now. Surely she could make a difference.

"I'm up to the task. How sweet of Daddy to pay for my outfit."

She'd tried on fifteen pair of shoes before she decided on the white patent-leather ones she now wore, with a matching purse dangling over her shoulder.

"Daddy was right," she mumbled, as she walked toward her set of luggage setting beside the tracks. "I brought too much stuff."

She stood by the luggage, gazing after the train as it pulled away and until it became a distant sound. She again scanned the surroundings. The two boys stuffed marbles in their pockets as they walked slowly toward her. Perhaps she could introduce them to a more refined game, chess.

"Hello." She offered her warmest smile.

"Howdy, ma'am. Needin' some help?" the taller of the boys responded, without reciprocating her smile.

"Yes sir, Mr. ..."

"Emanuel Ray Allen, ma'am. Friends call me Manuel. This here's my little brother, George Daniel Allen. Goes by George. Can we help some?"

"Yes, thank you." She glanced at her luggage. My name's Nancy York. I'm the new schoolteacher."

"We've been 'spectin' you, Miss York." Manuel looked at her luggage as if appraising its contents.

She couldn't sense if they were glad to see her, for they showed no facial expressions.

"I'm needing a temporary place to stay, until I find a more permanent residence, of course. Is there a hotel close by?"

Manuel's expression remained blank. "Ain't no such place round here at all, Miss York."

"You mean there's no place for a traveler to stay? Oh, dear." She brushed back a flowing strand of hair.

"Didn't they tell you who you'd be staying with, ma'am?"

Who I'd be staying with? Why didn't someone tell me there were no motel rooms? I can't believe I overlooked such a detail.

Manuel began arranging her luggage in an orderly fashion. She was impressed.

George kept his hands stuffed in the pockets of his faded overalls, half hidden behind Manuel. His burred hair stood straight out from his head.

Why doesn't he speak? She didn't want to stare, but his light blue eyes captured her attention as they reflected the color of her suit. He resembled a frightened porcupine cartoon character. Nancy smiled at him, wanting to ease his reluctance, but also remembering the cartoon. He scratched the calf of his lanky left leg with a dirty, bare foot. She noticed a red rash on his leg. Has he gotten into a patch of poison ivy? Does he even own a pair of shoes? She glanced at her shiny patent-leather shoes and suddenly felt nauseous.

"You best talk to Ida Mae Deaton. She's the woman in that store over there." Manuel pointed toward the building. "She can probably help you if'n anybody can."

"Thank you, Manuel. George."

George still hadn't acknowledged her.

"Don't pay no mind to Sigel Diddle. He's just plumb crazy." Manuel nodded toward the man sitting on the porch. For the first time Manuel's face displayed some hint of emotion.

She glanced toward the front porch. "You'll watch my things for me?"

"Yep." Manuel continued to stack the luggage.

And I look forward to having both of you soon in class."

"We'll be there, teacher," Manuel said.

"How about you, George?" Nancy smiled at him. "Will you be coming to school?"

"Yea. First time."

She fought back the urge to rub his burred hair. "I'm glad. Nice to meet both of you." She walked slowly toward the building, reading a faded sign attached to the front: US Post Office, Copeland, Kentucky; L&N Train Depot; Deaton Store. Certainly a multipurpose building.

The wooden steps creaked as she ascended. A napping dog opened his eyes, stood up, moved a few inches and turned in circles before laying down again in her path. A tangled tail swatted at gnats that swarmed around him; a pungent odor and matted fur revealed he wasn't an indoor pet. She stepped around the dog, and in so doing, stepped too uncomfortably close to the raggedly dressed man

Manuel called Sigel Diddle. The wooden RC Cola crate on which he sat leaned precariously against the wall. He tossed her what seemed a contemptuous glance. She smiled at him. He didn't smile back.

Nancy opened the screen door and stepped inside but hesitated until her eyes adjusted to the dimly lit room. She removed her sunglasses. The snap of the screen door shutting startled her.

A single, unlit lightbulb hung from the center of the ceiling. A potbelly stove occupied the middle of the floor, the focal point for the small room. She reasoned the odd smell to be somewhere between linseed oil and pickle juice. She remembered the smell from an old-fashioned general store her grandparents had taken her to back in Cincinnati when she was a child. Or was it dead mice? She frowned. Perhaps she was partially right, as a large jar of pickles set on a countertop. Her nose had not deceived her. She walked gingerly across the hardwood floor coated with a grimy film, and more than likely it produced the linseed oil smell.

A heavy-set, elderly woman Nancy assumed to be Ida Mae Deaton stood behind the counter, her backside pressed against the shelves that lined the wall. She swayed from side to side against the shelves, as if to scratch an itching back.

"Mornin', miss. Ain't seen you 'round these parts before. What can I do for you?"

"Are you Mrs. Deaton?"

"That'd be me, alright."

"I was speaking with the two young boys outside…"

"That'd be Manuel and George, 'course George probably didn't say much."

"Yes, those two, and yes, George didn't say much." She paused. "I'm needing a place to stay, but it seems I might have a bit of trouble finding it." Nancy tried to muster a determined demeanor.

"Don't worry your purty little head none, child. We'll find a place for you before bedtime. Now, what did you say your name was, miss?"

"Oh, I'm sorry. My name is Nancy York. I'm here as the…"

"Oh, my!" Ida Mae interrupted her. "You're the new schoolteacher from down Cincinnati. Shore look awfully young to be tackling a one-room schoolhouse. First assignment?"

"Yes, but I think I'm up to the challenge."

"I'm sure, dear. How old are you?"

Nancy hesitated.

"Don't have to answer that, dear. Rude of me to ask."

"No, I don't mind. I'm almost twenty-three."

"Thought so as well. I was in Cincinnati this summer with my husband, Bill. He's the old schoolteacher. Retired last year. We went down there to buy some hardware for the store. Bill was afraid they wouldn't find a replacement for him soon enough for the fall. He's taught for nearly forty years. Glad you've come up here to take over the school."

Cincinnati is north of Copeland, so Nancy traveled south to get there. Shouldn't here be considered down instead of up?

"I actually came down from Cincinnati by way of Lexington."

"Right. But us hill-folk's concept of geography has its own interpretation. Elevation, not direction, matters mostly to us. Everything is up if you're coming here, down if you're leaving here. So we say we're going down to Cincinnati or down to Lexington."

"I see." Though she'd tried to offer a subtle lesson in geography, she suddenly felt like a student again as Ida Mae rattled on about this part of the country.

"From up here you look down to the rest of the world around you. This is the Appalachians — the Cumberland Plateau of eastern Kentucky. You're up here in the hill country, dear. Close to the stars and the sky, where the air smells of honeysuckle and pine, still unpolluted by factory emissions like y'all have in the valley around Cincinnati and down around Louisville."

How poetic! Nancy hesitated. "I'm looking forward to the fresh air and open land." She tried to hide a yawn with the back of her hand.

"You look tired, child."

"I am."

Ida Mae retrieved a wooden chair from the corner of the room and slid it behind Nancy. "Here, sit down and I'll get you something to drink."

"Thank you."

Ida Mae wobbled to a red metal cooler against the wall. Its letters were faded, but a white crown revealed its contents. She retrieved a bottle of RC Cola and wiped it with the bottom of her dress. She popped the lid with an opener attached to the side of the cooler and handed the bottle to Nancy.

"Thank you, again. How kind!"

"Think nothing of it, dear. Don't drink it too fast, though, for I'm gonna fix you something to eat to go with your drink. You like pickled bologna?"

"I don't know. Never had it."

"Let me fix you a sandwich, and you can try it, but you don't have to eat it if'n you don't like it."

"Thank you. I don't mean to be such a nuisance, Mrs. Deaton."

"Ida Mae, dear. Folks 'round here call me Ida Mae. Of course, they call my husband Mr. Deaton out of respect for him as a teacher. He's taught most everybody in these parts still under fifty. Mind if I call you by your first name."

"Not at all. That sounds rather comforting."

Nancy wiped the top of the bottle and took a sip. The fizz felt good on her throat. "Are those your relatives?" She pointed to a framed picture hanging on the wall in back of the counter.

"My folks. Couldn't have been more than your age when that picture was taken. Born and raised not too many miles from here."

Nancy stared at the photograph.

"You okay, dear?"

"Sorry. I was daydreaming. I can't believe it, but I'm already missing my parents. Is that vinegar I smell?" Nancy changed the subject.

"Yes. Preserves the meat." Ida Mae knifed a roll of the pickled bologna and pulled it from the large-mouthed jar. Her large callused hands welded the knife like a seasoned butcher as she sliced through the meat with a single stroke.

Nancy studied Ida Mae's every movement. Daddy is the strong personality in our family. I like that about him. He's tried to pass that along to me. I'm already missing his reassuring mannerisms. Daddy would have washed his hands before serving up a sandwich. She winced at the thought and was glad Ida Mae didn't notice.

Though the trip from Cincinnati was less than two hundred miles, she felt a thousand miles from home. The adrenaline rush had vanished; apprehension settled in.

Calm yourself. Everything will work out.

"Is there a telephone I can use? I just remembered I promised to call home as soon as I arrived."

Ida Mae laughed as she handed Nancy the sandwich. "No, child. We don't have such modern conveniences, not yet anyways. I'm the postmistress and I'll get your letters anywhere you want to send'em."

Nancy bit into the sandwich and chewed slowly.

"What do you think?"

"Good. Very good."

"Glad you like it. What made you decide on Copeland, Miss Nancy?"

"I'm interested in studying the culture of the Appalachian people."

"Really?" Ida Mae turned away, waddled across the room and squeezed back behind the counter. "I thought you were here to teach our children how to read and write and do math."

How curt of me. Are these people more sensitive to what outsiders think of them than I realized?

"I'm sorry. That was a poor choice of words. Teaching is my first love and my primary reason for being here. While here teaching your children, I want to take the opportunity to learn all I can about the culture of the Appalachian community: the traditions, the songs, as much of the folklore as time will permit."

"That makes sense." Ida Mae shook her head in affirmation.

"Right now I desperately need to find a place to stay."

Ida Mae waddled back across the room, placed her hands firmly on Nancy's shoulders and looked down, directly into her dark brown eyes. Nancy, though usually at ease with her five feet five inch height, felt rather petite standing so close to Ida Mae. Ida's consoling smile put her at ease.

"We'll find a place, miss. Don't you worry none. Hear?" Ida paused. "I know just the place. Family up the road could use a young gal like you to help out a little with the children. The daddy works long hours. The lady of the house is a little on the cranky side, so

21

you'll be a pleasant addition to the family. They've taken in boarders before. It's a big house with extra rooms, 'bout a quarter mile up the tracks, first house on the right. Just tell Nanny Sue I sent you."

"How many children, Mrs. Deaton?"

"Couple or so. You'll like'em."

CHAPTER SEVEN

Nancy stepped outside the store and paused on the porch to put on her sunglasses. She glanced at Sigel and realized he was looking at her, but he quickly closed his eyes. What is that unpleasant odor? The dog had left. Oh, dear! It's the man. She covertly covered her nose with the back of her hand as she stepped hurriedly past him and down the rickety steps toward her luggage.

Manuel stood beside her luggage like a bellboy. He seemed pleased with himself for such thoughtfulness. George was sitting on the track, tossing rocks into the weeds.

"Thank you, Manuel."

"You're welcome, Teacher. Where we goin'?"

"That way," she pointed. "First house on the right. How am I going to manage all this luggage?"

"We'll do it, Teacher. George, I need some help with the teacher's things." George quickly tossed a rock at some unidentified target in the weeds and scurried toward them.

"Do you know the people where I'll be staying?"

"That'll be our relatives from on their momma's side," Manuel answered.

"Oh, really?"

"All five of them. 'Course that don't include the adults."

Nancy mumbled under her breath, "A couple or so?"

"What's that, Teacher?"

She didn't answer.

Manuel added with pride, "The daddy, Wesley, he's a fine fella. Fought the Nazi's in the war. Shot him a couple I heard. Got wounded himself. Brought home some medals for courage."

Manuel led the way, walking in the middle of the railroad tracks, while George walked the rail, balancing his skinny frame with ease. Manuel rattled on, but Nancy wasn't listening. She spent the quarter-mile trip reflecting on her immediate situation. She'd envisioned this assignment quite differently: a self-contained private room with plenty of time to write and enjoy nature as she taught school by day and interviewed the hill people in the evenings. All paid for by a government grant. Instead, she was on her way to live with a family of five children in a community where the only communication back home would be by postal service, and that seemed slow at best. Her feet were killing her. She suddenly realized she had to get different shoes for walking on the railroad tracks.

As they approached the Taggart residence, a dog dashed toward them. Nancy hesitated.

"How you doing, Giggs?" Manuel called out to him.

Giggs' wagging tail consoled Nancy, and she was especially relieved when he leaped into the outstretched arms of George, who rubbed the dog's fur furiously.

The eastern windows of the white weatherboard house reflected the morning sun.

Nancy stopped and stared at the house.

"Big, ain't it, Teacher," Manuel said.

The size of the house surprised Nancy. Though it was average compared to the houses in Cincinnati, it was much larger than anything she'd seen since entering the hill country. The wraparound porch gave a charming effect.

"What's the last name of the family who lives here?" Nancy asked.

"Taggart."

The hinges squeaked as Manuel opened the front gate and led the way as if he lived there. A concrete sidewalk led from the gate to a wide set of steps to the front porch: dried blades of grass jutted from cracks in the concrete. The expansive yard, surrounded entirely by a white picket fence, though a step down from her Hyde Park lawn back in Cincinnati, was reasonably cared for. A colorful patchwork quilt hung across a clothesline in the side yard, airing in the morning sun, accompanied by a dozen diapers.

What a beautiful quilt! Nancy's grandma made her own quilts and used to hang them outside to air. Is that the Star of David? The quilt pattern looks similar to Grandma's. I don't like the looks of all those diapers.

Four curious faces lined the front porch, like stair steps in height. The inquiring blue eyes of the two shortest peeked between the white wooden bannisters of the wraparound porch. The tallest and oldest, a girl, her chin resting on the railing, peered from underneath bangs cut straight across the forehead. Next to her a young lad stood on the bottom of the railing and clung to the top, making his stature equal to the older girl's. A gaunt woman rocked a baby in a cane-bottomed rocker. She brushed back a graying lock of hair that had escaped the bun on the back of her head. The woman hesitantly stood as they approached.

"Howdy." Manuel sat the suitcases on the bottom step.

"Howdy, Manual. George." Her face remained stern.

"This is our new teacher and Ida Mae sent her to stay with you for awhile. Name's Miss York."

At the mention of Ida Mae, the woman's drawn face softened. "Howdy, Miss York."

"Hello, Mrs. Taggart. I hope I'm not imposing on you and your family."

The woman laughed. "Mrs. Taggart? My family? I'm way too old to be having young'ens of my own."

"I'm sorry. You are Nanny Sue?"

"Yes, ma'am."

"I thought Ida Mae meant you were the wife... "

"Just the housekeeper and a relative."

"Nice to meet you, Nanny Sue."

"The same, Miss York."

"Hello." Nancy acknowledged the children who stared intently but silently at her. She turned back to Nanny Sue. "Is Mrs. Taggart home?"

"No." Nanny Sue's response seemed awkward.

"Are you expecting her soon?"

"Mrs. Taggart passed on."

How assuming of me? How can anyone put their foot so far in their mouth? I've gone from bad to worse. For a moment Nancy didn't respond. She looked at the children. They stared blankly at her.

"I'm sorry. I feel like I'm intruding in..."

"No, Miss York. It's okay. I purty much run the house for Mr. Taggart. Ida Mae sent you here 'cause this is the only house big enough for an outsider to board. We take in travelers once in a while stranded when the tracks get snowed over or there's a breakdown. Doc Lewis sometimes stays when he's making house calls up here and misses the train back to Jackson. Mr. Taggart is certainly appreciative of having someone to teach his children at the school."

"I will need to speak to Mr. Taggart first. I assume he isn't home?"

"Right."

"When do you expect him?"

"Late tonight. He left early this morning. Train probably passed him a ways back. He was ridin' his stallion."

"I did see a man on a gallant black horse just north of the station."

The sight had caught her attention, the way he sat in the saddle, one hand holding the reins as he patted the neck of the jittery horse while the train passed.

"That was probably Wesley. That's Mr. Taggart's first name."

"I'll need to seek his approval of my boarding here."

"Mr. Taggart will approve. I can assure you of that."

Nancy wasn't sure how to interpret Nanny Sue's comment, and she certainly wasn't going to ask what she meant. She turned to Manuel, then back to Nanny Sue, then to the children. That's when she noticed the oldest boy smiling at her. She smiled back.

"How are you, young man?"

His smile vanished.

"What's your name?"

The lad didn't answer.

"His name's Gary Eugene, after his daddy's middle name," Manuel said. "He don't talk none since his mommy died. He'll be in your second grade class."

Nancy reflected momentarily on a college course on personalities. She thoroughly enjoyed that class. Gary seemed of the quiet nature, a blessing for a rowdy class. But Manuel? He'd certainly keep the class awake.

The child on Nanny Sue's knees whined. She repositioned the child onto her shoulder.

"Boy or girl?" Nancy asked.

"Boy."

"How old?"

"Goin' on two."

So young to lose a mother. The child will have no memory of his mother. Her death must certainly be affecting the children emotionally. If the man I saw earlier on the horse was Mr. Taggart, he must still be grieving.

The baby began to cry. "A mite fussy today," Nanny Sue said. "The twin boys are three. Gary's six and Joyce is seven."

"Be eight next month." She brushed back her bangs.

Nancy's mind raced. Why didn't I make prior arrangements? Even so, it probably wouldn't have made any difference, for the options in this community seem limited at best. Would I have accepted this assignment if I'd known these circumstances? Probably not, but here I am. I could turn around and go home. No. I must make the best of it. At least I now have a place to stay. Is it the right decision to board with the Taggarts? They seem like such a needy family.

CHAPTER EIGHT

~

W esley Taggart watched through a cracked and dirty office window as the workers scooped salt from stockpiles on the ground and loaded it onto a sled. Once full, the teamster cracked a whip over the ears of the pair of mules who pulled hard against the doubletree harness. The sled lunged forward as the mules' hoofs dug into the silt that littered the landscape. The mules knew the routine: the downhill trip to the tipple, where the salt was loaded onto a train car, and then the trip back, where they were watered and fed while workers reloaded the sled: six round trips in an average twelve-hour day.

Wesley tallied the loads. He shook his head. "The mine is slowing." The veins of salt were narrowing and they had to separate more waste than usual. He had already cut back on two employees, but the smaller margin of profit still concerned him. Though he felt guilty for the layoff, he had no other options. Thomas Fugate's failure to show for work the past week made him the next candidate. He could also sell one team of mules to cut overhead. He hated to cut another worker, for each had a family that desperately depended on the income from this employment. Perhaps he should pursue his venture at Troublesome Creek. He rubbed his furrowed brow.

Wesley closed the ledger. He stared out the window. Whose was the beautiful face peering out the train window this morning? He knew most faces in these parts, but he'd never seen her before. Why did she remind me of Nancy? Is she the new teacher? He knew the new teacher was a woman, but he had no details. Probably someone just passing through Copeland on her way to Hazard.

Another team of mules approached, pulling hard on the uphill grade. He checked his pocket watch, stepped from the office into the evening shadows and called out to the workers. "Last load for the day, men. Let's get it done and go home."

They nodded their heads in approval.

Wesley yawned. The long hours left him tired, but they were necessary for productivity. Modern means of salt mining had forced his profits down as prices dropped. He needed more up-to-date equipment. His workers were compensating somewhat by working longer hours for the same pay, but he was still concerned. He hoped the salt vein didn't peter out before his lease ended.

He'd get home late again, but the weekend would give him some reprieve from this hectic schedule. He could spend some extra time with his children. The long hours were a diversion. Still, though he loved and lived for his family, each day remained a struggle. He knew he had to somehow get beyond the meaningless existence he felt. But how?

CHAPTER NINE

~

Dawn peeked through the sheer curtains and teased Nancy awake. She lingered in bed, enjoying the comfort of the downy quilt and needing time to chase away the grogginess dulling her mind. Rising slowly, she sat on the bedside, reflecting the events of the previous day, apprehensive that Mr. Taggart hadn't arrived before she retired to bed. She wanted to make sure the boarding arrangements received his approval before she unpacked her things. The distant whistle of an approaching train motivated her to get dressed. She peered through the window and noticed young Gary on the front lawn.

Examining her face in the dresser mirror, she dabbed her swollen eyelids with a damp washcloth, brushed the loose black locks from off her forehead and pulled the hair into a simple knot, allowing it to flow across her shoulders on either side. Semi-satisfied with her appearance, she eased the bedroom door open and stepped into the hallway. Finding no one in the parlor, she tiptoed through the room and onto the front porch.

The train whistle blew again, long and even blasts. It was approaching the Copeland station. A part of her longed to be on the train, headed to Cincinnati, but most of her wanted to stay. A good night's sleep had rejuvenated her adventuresome spirit. Daddy would be proud, mother terrified.

She strolled the wraparound porch, observing the landscape. Inhaling slow and deep, she studied the unique smell of the country. She squinted from the morning rays bursting through the treetops. The reflection off the dew resembled diamonds scattered across the front yard.

A fog blanketed the river running in back of the property and drifted upward, cascading the tops of the cluster of conifers that lined the edge of the palisades overlooking the river. She made an entire circle around the house and stopped on the front porch.

Gary played in the front yard, tossing a lopsided ball into the air and catching it with a worn leather glove. Perhaps distracted by the approaching train he didn't seem to notice her.

"Good morning, Gary."

He turned abruptly, as if surprised. She started to apologize, but a smile broke over his face. She slowly descended the flight of stairs, and not wanting to invade his space, sat on the bottom step.

He seemed more interested in her than his game of catch or the approaching train. A lad his age would miss his mother terribly. What kind of woman was she? Had the elements aged her prematurely? What did she die from? Five children seemed a lot? How old was she?

"I look forward to having you in class."

He continued to smile at her.

"Last night Nanny Sue told me you finished the first grade, the youngest in your class, and that you made good marks."

He stepped toward her as if the noise of the approaching train drowned out her words.

She repeated the sentence and emphasized good marks.

The train couplings clanged together as the engineer decelerated. The brakes screeched a long, shrill sound; metal moaned and air hoses hissed. The locomotive reduced speed, then lunged, braked again and slowly stopped, like an elevator trying to match the desired floor. A stream of smoke and steam surrounded the engine, giving an illusion the train was on fire. The conductor gave a hurry-up warning, a loud blast from the train's horn, for any potential passengers. "All aboard!" The brakes released and the train jerked forward, wheels spinning, as it slowly gathered speed.

They waved as the train roared past; the engineer reciprocated. Gary studied the passing train.

"How many cars?"

He held up both hands, smiling. He was a smart one, but why could he not talk.

"I was wondering if you and Joyce would accompany me today as I get acquainted with the students of your community."

Gary rubbed his nose profusely with the back of the ball glove before nodding his head yes.

"Good. We'll get started after breakfast. Would you mind bringing in an armload of wood so I can start a fire in the kitchen stove? I'd like to help Nanny Sue cook breakfast. On second thought, maybe I can learn how to cook breakfast from Nanny Sue." She laughed at herself.

Gary glanced momentarily at Nancy, stared instinctively up the hillside that loomed across the tracks and then scurried off. She hoped to the woodpile.

Manuel had said Gary didn't speak since his mommy died. Did Manuel mean that literally? She was beginning to think so, for she'd spoken one-on-one with Gary, but he hadn't verbally responded to her. Not one word. Was he traumatized in such a way that he couldn't speak?

Nancy stood and dusted off the back of her skirt. She turned to ascend the steps but stopped abruptly. A tall, robust man stood at the top of the steps, staring at her. His dark wavy hair fell across his forehead, as if needing to be brushed back. Was that the same man she'd seen yesterday on the horse? She assumed him to be Mr. Taggart, but she'd been wrong about Nanny Sue being the wife. He looked directly at her, seemingly self-assured. Up close he looked much younger than she expected, being the father of five children.

"Sorry. I didn't mean to startle you. Miss York, I presume?"

"Yes."

"I'm Wesley Taggart. I understand you'll be boarding with us."

"Yes. I mean I will if that's alright with you, of course."

"I'm sorry I returned home too late last night to greet you."

"Nanny Sue said you wouldn't mind my staying here so…"

"It's okay. Mine is the only boarding house available in the community. I wasn't expecting—"

"Someone so young?" Nancy interrupted him.

"No."

"A female teacher?"

"No."

"Then what weren't you expecting?"

"Never mind. I spoke out of turn. I'm pleased you've accepted this teaching position, but I must warn you there are difficulties teaching eight grades in one room. My own son adds to the challenge. He hasn't spoken since…"

"The accident?"

"Yes."

She wanted to know details about the accident and Gary's refusal to talk, but she didn't want to pry. Mr. Taggart did not elaborate.

"I've had four years of teacher training. I think I'm up to the challenge."

"I'm sure you are, Miss York. I'm sorry if I insinuated otherwise."

"You still haven't answered my question, though."

"What question was that?"

"What you weren't expecting in me as the new teacher."

"Mornin', Miss York. You're up awfully early." Nanny Sue tied her apron as she spoke.

"Good morning, Nanny Sue."

"Miss York will be boarding with us, Nanny Sue. See that she's properly cared for. Good day, Miss York." He quickly retreated inside the house.

CHAPTER TEN

~

T he Taggart children took to her immediately. Nancy felt mixed emotions, for she knew she was filling a void in their lives. They walked hand in hand, Nancy and Joyce, talking and laughing. Gary tagged along, always a few steps behind, catching grasshoppers and tossing rocks he picked up along the railroad track, but never speaking, though she tried to engage him in conversation.

They stopped at each house where there were school-age children.

"Hello, my name's Nancy York. I'm the new schoolteacher. These are my assistants. I believe you already know them."

Joyce beamed with delight. Gary's smile remained somewhat subdued, never speaking, but Joyce covered for him, talking incessantly. She was quite learned for her age.

Nancy carried a spiral-bound notebook in which she'd jotted down general information of the community that Joyce gladly shared. Nanny Sue had helped some with the project. Each home they visited brought its unique set of questions. Where was the father? Why was the mother so shy? How could so many people live in such a small house? Nancy asked general questions but hesitated to ask some of the questions she really wanted to ask. The short time spent with Ida Mae had taught her the people may be poor, but they didn't want to be treated as such.

The community spread in either direction for a couple miles along the North Fork. The multipurpose Deaton's store served as the midway point. That Saturday morning they covered only the homes to the east. Arriving back at the Taggart's house for lunch, Nancy

34

sat on the front porch and made additional notations of each family. Joyce and Gary sat beside her, one on either side.

"Would you mind sharing information about the students we'll meet tomorrow? I'd like to be a little better prepared."

"Well, there's Shoog Sebastian and the Buggins family: Jimbo, Tiny, and Sissy. Then there's the five Tally children." She rattled off a list of names.

Nancy studiously checked the names Joyce used against the list of names she'd received from the school superintendent. She frowned as she scanned the list.

"Something wrong?" Joyce asked.

"Some of the names don't match my list."

"That's 'cause we mostly don't go by our real names."

"I've been meaning to ask about that. What are their real names?"

"Don't rightly know all their real names. Don't everybody use nicknames, though?"

"Not everyone." Nancy smiled.

"We mostly do." Joyce sounded proud.

"This student list sent to me from the school superintendent doesn't list the Tally family you mentioned. Are they new in the community?"

Joyce laughed. "Been here all their lives. Tally's not their real name, though."

"Really?"

"We call them that because their grandpa was Italian. That means they came from Italy years ago. It's easier for us to call them Tally instead of DePasqualies — or whatever their name from Italy is. Do you know where Italy is, Miss York?"

"Yes. It's the boot of the Mediterranean."

Joyce frowned.

"I'll explain when I can show it to you on a map."

"We like nicknames. Makes it easier to remember."

Gary remained close by. Nancy noticed he seemed interested in the conversation. "Do you have a nickname, Gary?"

He shook his head no.

How could the death of his mother cause him to loose his ability to speak? He doesn't seem to try. I'll need to continue to engage him in conversation.

"What's your nickname, Gary?"

"He don't have none. It's just Gary for him and Joyce for me. He does have a middle name. Eugene."

"Why no nicknames?"

"Daddy won't let us. He says it undermines a person's confidence, whatever that means. 'Course I like nicknames even though Daddy don't."

"Why do you like nicknames?"

"Like I said before, they're easier to remember, and it helps us understand each other better."

Nancy frowned and scratched her head, in a silly manner. This stimulated Joyce's conversation. Joyce cackled. Gary grinned. Nancy continued her facial expression, delighted to see the children happy.

Nancy's antics motivated Joyce, who pointed out various idiosyncrasies about the people of the community. She explained nicknames came about for lots of reasons: because of something someone did or didn't do, something about their size, or the color of their hair, or their occupation or aversion to work. Through the words of this small child, Nancy came to realize hill folks felt tolerable to one another, but being tolerant didn't mean they were blind to a person's faults, or that they were without an opinion.

Nancy smiled and nodded, encouraging her to continue, all the while writing furiously in her notebook.

"Daddy says a character flaw needs challenged like a flogging rooster needs de-spurred. Having an opinion ain't criminal so long as you don't bring emotional or physical harm to those who beg to differ."

"Really? Your daddy said all that?"

"Yes, ma'am."

Does she actually understand that? She sure does have opinions. Did she get them from her father? I've hardly seen them interact since I've arrived.

"'Course I don't rightly understand what all Daddy says. Do you?"

"Somewhat." She smiled at Joyce.

Joyce reached out and gently touched Nancy on the cheek. "You're beautiful, Teacher."

"And I think you are beautiful, Miss Taggart. And you, sir, are handsome."

Gary giggled. There was sound. He has the ability to make sound.

The conversation lasted into the evening. Nancy's many questions, eliciting Joyce's opinions, helped her draw some conclusions. After dinner she completed her days entry with some personal conclusions. She transliterated Joyce's childlike explanations into more adult terminology, but sometimes she used Joyce's words for their uniqueness. With her interests in history and current events, she evaluated how both had affected this community: good and bad. The community, without a road, was fortunate to serve as a depot for a spur of the L&N Railroad that took out their coal products, but also opened up a whole new world to them. With the railroad line they could ride the passenger train to the nearest town large enough for shopping. Jackson was twelve miles away. They could do their shopping and return home in the same day. The community had been hopeful back in '53 when news leaked the state was funding a road their way. While the rest of the world sat glued to their new television sets, watching the flickering black and white images of Britain's new monarch, local folks huddled at the store speculating about their first road. Unfortunately for the community of Copeland, the construction engineer chose the opposite side of the North Fork, leaving the majority of the community cut off from the road. So the locals still depended mostly on the passenger train, though a few folks on the opposite side of the river had purchased cars.

The misfortune of the road bypassing them didn't dash their community spirit. They knew all their neighbors and spoke to them often. They knew when a neighbor's child was sick or needed clothes. They knew if they went to church or not. They attended each other's good-bye parties when someone moved away to the city or one of their boys went off to serve his country in the military. They gathered daily at the post office and waited eagerly as Ida Mae sorted the mail and handed it out one letter at a time, calling every name aloud. During the winter they stood around the potbelly stove.

During the summer they sat together on the front porch, reading the mail and sharing the news of near and far. The annual arrival of the Aldens Catalog created quite a stir of excitement and more when a package of new clothes arrived.

The community truly was close, caring, and cooperative, but Nancy evaluated them as being too obsolete for the changing society around them. They were falling farther and farther behind the post world war society. Some suggested the only hope to get ahead was to move away; others vehemently opposed the idea. This seemed their greatest divide.

Joyce snuggled next to her. Nancy laid aside her notebook. "You've been very helpful today. I do have one question. You didn't mention the Callahan family. I have them on my list as having two children. Do they still live here?"

"Yep. That'd be Jack and his younger sister, Sherry Jane. Jack might come, but not his sister. She's a blue skin."

"A what?"

"A blue skin. You know, a child born with blue skin."

"I'm sorry, but I don't understand what you're talking about."

"You don't got no blue skin children in the city you come from?"

"No. I've never heard of this. Is it some kind of sickness?"

"Don't rightly know. Their skin is just blue. Like yours and mine is white, theirs is blue, as if'n they chewed on a mulberry and it colored their lips."

"Blue on just their lips?"

"Their whole body is blue."

"How strange! Are they being treated by a physician?"

"Don't think so. No need as far as I can tell."

"Is the blue skin contagious…passed from one child to another?"

"Nope. At least I don't think so."

"Then why would this keep them out of school?

"Some adults don't like them going to school with normal children."

"But why?"

"'Cause it's the curse of Cain I guess, or at least that's what Granny Combs calls it."

"Who is Granny Combs?"

"She's like a doctor, but she ain't been trained in school to be a doctor. She just teached herself."

"Really? Does your daddy take you to her?"

"No. She's too far away. Lives over on Troublesome Creek."

CHAPTER ELEVEN

~

Smoke drifted from the flues; smells of breakfast permeated the air. Doors opened on squeaky hinges and banged shut, as students ran from their houses, books in hand, and made their way to school, just ahead of the new teacher. She'd explained to Joyce and Gary she'd be walking with Mr. Deaton in order to discuss the first day of school. They seemed to understand and joined in with the other students.

"I can't believe I have butterflies." Nancy walked alongside Mr. Deaton, taking two strides to his one.

"They never leave."

"Really?"

"Especially the first day of school. You'll do okay, Miss York." He smiled and placed a hand on her shoulder.

"Thank you."

She stepped delicately along the railroad tracks, trying to pace herself to step on the ties and fighting back the jitters in her stomach. His steps cleared two ties at a time, years of routine evident in his demeanor.

"I'm very pleased you asked to accompany me the first day of school."

"A transfer of the torch. I'll introduce you and then sit back and let you take over. Tomorrow it's all yours."

Perhaps that's why I feel so apprehensive. Maybe it's not the students, but it's lecturing in front of a seasoned teacher.

Music drifted from a squawking radio, the words of the song hardly audible above the static.

Mr. Deaton whistled along with the song until they were out of hearing.

"Recognize the song, Miss York?"

"*Good Night Irene.*"

"Sad, huh?"

"Very."

"The mountain people love sad songs."

"Really? Why so?"

"Not sure. It seems to connect the soul to the creator, a dust-to-dust mentality. Since death is inevitable, and life at best is uncertain, and for sure temporal, skip the temporal and get death over with. If you pass death's test, then life on the other side will be much better."

A straggly-haired dog with a white circle around its right eye trotted toward them, barking.

Nancy stopped.

"It's okay, Miss York. Mornin', Spot." He retrieved a biscuit from his coat pocket and tossed it toward the dog, which caught it in midair and bolted it down. "Maybe Miss York will have something for you tomorrow."

"Do you give him a biscuit every morning?"

"Ever since he bit me a few years back." He chuckled. "Not that he'll ever bite you, Miss York."

"Thanks for the encouragement." They both laughed.

Shoog Sebastian, Mr. Deaton's great-nephew, followed behind them. Nancy had learned from Joyce he lived with the Deatons. Joyce didn't know what happened to his parents. Nancy reminded herself to find out. He seemed too old for grammar school, but he was finishing the eighth grade. Perhaps he'd failed a grade or two. He kicked rocks and occasionally flung one at a flock of swooping sparrows.

They rounded the curve and Nancy's adrenaline rushed when she saw the school, perched on a knoll of yellow clay overlooking the railroad and the North Fork.

"The schoolhouse sits on property once a part of the Noble farm. The Nobles deeded it to the county for a school. They also gave land for the community cemetery. It lays higher up the hill behind the school."

Nancy stopped and stared at the school. "Mind if I stop and catch my breath?" She breathed heavily.

"The first day is always the most apprehensive."

"How many times have you made this trip?"

"It seems a long time, perhaps too long. Time, like speed, doesn't matter that much here in Copeland. Take for example the Indy five hundred. With a speed of one hundred twenty-eight miles an hour this year, that means little to a community that has neither a road nor vehicles."

"I can't relate to the Indy either. It seems too dangerous."

"The Kentucky Derby is different. Our community can relate to this year's winner, Needles, and his jockey, Mr. Erb, for our young men pride themselves in their fast horses."

"Do you frequent the races?" His grasp of current events surprised her.

"Oh no. Just read about them in the paper I get from Lexington."

"How often do you get the paper?"

"Once a week. Comes in the mail. I read it word for word, kiver to kiver." He laughed at himself for his use of the colloquialism.

Nancy didn't laugh. "Then you're also aware of the bad publicity this area sometimes receives in the newspapers."

"Don't have to read about it, Miss York, I've seen it with my own eyes over the years."

"Do you feel the situation is still bad here, or is it getting better?"

"Bad? That's a subjective term. Bad compared to what?"

"Bad compared to…" She paused. "Compared to the Bible, The Ten Commandments and the teachings of Christ."

"The good book is for believers."

"Are you a believer?"

"Somewhat."

"How do you evaluate this community, according to the Bible?"

"The believers are doing a decent job believing and the nonbelievers aren't too bad when compared to some of the sinners of the scripture."

"What about Mr. Taggart? Is he a believer?"

"That sounds like a question you need to ask Mr. Taggart."

"I suppose so. Can I retract my question about Mr. Taggart?"

"What question is that, Miss York?" He smiled at her.

"Have you ever thought about becoming a politician?" She chuckled.

"Once. But my friends were all divided about what they wanted for this community, and I decided I didn't want to disappoint my friends. I just kept on teaching. Sad to say, I still disappointed some of my friends."

They both laughed.

Nancy glanced over her shoulder at Shoog, who had fallen farther back, sidetracked by a covey of monarch butterflies that landed on some milkweed plants. How beautiful! And intriguing. Resting in this remote area of the world on their way to Mexico. What wanderers! Not a care in the world as they flutter from plant to plant. With my love of studying nature, perhaps I can learn to love this natural setting, even with all its hardships.

A lone horse and rider approached from behind. Nancy squinted, curious. Is that Mr. Taggart? Probably not, since he left much earlier, before I got up. Not tall enough. Too thin.

"With the warm weather, we'll dispense with building a fire today," Mr. Deaton said.

She didn't respond.

"Miss York?"

"Oh, sorry. My mind had wondered. Did you say build a fire? I hadn't thought of a fire."

"Ever built a fire?"

"Yes. Well, at the boarding house I helped Nanny Sue the other day."

Mr. Deaton chuckled. "You'll need to assign the task to the students."

"Isn't that dangerous to ask them to build a fire?"

"Miss York, that's survival in these parts. Fire and firearms. Fire for cooking and firearms for hunting something to cook. And swimming."

"Why swimming?"

"Manliness."

"So girls don't necessarily swim?"

"Some do. Depends on their pappy."

"What does that mean?"

"Whether or not their pappy feels they should learn to swim."

The lone rider caught up with them.

"Mornin', Bill," the rider said.

"Mornin', Greenberry. Seems you're ridin' light today."

"I don't determine how much mail there is. I just deliver it. Christmas catalogs won't be out for another month or so."

Horse and rider kept a certain rhythm: the horse a set pace and the rider a rocking motion in harmony with the horse's pace. This produced a cadenced squeak of the leather saddle. The horse's hooves made a steady clopping on the cinder path, which ran alongside the railroad tracks. The horse's gait seemed to signify a long day ahead. The sounds and smells were unique to Nancy. She stared after the horse and rider.

"What does Greenberry actually do? Is that his last name?"

"First. Last name is Turner. Greenberry delivers mail to the hollows surrounding Copeland — rain or shine. He's one of the few horseback mail carriers left. He's the antithesis of the short-lived Pony Express created from an entrepreneurial spirit built around speed. Greenberry's route exists because of necessity rather than for speed — there's no other way for the mail to be delivered around these parts. He picks up the daily delivery that arrives on the morning passenger train. My wife sorts the mail for the locals and hands over the rest to Greenberry. He'll deliver all the letters and packages by nightfall. For some in these parts he's their only source of communication with a distant and unfamiliar world."

They walked on in silence as Nancy pondered this strange world into which she'd come. She followed Mr. Deaton past the waiting students and into the building. The wear and tear of life showed on the students' clothing. She didn't know how to respond to their disquieting stares. She glanced at her satin dress with gold colored buttons lining the front. It was one of the gifts purchased by her parents for her to wear on her first day as a new teacher. Perhaps not a good choice.

She scanned the classroom: a blackboard covered most of the front wall, with faded prints of George Washington and Abraham Lincoln centered above the blackboard; worn wooden desks and benches lined in rows, leaving room for the potbelly stove that sat in the center of the room; a huge oak desk with a matching swivel chair faced the students' desks; a square wooden table, on which a porcelain coated water bucket sat, stood against the back wall. A battered aluminum dipper hung from the side of the bucket.

Nancy shook her head in disbelief. She'd seen pictures of one-room schoolhouses; still, she was shocked by the crude and cramped quarters. She walked slowly toward the back of the room, her hand sliding across the backs of the benches. She wondered what her former classmates' teaching assignments were like back in Cincinnati. She thought of her mother and the forlorn look on her face when she told them she'd taken this assignment in eastern Kentucky. She also remembered the look of pride on her daddy's face.

A clanging startled her as Mr. Deaton waved a hand-held brass bell, announcing the start of the school day. She walked back to the entrance to greet the students. The children filed in timidly and took their seats, two students to a desk, youngest to the oldest.

"Good morning, Manuel. George. How's that poison ivy?"

"Almost gone," Manuel answered for George.

Nancy greeted each of the students, trying to recall their names.

Shoog dashed in past Mr. Deaton just as his chalk shrieked gratingly against the blackboard, writing the words: September 9, 1956; Miss York. He turned to the class, opened his Bible and read from the Gospel according to Luke.

Nancy walked to the back of the room and observed. The students chuckled as the door slowly opened and a raggedly dressed, lanky boy, unkempt and shoeless, gawked at the scene before he strolled in. He slouched into the room. It seemed to Nancy he carried a chip on his shoulder. Mr. Deaton cleared his throat, noticeably aggravated at the boy's tardiness.

"Think you could get up a mite earlier for school, Jack? If you want a job other than shuckin' corn in the bottoms all day, you best sharpen your mind the way you sharpen that knife of yours."

The boy said nothing. He turned his back to Mr. Deaton, strolled to his desk, and fell hard onto his wooden bench, knocking books and a lunch pail to the floor.

Nancy assumed the boy to be Jack Callahan, for that was the only family she hadn't been able to visit. The Callahans lived the farthest away from the community, and time hadn't permitted Nancy's visit. She looked out the open door; the boy's sister was not with him. Nancy's heart sunk.

Mr. Deaton walked to the door and pulled it shut, then turned back to the class and continued to read aloud, "'Be ye therefore merciful, as your Father also is merciful. Judge not, and ye shall not be judged: condemn not, and ye shall not be condemned: forgive, and ye shall be forgiven'.... Let's pray."

Nancy bowed her head, but she didn't close her eyes. She lifted her head slightly and watched the students, their heads bowed, eyes closed, some with their hands in a position of prayer. Her eyes fastened on Jack, his head held aloft, hands in his pockets. He withdrew something from his pocket. She stood flatfooted as he walked toward Mr. Deaton, holding an opened knife aloft.

"No." Nancy's scream came too late to warn him. Jack buried the knife deep into Mr. Deaton's upper left arm. He grimaced. Nancy rushed to him and attempted to clog the flowing blood with her new, fine-laced handkerchief. She turned to the class and tried unsuccessfully to calm the terrified students.

Shoog charged toward Jack; yelling and shoving ensued between them. The scuffle overturned a desk, knocking students and books onto the floor. Someone screamed. A small girl began to cry.

"You'll leave this schoolhouse immediately, Jack," Shoog demanded.

"I'll leave when I get ready and not a second before."

"Now!" Shoog demanded.

"Whose gonna make me?"

A couple of the older students slowly walked toward the front of the class. For a moment Nancy thought they were siding in with Jack, but they just stood there beside Mr. Deaton, stern faced. Blood covered the front of Mr. Deaton's white shirt. He continued to press Nancy's handkerchief against the wound; the blood flow seemed to be stopping.

"Jack, get your things and leave," Mr. Deaton pleaded.

Jack hesitated.

"Now!"

Jack stomped out, leaving the door ajar. As the sound of his bare feet against the wooden floor faded, the classroom fell silent.

Nancy stared at Jack as he stalked away. With one wildcat slash of his knife, he'd severed a link to a better life. In a way, she was glad to see him go, for she could see the terror on the faces of the younger children. She pitied but also feared him. If he could do that to a male teacher... Her thoughts trailed off as Mr. Deaton cleared his throat and held up a hand to quiet the students.

"This is your new teacher, Miss York, from down Cincinnati way. Please make her welcome to our community."

She felt embarrassed for Mr. Deaton, standing there with his clean, pressed shirt all bloodied and torn, his pride frayed a bit also. Both Jack and Mr. Deaton seemed to have lost the fight and maybe the war that had raged for the past few years. It happened on his last day as a teacher and her first day as the new teacher. What an ending for a career! What a beginning!

"They're all yours, Miss York. I'd best get home and tend to this wound." He walked toward the door but stopped abruptly and turned to her. "Above the door, Miss York, is a hickory stick. Don't hesitate to use it. Spare the rod..." He didn't finish the quote.

"Thank you, Mr. Deaton." Her voice quivered. "I doubt I shall need it."

Mr. Deaton started toward the exit. Nancy observed Jack sitting about fifty yards away, his back to the schoolhouse. Is he waiting for Mr. Deaton? Mr. Deaton stepped outside and pulled the door shut. Nancy turned to face the blank faces of the two-dozen students.

She hastened to her desk and half sat, half fell into the seat. That is when she noticed Gary, ashen faced, staring at her. Joyce had a consoling arm around him.

Nancy smiled. I must be brave. For him. For all the students.

"Today, class, begins a journey around the world in one hundred fifty days. Who would like to take that journey with me?"

Joyce's hand shot skyward. Others slowly rose.

"Good. Let's begin."

CHAPTER TWELVE

~

It pleased Gary Miss York was his new teacher. He wasn't sure how she heard about them. Mostly only kinfolks came from far away to visit, like his cousins, the Birchfields, from over Booneville way. Yet, there she sat, a total stranger a few days back, now like family, eating meals with them. She had her place at the head of the table opposite Daddy, and he and Joyce sat next to her, one on either side. He loved the sound of her voice, like Mamma's, soft and caring. It was unlike Mr. Deaton's voice, which was loud and choppy, like the raging, murky waters of the North Fork during flooding.

He watched her every movement: the way she maneuvered the tableware, the way she lifted her glass, the way she dabbed her lips with the table napkin. He lingered at the dinner table, relishing the adult conversation and Joyce's occasional input. He so much wanted to join in the conversation, but he was afraid to try.

"How was school?" Daddy asked no one in particular.

"Jack got into trouble," Joyce piped up.

"Nothing unusual."

"He stabbed Mr. Deaton."

"Is Mr. Deaton okay?"

"I think so," Nancy answered. "It was a horrible scene, Mr. Taggart."

"I'm very sorry for your sake, Miss York, and for Mr. Deaton. I'm especially concerned that my children...all the children were exposed to such violence."

"We're alright, Daddy. It was scary, though."

"You alright, Gary Eugene?"

Gary nodded his head up and down. Daddy seemed to be concerned. He generally didn't get much attention from Daddy.

"I must stop by and speak with Mr. Deaton. He might need to have the wound checked by Doc Lewis." Wesley tossed his napkin onto the table. "That man can be a stubborn soul. Why was he at school in the first place?"

"He came to introduce me," Nancy said

"That was thoughtful of him. I'm sorry about Jack. That boy's headed for trouble if he doesn't change his attitude."

"Jack's sister wasn't in school. Joyce said she has some kind of skin disease."

"Blue skin. Runs in the family." Wesley said.

"Is it contagious?"

"No. Mostly the Fugate clan, and some relatives by marriage have it. My speculation is it's the silver in the water they're drinking over on Troublesome Creek. Why can't Jack just behave himself? Now he's destined to be like...he's destined to grow up without an education."

"Yes, that is very sad," Nancy said. "Jack's behavior affirms what I've read about the Appalachian people."

"We're written about?" Joyce sounded surprised.

"Yes, quite often. That's how I first got interested in teaching here. I find it ironic this part of the county, so isolated from society, has gotten so much national attention."

"What does ironic mean?" Joyce asked.

"Sort of like the two don't go together," Nancy explained.

"Like poison ivy growing in a flower garden. It's out of place. It's not a compliment to us," Wesley said. "Unimportant folk like us don't make national news unless we're feuding."

Gary didn't like the tone of his daddy's voice.

"Where did you get your information about us, Miss York?"

"Newspaper articles. The Cincinnati Enquirer, the Chicago Tribune, the Washington Post and the New York Times, to name only some of the many papers who have written about this part of the world. Would you like to read some of the articles?"

"I don't need a national newspaper to inform me regarding local news. This community may not be perfect, but it's as safe, if not safer, than any of those cities of which you speak. They don't write about us because they care. It's sensationalism they seek, and to get it they have to sometimes stretch the truth."

"I disagree somewhat. The world does care what happens in these hills, Mr. Taggart. Seeing young Jack's behavior today, and observing the shabby clothing of the students, I don't believe the newspapers are exaggerating when they speak of this country's 'overzealous taste for revenge and underprivileged state of poverty.'"

"You've categorized all of us by these overstated articles."

"Mr. Taggart, in national papers, this part of the country is written about as much as other Kentucky cities, much larger, like Lexington, Louisville or Kentucky's own Little Chicago — Newport."

"Where's Newport?" Joyce asked.

"It's a rowdy river town opposite Cincinnati, where the Licking River flows into the Ohio. Over the past few years it has gotten itself a bad reputation," Nancy explained.

"So you've come to save us, Miss York?" Wesley asked abruptly.

Gary didn't like this conversation. He resented the way Miss York spoke about his world. It troubled him the way she and Daddy spoke to each other. He didn't understand all the big words she quoted from the articles: savagery, affrays, barbarism, consanguineous marriages and anarchy. He thought they must be bad. Why does Miss York believe the bad things the people write about us. With all these dreadful things strangers write about us, it's a wonder any outsiders ever come here, especially Miss York. If she leaves, then what'll we do for a teacher?

Nanny Sue interrupted, "You've got to admit, Wesley, we've got a lot of souls needin' saved around here. Just the nickname of our county says something: Bloody Breathitt! Why? Cause men prefer guns from a distance over workin' out their problems face to face."

Are Miss York and Nanny Sue right? Gary squirmed in his seat. Bobby Combs and Tommy Spurlock did meet on the Haddix Bridge over near Troublesome just last year and shot and killed each other. Is that what Miss York means by barbarism? They buried them the next day. Their widows cried and cried at the funeral. Why did they shoot each other, and what does it feel like when a bullet goes into your body?

Nanny Sue continued, "In the two-year period during the time my daddy was killed, twenty-seven men died from gun battles as vengeance tore apart our community. It was all because Daddy didn't keep quiet about their moonshine dealings. What did it gain him speakin' up? Daddy left Mamma to raise ten children by herself!"

"That was before I was born, Nanny Sue. It's different now." Wesley argued.

"Ain't that much different. The days leadin' up to 'lection day have a way of revealin' the demons in a man, as if politicians are the lords of the universe. Moonshine and 'lections are a bad lot."

Gary noticed Miss York scribbled in her notebook. Why does she keep writing about us? Is she taking sides with the others that don't like us? I don't like that about her. Why does she have to write things down? I'd like to tear the pages out of her notebook and burn them in the woodstove.

Wesley refilled his coffee cup. "Things have calmed down since then, Nanny Sue. That was forty...fifty years ago."

"Daddy's cousin, William Brewer, was shot and killed on 'lection day, too. It was a senseless thing. Left another family for his wife to raise alone. Seems like 'lection day don't do us no good a'tall."

Nanny Sue usually didn't talk that way to his daddy. Gary wondered what had gotten into her. It was the teacher speaking her mind that got Nanny Sue all riled up.

"Death is a fact of life, Nanny Sue. Who should understand that more than you?" Wesley said.

"But such senseless deaths are incomprehensible," Nancy challenged.

Gary didn't understand what the teacher meant, but he assumed it was against his daddy.

"So you have come to save us, Miss York."

Gary did not like the way Daddy talked down to Miss York.

"I'd like to think I can help."

"Then let me give you some history of this land. Others have come and gone for years before you, but their selfish interest seemed to be their motivation. They came for the virgin timber, tall, mature and plenteous. They ravaged this land for years before leaving it barren and exposed to the elements. Afterwards, the coal kings and their courts reigned over this land, stripping the native queen highlands of her dignity. The misty morning mountaintops, majestically crowned with jewels of dew, with valleys clothed in downy fog, and lush rolling meadows, succumbed to their erosive means of mining and their personal scorn for the land. Such disregard for nature left the local men with a residue of blackness coating their lungs and cutting off their lives, but worse, it stained their souls with a darkness of despair."

The room echoed as Wesley's voice rose above the normal mealtime conversation. Gary had heard this story before. Daddy spoke as if he was reciting a rehearsed speech, or reading from a well-read book.

Gary stared at Miss York. She'd touched a sensitive spot in his daddy's soul, and he wasn't finished talking.

"The interloping and clever entrepreneurs bought mineral rights from generational landowners who couldn't read or write or understand anyone owning the land except God. The promise of enough money to pay their spring taxes on the land tempted too many into placing their 'X' on a page filled with confusing legal terms, but which suave lawyers explained with promises of future fortune. The conglomerates gave little but took much—then left, leaving nothing. The sun that once shined bright with promise on our ole Kentucky homes dimmed with the prosperity of foreigners who didn't even care to own a home in our beloved highlands."

"I'm sorry for your disappointment, Mr. Taggart, but I haven't come with any such intentions as those of which you speak."

"Then why have you come? I've observed your continual note taking. It seems obvious you have more in mind than teaching our children to read and write. What deliverance from bondage do you offer? To what promised land do you direct us?"

Gary wanted to speak, to agree with his daddy. His daddy's hand gestures resembled Preacher Charlie's when he got very excited during one of his sermons. Gary couldn't understand the meaning of everything his daddy said, but he could tell by the way he spoke he disagreed very strongly with whatever Miss York had in mind for them. He figured his daddy was defending their honor. That made him proud.

"I didn't come to save you. I've come to educate your children and other children in this community. It's obvious, Mr. Taggart, you received a good education. Your vocabulary…"

"I didn't receive my education here alone. I was fortunate enough to have some caring instructors who mentored me and saw to it I went on to college."

"Your children deserve just as good an education as you received. I want to help. That is why I have come. As for my continual note taking, I hope to enroll in graduate work, and I believe this will facilitate my application."

The room grew quiet, except for heavy breathing.

"Forgive me for such presuming statements. I hope you can make a difference. I must admit, you've already made a difference for my family. For that I'm very grateful."

His daddy's tone softened. He was glad.

"Thank you."

They seemed to come to some agreement. The edginess cleared. Gary was glad.

"I hope I can make a difference with all the children, not just your sweet family."

"That may not be as easy a task as you think. Not that you lack in ability. Some folks around here hold education at arm's length. They view educated people without local job opportunities as bound to move away. This seems too high a cost for an education—having to move away from the land. Roots grow deep in Appalachian soil. The earth, though full of toil, has given us life. Most of these people are poor, but they have a heritage. They don't wish it to vanish. This is their land. They're free here. They don't want to be in bondage on someone else's land just because it offers a few more conveniences in life."

"Nostalgia and dreams could well blind this community from reality. Compared to the majority of this state, this is a dying world here. The future of your children is certainly at stake."

"I believe we have a future here, and we'll make it. Outsiders have come to help us before, but always conditionally. They never liked us for what we were, but for what they could get out of us. We were merely projects. Their salvation demanded change, but it was a change we were reluctant to accept. It was a price too high for the highlanders of eastern Kentucky."

"You are the foreigners to those outside these hills," Nancy challenged.

"I admit, we are different, but we're not foreigners. We're true Americans: white Anglo-Saxon Protestants with a bit of superstition mixed in. We may be called hillbillies, but we're not stupid. We have our traditions, mixed with some carryover from English and French ancestry. We're not as needy as many outsiders perceive. Our philosophy has worked so far."

"And what philosophy is that?" Nancy reached for her notepad.

Wesley smiled. "Aide-toi, le ciel t'aidera."

Nancy raised her eyebrows but didn't respond.

"Does my French surprise you?"

"Yes, I'd have to say it does. Help yourself and…" Nancy paused.

"Heaven will help you," Wesley finished the translation.

"Where did you learn French?"

"I spent two years in France. No, these folks don't speak French. They lost their native languages long ago, but the philosophy lives on, and they understand it. They don't depend too much on outsiders."

Gary was glad his daddy and Miss York were speaking nice to each other. She'd become one of them, eating at their table, playing tag, hula-hoops in the evening and catching fireflies at night. He viewed her differently than the others Daddy talked about.

"Life seems so difficult here." Her voice lowered to almost a whisper. "You don't even have a road to your community. It's like circumstances have shut you out, or else penned you in. What about the future of your children? Will someone teach them French? Can they cling indefinitely to such a philosophy in the face of poverty, especially if they realize the rest of the world is advancing with opportunities galore? Do you honestly believe this community has a future for these children?"

"We're trying to catch up. The county commissioner has received funding to build a bridge across the North Fork and connect us to the new road. We'll furnish the labor—jobs for some of our men. Once the bridge is completed, it'll open our community for new opportunities, right here in Copeland. Our school will flourish, and we have the right teacher to make that happen."

"It's too late for your community." Nancy lowered her voice.

"What do you mean?" Wesley stared at her.

"The school district has already decided to close your school. I'm the last teacher that will ever come to this community. The new bridge isn't going to keep these children here. It'll be their opportunity to escape. They'll be bused to larger schools with greater opportunities."

"You know that for a fact?"

"Yes. I'm surprised they haven't informed you. Consolidation is the wave of the future."

Miss York's abrupt announcement stung Gary like a bumblebee. He jumped from his chair, knocking it backward, and ran from the room.

CHAPTER THIRTEEN

~

Gary fled from the house and out the front gate. He didn't stop until he'd climbed to the plateau of Coffin Rock Mountain. The climb exhausted him, and he crumpled to the ground gasping for air.

He couldn't believe what Miss York had said. Why would they close his school? Miss York would have to leave. He'd never see her again.

He lay on his belly, his chin resting in his open palms, and stared across the North Fork valley. Ridges of forests rimmed the tiny valley with an array of golden colors. The few houses scattered along the railroad tracks looked like miniature models; the people seemed as small as ants. He could see the North Fork as it snaked along the countryside.

I will never leave this place.

He rose from the ground, searched until he found a suitable walking stick and continued his journey, this time at a slower pace. The coffin rock lay just ahead.

Miss York was the enemy. It was good to be shed of her, to be on his own again, to do men things for a change, rather than tagging along after a nosey woman snooping around in other people's business. He still liked most things about Miss York; of that there was no doubt. He enjoyed the smell of her perfume when she entered the room and the way her smile cheered him. She reminded him of Momma. He resented that Miss York didn't like his daddy the way Momma did. Momma never spoke mean to Daddy. Should I dislike her for that? He felt confused. Coffin Rock will be a good place to get my thoughts together, to shed the foolish talk of Miss York.

He slowed his pace. Local stories about the rock made him curious, yet cautious. Tales abounded about the Indians of this area. Some said it was a place where the Cherokees made human sacrifices, and that the blood of victims left a stain upon the rock. His daddy didn't believe any of those things.

He'd never ventured this far before. Daddy promised to show me the rock someday, but he's too busy working the salt mine. Daddy needs to work hard to make a living for our family.

He'd listened as the older boys talked about how to get to the rock. He followed their directions, and the worn trail, approaching cautiously. The older boys talked about the Indians who came here long ago. They traveled the warriors' trail not far from here but mostly for hunting. His daddy told him no Cherokee had been seen in these parts for over a hundred years, ever since the Trail of Tears to the Oklahoma territory, which he knew followed the setting sun for a long way. Daddy said some still remained in North Carolina. Someday he hoped to take him there and see them. He was curious. His daddy also told him he had some Cherokee blood from his momma's side.

He paused to catch his breath. He guessed the rock was just ahead. He wiped his brow with the back of his shirtsleeve and started out again.

He saw it for the first time, but he could hardly believe it. It did resemble a coffin, laying north and south, with the northern most point looking like a roughly carved head, perhaps the carving of a famous Indian head. The chin pointed in the direction of the North Fork, probably on purpose to show direction.

He scurried onto the rock but froze in his tracks. The center of the rock was covered with blood, but it wasn't an old bloodstain from the Indian stories. It was fresh, real and swarmed by blowflies.

Gary covered his mouth and dropped to his knees, heaving. His body convulsed and his supper spilled onto the ground. The heaving stopped. He wiped at the front of his shirt and cleaned his hands on the moss covering the rocks.

Something bad has happened here. Has someone been killed? Somewhere nearby there might be a dead body. What should I do? He tried to unscramble his emotions.

He circled the rock, slowly casing the area, fearful he'd stumble upon the body. Nothing. He found a moss patch and lay down. A dark cloud drifted from the southwest, blocking the warmth of the sun. He listened and watched: a squirrel scurrying through the leaves, an acorn falling to the ground, a Blue Jay chasing another bird. His daddy had taught him the ways of the outdoors. The sounds of the forest were many and each had its place. Daddy said a displaced sound in the forest is like a sinner sitting on the front pew in church. Sinners sit on the back row, not on the front. A sinner on the front row spells trouble; he either wants a handout or else he's drunk.

Gary's stomach felt better. He closed his eyes and counted the various sounds. His body relaxed.

A dozen sun-bronzed and painted warriors approached, stepping quickly, glancing from side to side. They carried a body and laid it on top of the rock. They watched as an older man, slightly hunched, danced around the fire they'd built, rattling a gourd with each hand, in rhythm with his shuffling moccasins. He wore a frightening mask; strange emblems tattooed his chest and arms. A frayed belt, entwined with pinecones, flowers and herbs wrapped his waist. He danced to the steady beat of a stick struck against skin tightly stretched over a hollowed out log. He waved what looked like turtle shells filled with something that rattled softly in time with the drumbeat. He removed a powdery substance from his leather bag and tossed it into the flame.

Gary watched from his crouched position in the underbrush. He couldn't understand what all this meant, but he figured it was an Indian funeral. He did recognize the smell of tobacco smoke mingled with the hickory smoke of the flames that drifted upward. The dance, the fire and the chanting continued. Suddenly the others joined in the dance. Was it okay to dance at death? He didn't dance at Momma's funeral. He remembered Preacher Charlie's words, cry at a birth and laugh at death. Why? That confused him.

Sparks from the flames shot outward, with no apparent aim; a cloud of smoke rose rapidly and disappeared into the forest of tall oaks and pines. A blood-curdling howl from the medicine man scared him, but the warriors joined in the chorus; their voices attracted the attention of a pack of wolves, which echoed the wailing.

Gary sneaked closer to get a look at the dead Indian who lay still on the partially moss-covered stone, evidently killed in battle. Blood seeped from a wound in his side and flowed onto the stone. A bow, a quiver of arrows and a flint hatchet were positioned beside him. His haggard dog lay nearby, its front paws crossed and pointed toward its master. A whippoorwill called out in the distance. He paused and called out again. Another answered. Clouds darkened the face of the moon. Far off, lightning flashed; five heartbeats later thunder rolled across the sky towards the warriors. Raindrops fell into the fire and hissed as they vaporized and rose again. The warriors sought shelter in a grove of pine trees.

The descending raindrops beat away at the bloodstain of the slain warrior. The red-tinted water ran off the rock and onto the ground where it mixed with a rapidly forming stream.

Drops of rain peppered Gary's face. His eyes blinked open. His heart raced, but there were no dancing Indians. He remained very still and slowly scanned his surroundings. "I must have fallen asleep," he muttered as he wiped at the rain on his face.

He suddenly sat upright. What is that sound? His senses piqued. Was it a deer stepping carefully between twigs? Or a squirrel among the leaves? A wolf stalking its prey? No, it was none of these. Like Daddy says, there are some sounds that are out of place in the woods. He quickly slipped into some underbrush and waited. Time passed slowly, like melting icicles hidden from the spring sun. The sounds grew louder and obviously closer.

CHAPTER FOURTEEN

~

Back and forth they rocked, a slow cadence. Nanny Sue held the baby. Nancy balanced a book on her lap; she wasn't up to reading. The sun dipped quickly over Coffin Rock Mountain. Mr. Taggart had left over an hour ago, without comment, in search of Gary. Nancy helped Nanny Sue with the dishes. The task somewhat distracted their distress. Joyce had sat with the twins until they'd fallen asleep. She now sat on the tracks in front of the house, digging her heels into the granite gravel. They sat in the rockers, waiting and worrying.

"I'm sorry, Nanny Sue. I've made a mess of things."

"Don't go beatin' yourself up, dear. Wesley's partly to blame. He egged you on."

"I started it."

"I'll share a secret about Wesley. He loves to argue, just doesn't have anyone with his intelligence around here to argue with. That is till you come along."

"I've got to learn to shut my mouth, especially since I'm a guest."

"A boarder, dear, payin' to stay here. I reckon you have a right to speak your mind."

"I wasn't just speaking my mind. I was attacking my opponent, defending my honor and demanding the enemy surrender."

Nanny Sue laughed. "Wesley ain't your enemy, child."

"I dare not imagine what he's thinking of me right now."

"He respects you."

"Sounded like he despises me. A pushy, loud-mouthed city woman is what he's thinking."

60

"He disagrees with you, but he don't despise you."

"How can you tell?"

"Oh, I don't know if I can rightly put it into words. But I know Wesley."

"Daddy's coming," Joyce called out.

Nancy stood and with the book shielded her eyes from the piercing sunset. Wesley was alone. Her heart sank. Was she to blame? Vacillating thoughts tore at her heart. She wanted to run, but that smacked of cowardice and acknowledged guilt. She could apologize for any contribution she had to Gary's running off without permission or explanation. She could go to her room. Go to her room and what? Pout?

He walked in the manner he rode his stallion, tall and head erect. He carried a walking stick but wielded it more like a weapon than a cane. With each step he pivoted the tip of the stick upward and forward, then quickly flicked it downward onto the next railroad tie. The stick made a rhythmic thump against the tie.

Something about Mr. Taggart reminded her of her daddy. What would Daddy do if he was in her place? No, what would he want her to do? May you play the game of life warily, for your opponent is full of subtlety, and take thought over your every move, for your soul is at stake.

She quickly descended the steps. Nanny Sue says Wesley's not my opponent. Is he? If so, it's of his accord, not mine. She rushed to meet him.

CHAPTER FIFTEEN

~

Nancy braced herself for the confrontation. Wesley didn't alter his stride as he headed straight toward her. Her mind raced. Be civil. Do not attack him again. I cannot surrender my beliefs just to appease his affection for this community. What kind of chess match would that be? "Never let me win again, Nancy." Her daddy's words echoed in her head. She toyed with a strand of hair falling across her forehead.

"Did you find Gary?"

Wesley stopped, stuck his hands in his pockets and tilted his head toward the ground. "No, I didn't find him."

"What are you going to do?"

"Wait."

"Wait? It'll be dark in an hour. You can't just wait."

Wesley slowly lifted his head and stared into Nancy's eyes. They'd never stood this close. She wasn't sure what to do. She wanted to take a step back, to distance herself. She didn't.

"Miss York, unless you have a better idea, which I will gladly consider, I'm going to wait until he comes home, then he and I will have a talk until we can reach an understanding of what his actions have done to all of us."

His blue eyes seemed kind enough, but the elevated tone of his voice cautioned her.

"I am to blame…we are to blame, Mr. Taggart, for his running away."

"You and I were in a heated debate, but that's no excuse for Gary leaving these grounds without permission."

"I disagree."

"You're entitled to your opinions, Miss York, but we need to be mature enough to admit it when we realize we're wrong."

"Wrong? When a six year old is out there somewhere in the wild, alone and soon in darkness, isn't it right to search until you find him?"

"There's a difference in being lost and not wanting to be found. Gary's quite familiar with the community. He's not lost. Troubled, but not lost. The animals need fed. They can't do that on their own, can they? Gary can come home anytime he pleases. And he will."

"So he has run away before?" She instinctively reached out and gently touched his shoulder but quickly withdrew her hand.

"No, he's never run away."

The answer surprised her. "So how can you be sure he'll come home?"

"For six years I have given him my unconditional love. Anything less and I'd be worried. Love will win in the end." He paused. Nancy didn't respond. "I must be going. There are chores to do."

Nancy didn't know what to say or do. *Should I follow him? Should I go search for Gary?* She did neither. Rather, she simply stared after Mr. Taggart as he walked away, his head erect. *His steps seem sure enough. But his heart? What about his heart? Is it hardened? Is it aching? Broken?* She couldn't tell.

CHAPTER SIXTEEN

~

They came without hesitation. Their steps crushed leaves, snapped fallen limbs and scraped the briary thickets. They headed straight for the rock. Gary crouched lower in his hideout, trying to bury his body in the leaves.

Gary could hear their heavy breathing, winded from the climb. He slowly moved his head into a position in which he could see who they were. They climbed onto the top of Coffin Rock and sat down in a circle, cross-legged, Indian style. Worn stocking caps with holes cut out for eyes and mouth concealed their faces. Why? They weren't real Indians.

Someone finally spoke. "If' anyone tells, they're gonna pay. Understand?" The stocking cap muffled his words.

Evidently he's their leader. But who is he? The voice seemed familiar.

Gary scratched at the tip of his nose with his shirtsleeve, careful to make no noise.

"We're all in this thing together," the leader said demandingly. "Nobody can back out now."

He sat with his back toward Gary, and it was difficult to catch every word. The others hardly spoke. When they did, it was mostly in agreement with the leader.

Sweat trickled down Gary's forehead, the salt stinging his eyes. A bee buzzed around his head, while a mosquito buried its sucker deep into a vein in his right arm. He wanted to swat at both, but he dare not make any sudden movements. He tilted his arm against the leaf-covered ground, and the mosquito took flight. He blew at the bee, but it would not quit buzzing his head.

The scene of the blood on the rock flashed before him. Saliva formed in his mouth. He felt queasy again. Not a good time to throw up. His skin itched everywhere. He wanted to be home. He knew his family would wonder about him. Nanny Sue would have a dozen questions. What would Daddy do? He'd never run away before.

The leader stopped in mid-sentence as a commotion broke out down the hillside. The group hustled to their feet and waited—obviously anxious. Gary craned to see what was happening. Soon another hooded boy crashed through the brush toward them, waving frantically. Is he their lookout? What's happening?

"Someone's comin' up the hill right over yonder." He pointed. Gary instinctively turned in the direction he was pointing. Nothing.

"Follow me," the leader commanded.

They leaped from the rock and scrambled through the brambles faster than a rabbit chased by a hound dog. Gary could hear them yelping a good hundred yards off as briars slashed their arms and cut through their pant legs.

He waited in the underbrush. The lookout was right, for footsteps crushed the leaves, coming his direction. He breathed slowly as he raised his head ever so slightly, trying to see who, or what, approached. A bedraggled Sigel Diddle meandered up the path. Gary was somewhat relieved it wasn't a stranger, but he didn't trust Sigel. Folks talked about him having a mean streak in his docile nature, whatever docile meant. He knew it couldn't be good when talking about Sigel.

Sigel carried a brown paper bag in one hand and a walking stick in the other. He stopped at the rock, laid the sack atop it and propped the stick against the mossy side. He climbed onto the rock, took one look at the blood and climbed back down. He grabbed his paper sack off the rock and looked around, finally choosing a smaller rock on which to sit.

Sigel deliberately opened the paper bag, reached inside and pulled out its contents.

Gary smelled the pickled bologna even from a distance. He felt queasy again. He liked pickled bologna, but he couldn't get the sight of the blood out of his mind, so he couldn't imagine eating bologna ever again. The crunch of crackers, what Nanny Sue usually gave him for an upset stomach, made him squeamish.

Sigel smacked his lips and licked his fingers. He cleverly snapped the cap off an RC Cola bottle by using the edge of a rock. He chugged half the contents in one swig. Sigel wiped his mouth with the back of his hand. He drank the last of the RC Cola, wadded the paper bag and tossed it onto the ground and stuck the empty bottle into his hip pocket. Gary suddenly felt thirsty. He had never known a meal to last so long. His cramped body longed to straighten.

Sigel pulled a pouch of tobacco from his shirt pocket and slowly rolled and lit a cigarette from which he inhaled deep and long. Rings of smoke drifted upward as he allowed puffs of smoke to escape his oval-pursed lips, like a catfish blowing bubbles as it scavenged along the river bottom.

Gary knew he couldn't hold out much longer in his cramped and motionless position. How long will he stay here? Perhaps I should come out of hiding and pretend nothing is wrong. What would Sigel think about me being here at the rock? How could I explain the blood on the rock? Would Sigel accuse me of something bad? He couldn't defend himself. His head spun. All this was too much to think about.

The sun dropped behind the distant mountain. Darkness would come quickly.

Sigel stood, inhaled one last drag, flipped the burning butt onto the ground and continued along the path. Gary felt relief, then panic. Flames quickly spread in the dry leaves. He wanted to call after Sigel for help in extinguishing the flames, to let him know he'd started a fire. He couldn't. Words simply wouldn't come out of his mouth. Then again, for some reason, he feared Sigel. Maybe Sigel intended to start the fire for meanness.

Gary raised onto all fours, inching forward quietly. When Sigel was a good fifty yards distance, he sprang from his hiding place and stomped furiously at the flames. The fire spread quickly in the dry leaves, leaping upward from the leaves and onto the low brush, chasing him back. He couldn't control the rapidly spreading flames. He needed help. He needed to go for help. What if someone thought he started the fire? How could he explain? Would they believe him?

He started down the path but chose to abandon the curving trail and take the shortest route, straight downhill. Prickly shrubs slashed at his face as he dashed through the brambles. He didn't stop until the house was in sight. Nanny Sue rose to meet him as he rushed into the yard. She descended the steps and he leaped into her outstretched arms.

"About time you returned," she said gruffly. "I was startin' to worry. Where you been at, child? Your daddy's been huntin' for you. Might as well go get your own switch."

With everything in him, he wanted to speak, to tell the truth. He wanted to get help to put out the fire. He couldn't speak, and if he could, he was afraid to tell the truth, for he was afraid no one would believe him. They'd think he set the fire for spite.

Nanny Sue's mixed expression of anger and concern suddenly changed to surprise. "Oh no." She pointed toward the cloud of smoke billowing from the mountainside. "Lordy have mercy. There must be a fire on Coffin Mountain. Gary, go fetch your daddy. He's at the barn feedin' the black. He'll know what to do"

Gary glanced at Miss York who exited the front door. He watched her walk to the edge of the porch, staring up the mountain. As she descended the steps, her eyes fastened on his. He couldn't help but notice something peculiar about the way she looked at him as he hurried past her to get his daddy.

CHAPTER SEVENTEEN

~

Nancy stood vigil late into the night. Wondering. Praying. A welcomed thunderstorm enhanced the efforts of the volunteers; by midnight the fire succumbed to the downpour and the efforts of the ragtag crew. The morning light revealed an area of scarred black mountainside with patches of smoldering logs, but the community was fortunate the entire mountain hadn't been lost.

Due to many of the older boys fighting the fire, she canceled school for the day. Wesley didn't go to work, a rarity. After breakfast Nancy joined Gary on the front porch where they sat alone. She broached the subject of the fire. "Too bad about the fire. Lots of trees were lost. Could have been worse."

Gary wouldn't look at her. He busied himself with a logroller, practicing a backspin.

"You need to take care of those scratches on your arms."

Gary didn't seem to hear.

"When you returned home yesterday, your face had what looked like a soot mark, and your shoes were covered with black ashes. How do you explain that?"

Gary stared at the ground in silence.

"You were gone a long time yesterday, returning home just before Nanny Sue sighted the fire. Do you know anything about how the fire got started?"

The anguished look on Gary's face revealed guilt. Nancy wished he could speak to her, to offer some explanation for the fire. Surely it was not deliberately started.

"A simple headshake yes, or no. Do you know who started the fire?"

No response.

"Did you start the fire?" she prodded.

Distress showed on Gary's face, but he shook his head no. He hadn't started the fire.

"Then how do you explain the soot on your face and the ashes on your shoes?"

Gary stared toward the mountainside.

Nancy didn't hide her displeasure.

He wiped at his eyes.

"I have to tell your father."

His mouth opened as he tried to speak. Silence.

"I'm sorry, but such an act cannot go unmentioned."

"Nnnn...nnnn...nooo!" Gary managed a slightly audible response.

Nancy was taken aback. She was shocked and pleased. She was also disappointed.

"So you can talk when you want."

His mouth opened again, but no words came out.

Nancy embraced him. His body stiffened. "Gary, I'm thrilled to hear you speak, even if it's only one word, but that doesn't change the fact I believe you started the fire, maybe not deliberately, but nonetheless you started it, and your father should know."

Gary turned away from her.

"What if someone else gets blamed for the fire? Jack will probably be blamed. He already has two strikes against him."

Gary clenched his fists and tried to speak, but nothing came out. He ran up the steps and into the house. Nancy heard him slam his bedroom door just as Wesley appeared in the front doorway. Having dropped dead tired onto the sofa from the exhausting firefight, his face still showed soot smears; gray ash frosted his otherwise dark wavy hair. He rubbed at his bloodshot eyes.

"What was that all about?"

"We need to talk. Can we take a walk?"

"I'd be delighted. Have you ever seen the black up close?"

Nancy hesitated.

"Have you ever touched a horse, Miss York?"

"No, I haven't. Can you believe that?"

"Then it's time you made a new friend."

CHAPTER EIGHTEEN

~

Nancy and Wesley strolled the narrow river-stone path that led to the barn. Neither spoke. Surprisingly, Wesley hummed a tune as they walked side by side. *Love Me Tender*. She recognized the tune, having recently heard it on the parlor radio. The DJ had announced a million fans had pre-ordered Mr. Presley's single release. Wesley must have heard the song also. She couldn't be sure Wesley's tune was *Love Me Tender*, for it could be *Aura Lea*, the tune of a Civil War song of which Mr. Presley's song was fashioned. That was more likely what he hummed, for he was too busy working to be listening to the radio. Still, he could be humming *Army Blue*, the marching band version, for after all, he had been in the military. Was it *Love Me Tender*? She felt her face blush; she tried to conceal such by looking away from him. Why was she blushing?

The stallion whinnied as they approached the barn.

"The black actually likes me to hum to him," Wesley said. "It seems to settle him right down."

"Really?"

So he was actually humming to his horse? Why would I assume he was humming for my benefit? Why should I care? He's probably ten years my senior. But why do I care? I hope my face doesn't reveal my annoyance.

"Good boy, black." Wesley patted the horse's neck. The black stomped the straw-strewn dirt floor, as if ready to be off. "What's on your mind, Miss York?" Wesley continued a slow stroking of the black's mane.

Nancy straightened the sleeves to her blouse, searching for the right words. He's not ready for this. For once he seems happy, but now this. Oh, well. Here goes.

"It's Gary. I'm concerned about him." She paused. Wesley looked straight at her. "I'm concerned he…"

A commotion from the house interrupted Nancy's sentence. They exited the barn to see Nanny Sue rushing toward them.

"Something's wrong." Wesley dashed to meet Nanny Sue.

Nancy hesitated. What can the emergency be? Has Gary done something to himself? It's my fault. "No, Lord, please let Gary be okay," she muttered as she chased after Wesley.

Nanny Sue had stopped partway down the path. Wesley hovered over her, waiting for her to speak. She held up a hand as she gasped for air. Wesley patted her on the back, waiting.

"Asthma," Wesley explained. "You know better than to run like that, Nanny Sue. You're pale as a ghost." She continued to gasp for air. "Relax. Slower breathing."

"What can I do?" Nancy had never seen such gasping for air.

"She'll be okay."

She held up a finger, her gasping subsiding, and straightened from her bent over position. "Sorry. I'm…sorry to…give you…such a…fright…Miss York."

"What's happened?" Wesley asked.

"Is Gary okay?" Nancy blurted out. Wesley looked at her quizzically. She averted his gaze.

"Gary's fine…but Granny…Brewer…she's gone." She still struggled for air.

Nancy felt relief Gary was okay. Still, she empathized with Nanny Sue's obvious sadness. She gently embraced her wheezing body. Wesley stared into the distance. Silent. Stoic. What is he thinking? Nancy couldn't detect any sign of emotion in him. That puzzled her.

CHAPTER NINETEEN

~

Granny Brewer was the late Mrs. Taggart's mother. Though Wesley invited her to live with them, she preferred her independence and kept house south of the community. Nancy hadn't met her, and for that she was sorry, for the family spoke often of her and with affection. Neighbors stopped by the Taggart residence to express their sympathy and to drop off a covered dish. Nancy observed. And wrote. She questioned Mr. Taggart's reticent demeanor. Why no expression of sorrow? I can tell he's hurting, yet he doesn't express his pain. Is this a male thing? How would Daddy respond? She had no occasion to know, for her family had lost no one close. This was unchartered water emotionally and culturally.

Joyce, being the antithesis of her father, talked relentlessly. Her affable nature worked like a magnet, drawing children and adults into conversation as they stopped by to share their condolences. In between guests she shared with Nancy information about her grandma and how much she loved her. Talking seemed to help her deal with the death.

Nancy's gravest concern was for Gary. Teary eyed, he remained by himself on the front porch. If only he could express his sorrow. Her heart ached for him. He had lost his mother, now his grandmother, both within a two-year span. The two women most meaningful in his life were gone. Suddenly.

Nancy tried to imagine how Gary's young mind interpreted death. The look on his face reminded her of the facial expressions she received from children when she taught geography, pointing out states and rivers and countries and the world as thread-sized lines scribbled across a map. Her lesson simply drew blank stares from younger students. It was very difficult for a child to visualize the vastness of the world. The river flowing past the back of Gary's house was no small stream, yet a thin line represented it on a geography page. That line could never begin to represent all that had transpired along its banks. Likewise, how could life, with all its purpose, end so quickly? How could a preacher's prayer begin to finalize a life? How terribly confusing death must be for a child! Nancy scribbled notes, but erased much, for how do you capture the emotion of death with pen and paper?

Though she had never lost a close family member, she found it quite natural to empathize with the Taggart family. She climbed onto a wagon pulled by a mule team to travel with the family to Granny Brewer's residence. She sat beside Joyce, who snuggled close to her on a bench in the middle of the wagon. Gary rode beside his father in the front. Nanny Sue sat in the back on a chair, holding the baby. The twins sat on a stack of boards Wesley had loaded onto the wagon, boards with which to make the coffin.

Caring neighbors met them: the men unloaded the lumber and the women helped with the children.

It seemed irreverent to ask questions as Wesley and Fulton Noble built the coffin in the front yard, and so a hundred questions remained unanswered. Why had not the undertaker removed the body? What sort of emotional damage did this scene cause the children? Where was the pastor? Had the difficulties of isolated society calloused their souls?

Joyce remained by Nancy's side, while Gary played nearby, occasionally offering a puzzled glance at the development of the coffin. Once finished, they carried the coffin to the porch, where Isabelle Clay waited with needle and thread. With gnarled and rigid fingers, she carefully lined the wooden coffin with white satin shirring, offering a trace of decorum to a wooden crate. The manner in which she folded and tucked the lining revealed this wasn't her first. A shroud of the same material draped the banister, awaiting placement around the body.

Nancy had never experienced a scene so riveting yet repellent.

The layout took place in the living room of Granny Brewer's residence. Friends and neighbors from all around came and went during the day and into the evening, bringing food and offering their condolences. The elderly sat in chairs that lined the flowery-papered wall, in no hurry to leave. A line formed at the casket and stretched into the front yard. Each consoled the other with a sincere, "She's in a better place," and "If'n anybody makes it she'll be in heaven."

Nancy endured an emotionally charged church service in the same room where the coffin sat, with a quilt Grandma Brewer had made tacked to the wall as a backdrop. Neighbors crammed wall-to-wall and overflowed into the kitchen and onto the porch.

"Is it like this in Cincinnati?" Joyce asked.

"Somewhat." Nancy stroked the locks of her soft brown hair. "Are they friends of the family? I don't think I've met them."

"Not really. Same folks always sing for funerals. Don't have to ask, cause folks know who they are and always expect them to honor the dead."

The singers seemed more than willing to perform—perhaps too eager under the circumstances.

Tradition demanded someone stay with the body all night. It was unthinkable to leave the body alone. It seemed a silly superstition to Nancy. Certainly the body wasn't going to sneak off in the night, and it was quite doubtful anyone would steal the body. More than likely, guilt was the underlying motivation. Did I do enough for them while they were alive? Perhaps if I stay with them now they'll somehow know how much I cared about them. It surprised Nancy when Mr. Taggart stayed all night with the body. She and Nanny Sue took the children home.

The official funeral took place the next day. Folks arrived early and stayed for the procession to the cemetery. Nancy stood with Joyce and Gary near the casket as Wesley mingled through the crowd thanking the folks for coming.

Joyce and Gary shadowed Nancy's every move. She caught Wesley's glance. "Thank you," he mouthed. She nodded and smiled.

"Miss York, what is death like?" Joyce asked.

Joyce's question stunned her. They huddled at her side. Without speaking she gently placed her hands on their shoulders; she could sense their confusion but plausible words eluded her. They never discussed this in college.

Joyce began to cry. Gary buried his face into her side. They seemed to sense the end.

Wesley looked their way. "Help," Nancy mouthed to him. She knelt beside Joyce and gently wiped her tears.

Joyce's body shook. Her words came between sobs. "Miss… York, when death…took our…momma, people said…she was in a… better place. I…don't know…what death…is like. Do you think…it's a…better…place?"

"Yes, heaven is better."

"What makes it better?"

"A number of things, dear."

"Does that mean Momma didn't like it here on earth? Or do people really know, cause none of them that told me heaven is better have ever been there?"

Joyce's maturity impressed her, even challenged her. Is such ripeness of mind a result of the passing of Mrs. Taggart and her having to assume an adult role within the family? Then again, perhaps Mrs. Taggart was such a wonderful mother she facilitated such advanced thinking.

"We can trust the Bible, and it says heaven is a better place." Nancy felt quite inadequate at explaining the afterlife.

"I'm scared of death. I'm scared of being alone, being without you and Daddy and Gary."

Wesley eased beside them.

"Thank you," Nancy whispered to him. "Joyce is wondering about death, and I was trying to explain it to her."

Wesley knelt and cupped Joyce's face with his hands. He hesitated a long moment, as if collecting his thoughts. "Death is like a journey, sweetheart. The journey isn't exactly the same for all, but I can tell you what it's like for your Granny Brewer and for your momma, and someday for me and you."

"I don't like death, Daddy." Joyce's tiny shoulders heaved with each sniffle. Wesley dabbed at her tears with a handkerchief.

Nancy wiped tears from her own eyes as she placed an arm around Gary's stiff shoulders and pulled him gently to her side. His body relaxed against her.

"It's okay to not like death. But don't be afraid of death. The Bible says we're buried with Christ by baptism and if we're buried with Christ we shall live with Him. Your granny was a Christian, like Momma, both baptized by Preacher Charlie. They are both in heaven with Jesus, just like the Bible says."

Wesley paused. Joyce buried her face in his chest and continued to cry. Wesley combed his fingers through her hair.

Wesley's gentle mannerisms impressed Nancy, but she questioned his theological approach to a child's confusion. She started to speak when he, too, seemed to realize his theology was way over her head. He looked at Nancy as if needing help. She offered an assuring smile.

Wesley again cupped his hands around Joyce's tear streaked face. He spoke softly. "Sweetheart, do you remember the first time I took you to town on the passenger train?"

"Yes."

Gary's face remained buried in Nancy's side. She felt his tears soaking through her black, taffeta dress. She brushed his burr cut hair with her fingers, trying to comfort him.

"Do you remember the train going through the tunnel and the passenger car becoming suddenly dark?"

"Yes, Daddy."

Nancy listened with fascination, wondering where this story was leading. She knew about the tunnel, some neighbors had told her about it. Such stories gave varying accounts of how the train company brought in Negro workers on boxcars from down south, bodies crammed inside like cattle. They dug the tunnel with picks and shovels through the mountain just outside Jackson. When they finished, the railroad company took the Negroes away, but the fact the black men dug the tunnel left lingering, irrational tales among the hill folks. The spirits of the Negroes killed by the torturous labor still wander that dark and damp tunnel in search of their far away home place.

Wesley's consoling voice recaptured Nancy's wandering thoughts.

"Do you remember we soon escaped the darkness of the tunnel, into light—a radiance that seemed suddenly brighter than the morning sunrise?"

Joyce nodded. Her sobbing had ceased.

Wesley paused and gently dabbed the tears streaking Joyce's red-blotched cheeks.

"It was but a brief moment, and we exited on the other side of the mountain." His voice was soft but certain.

"I remember, Daddy."

"That's what death is like. It's a journey through momentary darkness to exit into brilliant light on the other side of the mountain."

"Is that heaven?"

"Yes, dear. That's heaven. Granny is with Momma in heaven."

Joyce smiled. Nancy was glad.

Conversation from the crowd suddenly subsided. Preacher Charlie stood near the casket behind a makeshift podium. He cleared his throat. "Could ever' body take a seat?"

The people hastened to the various assortment of chairs crowded into the room. Some stood along the walls and in doorways. The funeral singers sung again. And again. Preacher Charlie began his funeral message with a passage of hope from one of the Apostle Paul's epistles, weaving the verses into a eulogy of "Sister Brewer's faithfulness to the Lord after she was converted." He closed with prayer, then turned to Wesley, who organized the pallbearers around the casket. Preacher Charlie led the procession, filing past the wall of staring faces. They struggled getting the casket through the front door but successfully maneuvered the casket and loaded it onto a sled harnessed to ole Jack, Preacher Charlie's funeral mule. A neighbor, Saul Clay, held the reigns.

The crowd trailed the sled as it glided over the moist ground. Half an hour later the procession passed through the dilapidated wooden gate of the cemetery. Stately pine trees, like seraphim, kept watch over the sacred ground. A gnarled and knotted pine, lightning struck and wind whipped, gave witness to the reality of life. Death.

"Whoa," Saul Clay pulled back on the reigns. Otherwise, silence reigned.

A mound of freshly scooped soil, with shovels standing erect, identified the gravesite. The men lifted the pine box from the sled and placed it on boards laid across the open grave dug by volunteer neighbors.

Saul and Fulton Noble removed the lid from the casket. Everyone filed by a final time, slowly, expressing their grief in various ways: a gentle touch of Granny Brewer's clasped hands, a sudden outburst of tears, a stoic stare. Wesley, Joyce and Gary were the last to file by. At the children's insistence, Nancy walked with them. They took their place at the front of the crowd. Workers replaced the lid on the casket, and Fulton sealed the box shut with the horseshoe nails that rattled in his coat pocket with each hammer blow. Joyce clung to her daddy's hand. Nancy soothingly stroked Gary's back as he hid his face against her side. Preacher Charlie prayed. Calloused hands lowered the box into the hole. Nancy felt Gary's body wince at the sounds of clumped dirt hitting the casket.

The crowd slowly dispersed. The Taggart family lingered, gazing at the mound of dirt.

"We best be going," Wesley said. "Nanny Sue probably needs us by now." She had stayed at the Brewer residence with the younger children

They left Granny Brewer there in the yellow clay alongside the grave of Mrs. Taggart, high on the hilltop overlooking the Noble Farm.

Wesley carried Gary atop his broad shoulders. Nancy walked hand in hand with Joyce, a few steps behind. She dreaded telling Wesley about Gary starting the fire. She knew she must, but it could wait until a better day.

CHAPTER TWENTY

~

Saturday brought routine back to the North Fork. Nancy appreciated the opportunity to reflect and write. She sat quietly observing the nearby activity. Across the tracks, Silvia Combs, clothed in a faded, feed sack dress, and shielded from the sun by her favorite bonnet, shucked corn alongside her aging husband. A child cradled a Raggedy Ann doll as her "bubby" pulled her in a beat-up Radio Flyer along the cinder path alongside the train track. The last of the migrating butterflies, the orange and black monarch, fluttered about a patch of milkweed. Nanny Sue sat on the front porch vigorously churning the cream scooped from the top of a milk jar. She seemed in a foul mood, an uncommon disposition for her. Giggs' barking had awakened the household too early for a Saturday. Nanny Sue had commented she was sure it was George Lee that disturbed the dog. "Trespassing again," she had grumbled.

Gary sat on the front steps. His fishing pole lay across his lap, a forlorn look evident on his face.

Joyce sang softly to the baby as she rocked him in a cane-bottomed oak rocker on the front porch. The twins twirled in circles on the front lawn, hand in hand, like a dog chasing its tail.

Nancy observed these events from the homemade swing that dangled from an apple tree in the front yard: Nanny Sue stewing, Joyce developing her motherly instincts, the twins frolicking on the lawn and Gary cradling his cane pole, glancing occasionally in the direction of his father's salt mine. Wesley had left early.

Today was the last of the weeklong challenge of their annual fishing contest. Wesley had enthusiastically explained it always ended with a neighborhood fish fry in the evening. Per Wesley's explanation, he had entered his name in the contest but had endured a hectic week at the mine without even baiting a hook. Rumor had it George Lee was in the lead by a few dozen fish. Was Wesley working or fishing? If fishing, why didn't he take Gary along? The lad needed his father's attention.

Nancy had enjoyed Wesley's dinner conversations about the annual event and how he won on occasion. He gave her an insightful geography lesson of the North Fork. Of all the places along the hundred and twenty-five miles of the North Fork, the Taggart property bordered one of the best stretches for fishing. In many places the North Fork flowed shallow in the dry season; pools of tepid and stagnant water hailed as mosquito havens. Conversely, the stretch of water running along the Taggart property ran cool and deep through the palisades, shaded by the stately pines perched atop the towering cliffs overlooking the water. It was good to talk about something less controversial.

Nancy couldn't help but chuckle as Nanny Sue inserted her opinions about the contest. George Lee claimed to be the best fisherman in the community. Somehow, he could catch fish when others couldn't. He never offered to share, but he did like to brag.

Today Nanny Sue was rankled and in no mood for a braggart, especially one that had awakened them before sunup and had caught his fish from the Taggart riverbank.

Giggs' ears perked. George Lee soon appeared from the riverbank, walking across the Taggart's property. He held up a string of fish. "What do y'all think of these beauties?"

"I think you're the next thing to a thief, George Lee, fishin' from Wesley's riverbank while he's working all day." Nanny Sue snapped.

"What do you care if I catch your fish? Y'all don't never fish none. Anyway, you're just disappointed 'cause I outfished Wesley."

"If you'd get your lazy bones a job and do a real-to-goodness honest day's work like Wesley Taggart, you wouldn't have time for loafin' on the river bank all day." Nanny Sue continued to hit him square between the eyes with her condemnation. She probably wanted to use the churn handle, but he was a safe distance from her reach. Boy was she ever ticked!

George Lee changed the subject quicker than a chased rabbit in a cabbage patch changed direction. "When's Wesley comin' home?"

"What you wantin' to know for? You needin' your corn shucked?"

"Didn't mean to upset you so, Nanny Sue. Just wonderin' if he'll make it for the fish fry."

She momentarily stopped churning, though her hand held a firm grip on the handle. George Lee mumbled something about his bad back and skedaddled toward home.

Nanny Sue settled back into her churning.

Nancy smiled to herself as she scribbled in her notepad.

"Nanny Sue, can Gary go fishin' today?" Joyce interrupted the silence.

"Too young to go fishin' by himself."

"He's almost seven. Lloyd Combs is seven and his momma lets him go fishin' alone."

"Lloyd Combs' momma can do what she well pleases, but I ain't her and Gary ain't him."

"Shucks. Can't you see he's bored out of his tree?"

"Your daddy told you not to use that word, child. Too close to cussin'."

"Sorry. Can't Gary go just this once?"

"How could I ever face your daddy if he drowned?"

"He ain't gonna drown."

"I'd feel better if your daddy was here."

"You know Daddy don't never have time to take him fishin'."

"Don't you talk mean about your daddy."

The argument subsided. Joyce continued rocking the baby.

A sudden explosion shattered the tranquility of the otherwise perfect afternoon. A thousand birds took to the sky and a million katydids abruptly stopped their tune, as if the conductor had stopped the orchestra in mid concert. The explosion came from the direction of the river, upstream. Nancy and Nanny Sue rushed to the frightened twins, Joyce cradled the screaming baby, but Gary dashed toward the river.

"Wait up," Joyce yelled, handing the baby to Nanny Sue, and dashing after Gary.

"I'll stay with the children," Nanny Sue said to Nancy.

Nancy chased after Joyce and Gary, who scrambled down the embankment ahead of her. Once at the water's edge, they huddled. Nothing seemed amiss. Minutes passed before they saw an array of approaching objects floating from upstream: pieces of wood, various shapes and sizes of plastic bottles and a black container bobbing sideways as it took on water.

"Isn't that Daddy's lunch box?" Joyce asked.

"That could be anybody's lunch box." Nancy tried to calm their fears.

The black container drifted toward them like the sole surviving flagship of a shattered armada. Nancy found a slender stick, slipped off her shoes, waded knee deep into the water and retrieved the crumpled lunch box. She held the container for the others to see.

"Like I said, this could be anybody's lunch pail." She turned the box upside down, inspecting it. The initials W T appeared on the bottom.

"It's Daddy's lunch box," Joyce said. "Something's happened to Daddy."

Nancy didn't answer. Her mind raced with multiple questions as she stood in the waters edge, cradling the box.

The splashing of water and the scraping of wood against wood caught their attention. They stared upstream and soon spotted a boat rounding the bend.

"It's Daddy," Joyce exclaimed.

Wesley sat in the stern of the boat, brandishing a victor's smile. The gunnels rode low in the water and a pile of fish filled the center of the boat. His fishing line trawled behind, a red and white bobber popping under and out of the water intermittently.

Their suspense turned to cheers. Nancy's apprehension turned to tears. Gary waded into the water alongside her, grinning profusely. Wesley paddled the boat toward them. Gary grabbed the front end and guided it to the shore.

"Need you to get me a couple wash buckets, Joyce. We're going to have the best fish fry ever tonight."

Joyce clapped her hands with delight while Gary began to unload the fish onto the sand.

"Scared us half to death, Daddy. Why didn't you tell us you was going to use dynamite? We heard the explosion all the way to the house. You okay?" Joyce asked, short of breath.

"I was careful, sweetheart."

"How did your lunch box get so mangled?"

"I accidental knocked it off the boat before I set the charge."

"I'm glad you're safe." Joyce hugged him around the waist. He patted the top of her head.

"Mr. Taggart, I can't believe this," Nancy scolded. She tossed the lunch box into the boat.

"I was careful, Miss York. As a geologist, I'm trained in explosives."

"Not that, sir."

"Then what?"

"That you stooped to such means to get these fish."

"Necessity is the mother of invention, don't they say?"

"This is not invention, Mr. Taggart. This is…this is horrible."

"Invention or not, Miss York, this community will have plenty to eat tonight. Not one of these fish will be wasted."

"Now go get those wash buckets, Joyce."

Joyce started toward the house. Nancy turned abruptly and ascended the path after her.

CHAPTER TWENTY-ONE

~

The evening grew hot and humid. Folks from all around gathered at the Copeland station where kettles sizzled as the men dropped battered fish into boiling lard. Groups formed and some lounged on blankets spread on the lawn; a few brought chairs. A dozen sleds and wagons dotted the landscape; the horses and mules grazed alongside the railroad track, tethered to a makeshift hitching post.

After the meal, the adults gathered in conversation groups while the teens formed a circle and played drop the hanky. The children played tag. A few of the boys engaged in a heated game of marbles. Gary wandered from group to group. Listening, but never engaging. He knew people saw him as totally occupied with the whittling he started doing lately. But he was more than whittling. It was a way of figuring out things in his mind. He could whittle and listen at the same time, and nobody seemed to notice.

"Never sold so many notepads in my life," Ida Mae commented to Nancy. They sat with a group of women who seemed eager to learn more about the new school teacher.

"I find it fascinating to write about this community, Ida Mae. I've never attended a fish fry."

Nancy talked with the students' mothers, each shaking her hand and thanking her for teaching her child. Most everyone posed for a picture with her, reluctantly, talking about how their hair was a mess, or their clothes weren't pretty enough, but always seeming pleased to have their picture taken with the new teacher. Gary hoped all this excitement made Miss York forget about the fire on Coffin Rock Mountain.

"Nancy, you've got to promise we'll all make it into your scrapbook." Ida Mae's excitement was obvious. "I hope you speak kindly 'bout us in your writings."

"She will, Ida Mae." Throughout the evening Joyce hadn't left Nancy's side.

Nancy smiled.

Gary remained a short distance, always in earshot. Observing.

"Can we talk privately," Joyce whispered to Nancy.

Nancy took Joyce by the hand and they stepped away from the crowd. Gary inched close enough to hear.

"You was a little rough on Daddy, today."

"You think so?"

"I do."

"So do you approve of such techniques of fish massacre?"

"Not what you think."

"Not what I think? I saw it with my own eyes. He slaughtered a whole school of fish with dynamite. That's got to be illegal, and if not illegal, it's certainly unfair sportsmanship."

Gary wanted to defend his daddy. Tell her what really happened.

"You saw a boatload of dead fish. Daddy didn't kill them intentionally. He went to catch some fish for the fry and found them trapped in a swamp by last spring's driftwood, going to most likely die. So daddy just blew open a path so they could escape into the main stream. Things didn't go quite like he planned and, of course, a lot of fish got killed, but a lot of them escaped into fresh water, too."

Nancy stared at Joyce. "I can't believe I jumped to such conclusions. Forgive me, dear. I'll apologize to your daddy."

"He thinks it's funny."

"Really?"

"Yes." Joyce laughed.

Nancy smiled but didn't respond.

Gary was proud of Joyce for standing up to Miss York. He followed as they walked back to the crowd, walking slowly, trying not to be noticed. Whittling. Listening. Figuring. Wondering. Miss York glanced at him and smiled. He stopped whittling. Maybe she isn't going to tell Daddy about the fire. He smiled back and continued his whittling.

I'm glad Miss York realizes she made a mistake about Daddy. Maybe now she'll figure out she's made a mistake about me starting the fire. He continued to carve at the piece of driftwood he'd taken from the water the day he helped his daddy unload the fish.

The wind picked up. A storm threatened. Dark clouds rolled over the mountaintops, dropping heavy air into the valley. An uncanny darkness prevailed. The party came to a halt as some of the neighbors hastened home, trying to beat the rain, while others sought shelter nearby. Gary paused from his whittling, closed his knife blade, placed it into his front pocket and stuck the driftwood into his hip pocket. He hastened to shelter underneath the porch of the Deaton store. The adults ran up the steps. Gary could hear the clicking of the ladies' heels against the hardwood floor of the general store, while the men stood on the porch spinning yarns about the worst storm they'd ever endured. Their volume rose louder as each tried to be heard over the pounding rain. Some of the boys joined Gary's shelter. It felt awkward to him as they crowded underneath the porch. He liked being alone, for he didn't have to try to talk. Now they'd ask him questions and laugh at him when he tried to answer. He wanted to leave, but the blowing wind and rain was frightening. Hailstones the size of marbles beating onto the metal roof sounded like a thousand drums. The boys occasionally pushed an unsuspected one into the downpour, then tried to keep him from reentering the shelter, all the while giggling and taunting good naturedly.

The rain stopped as suddenly as it came. The air heated back up quickly. Steam rose from the railroad tracks. It reminded Gary of the dust clouds that formed when Nanny Sue beat the rugs hung out on the clothesline. The younger boys left the sanctuary underneath the porch. The games resumed. Gary resumed his whittling underneath the porch. Listening to the conversation above him.

"Me and the wife like her a lot, Wesley, but we just don't quite know what to make of her 'sinuations that we suffer emotionally and intellectually from isolation," someone said.

"She's suggestin' things that would make life hard for us: like our pigpens located farther from the house. Why walk a mile to slop hogs when you can throw food to them over the back fence?" another argued.

Gary listened intently from underneath the porch. Are they talking about Miss York? He didn't want to think badly about her, but he also felt she sure got nosey at times. When he thought like this, he wanted to run away. He thought again about Coffin Rock, about the blood, about the secret meeting and the fire. It hurt him that Miss York thought he started the fire. He wished he could explain it to her. Would she believe me?

Bottle rockets suddenly streaked across the sky and exploded in midair. Somewhere in the distance someone lit a whole pack of firecrackers. The sky blazed with celebration. The traditional fall fish fry was another success.

Gary observed from underneath the porch. He felt safer there. He didn't need to be with the other boys; he didn't have to endure others talking down to him. He suddenly realized the men had stopped talking.

Gary looked about. A lone figure emerged from the darkness, walking briskly toward them along the railroad tracks.

"Walks like Hiram Callahan," someone overhead said.

Gary's pulse quickened. He felt his heart beating in his ears. Boards squeaked overhead as men stood and walked to the edge of the porch, probably getting a better look at the approaching stranger. Gary peered from underneath the porch trying to see his daddy. He glanced in the direction of the approaching figure looming from the darkness.

"I heard he was up for parole," his daddy said.

"If I never seen him again in this community, it'd be all right with me," another commented.

"You okay, Wes?" someone asked.

His daddy didn't answer.

CHAPTER TWENTY-TWO

~

It pleased Nancy to be in church again; it especially pleased her to have Joyce snuggled beside her. Gary, though beside her, kept a cool distance. Wesley had left early for work at the mine. That concerned her, not only his absence from church on the Lord's Day, but the long hours at work and his absence from the children. She knew she had to speak to him about Gary starting the fire.

"It's 'bout time to start the service." Preacher Charlie stepped to the crudely built wooden pulpit. "We're askin' the singers and musicians to take their places and get us started."

Nancy recognized the singers; they were the ones who sang at the funeral. She reached for a hymnbook that rested in a rack on the back of the rough slatted benches. The inside of the book fell to the floor, leaving her holding the cover. Gary scurried to her rescue, retrieved the songbook and handed it to her.

"Thank you," Nancy mouthed to him.

He smiled.

"We wanna thank everybody for comin' out this mornin'," one of the singers said.

The musicians did a last minute tuning of their guitars as one of the singers exhorted the folks to worship.

Nancy surveyed the humble building. The potbelly stove in the middle of the room partially blocked her view of the platform. The water bucket sitting on a table in front of the pulpit amused her. She could have assumed it to be a part of the religious ceremony, perhaps for communion, had not it looked exactly like the one at the schoolhouse, plus the children were constantly enjoying its contents. She thought of her home church back in Cincinnati and envisioned her mom and dad sitting in the same pew her grandparents had occupied since the congregation erected the Gothic style building in 1927. As a teenager, Nancy enjoyed studying the colorful "Living Christ" stained glass window over the altar. She had attended the same church since childhood.

A "Praise the Lord" and a "Hallelujah" ricocheted from the unfinished hardboard ceiling of the church. A sleeping baby, startled awake, joined the fray. Nancy impulsively placed her arms around Joyce and Gary, pulling them closely to her side. Is it my responsibility to protect them, or to ease my personal sense of discomfort? She brushed the thought aside as being silly. It is neither. She released her grip on their shoulders and tried to relax.

Nancy flipped through the hymnal; she recognized some of the more traditional songs.

A tambourine jingled. Nancy smiled. The Wurlitzer in her home church boasted four manuals and ten thousand pipes.

The singing began, but not from the hymnal. It seemed a medley of *My Mother's Bible, Hide Me Rock of Ages* and *Where the Soul Never Dies.* The tempo didn't change; neither did the key. Two guitars and three tambourines kept the pace lively.

Testimony time followed. Joyce stood.

"Joyce, you wanna say something for the Lord?" Surprise showed on Preacher Charlie's face.

"I want to thank the Lord for our new teacher." She sat down quickly.

"Praise the Lord," a few shouted. Others replied with a hearty "Amen."

A dozen heads turned and stared at Nancy. She didn't know if she should respond. She wasn't accustomed to a testimony service. She smiled at the audience and nodded a greeting.

The audience clapped. Nancy blushed.

A few adults stood and testified of the goodness of the Lord. Some talked about their problems. Preacher Charlie looked at his pocket watch and cleverly changed the order of the service. "Time to take the offering." Nancy heard the clinking of change as parishioners walked to the front and dropped their offering into small baskets Preacher Charlie set on each side of the podium. Nancy opened her purse and handed Gary a dollar and nodded toward the offering. He rushed to the front with the offering and returned smiling. The singers returned for *Amazing Grace*. Nancy joined in; her participation seemed to please Joyce and Gary.

Preacher Charlie rose again and walked slowly to the pulpit, where he placed his large unopened Bible onto the podium.

"*Jonah, the Whale Bait,* is my sermon title this morning."

Interesting title. Nancy suppressed the urge to smile.

He opened his Bible and methodically thumbed through the pages and began reading from the Book of Jonah. Nancy opened her Bible and found the passage. She shared her Bible with Joyce and Gary.

The sermon began at a slow pace: Jonah's background, occupation and call to preach to Nineveh, but it gained momentum as the rebellious prophet of the Lord stepped foot on the wrong boat. The ability of Preacher Charlie to make the story so animated surprised Nancy, whose imagination perked up. The narrative took her back in space and time, where once again the waves crashed against the ship bound for Tarshish, crushing man and mast, spewing froth and seaweed, generating terror beyond reason.

With his fist punching skyward into the atmosphere, Preacher Charlie punctuated the damnation of those who flout God's commands, and he pronounced judgment to the defiant.

"God calls to the Jonahs of this day also. The largemouth whales of hell are on their way to claim their prize. You ain't nothin' short of whale bait if you don't turn your life around and give your heart to Jesus."

A moment of silence passed as Preacher Charlie gulped in needed air. It gave room for a supportive "Amen" from the congregation.

"A fathomless sea of red hot fire prepared for the devil and his angels 'waits the disobedient; the fated ship of stubbornness will carry you there."

Sweat coursed down Preacher Charlie's face as if he, instead of Jonah, stood on the deck of the sea-sprayed ship tossed about like a twig in a vortex. Moans from the audience simulated the hopeless state of the doomed on board this hell-bound vessel.

Preacher Charlie abruptly stopped. He stepped from behind the pulpit and made a final plea to the sinners. The room grew quiet. "Let's pray."

Nancy bowed her head in reverence but sneaked a peek at the audience. An ashen-faced Jonah, Nancy didn't know his real name, slipped from the pew, made his way to the deck of the ship and knelt at the captain's feet. With lips quivering like a pin oak leaf in winter, he confessed.

"It's me. I'm the lowdown scoundrel that's been a runnin' from the Lord. I'm tired of runnin'. I ain't gonna run no more. If God will forgive me now, I'll never run again."

Preacher Charlie quoted Jesus' instruction of heaven rejoicing over one sinner coming to repentance. The audience reflected the response of heaven, and they gathered around the repenting man to extend a hand of hope. Preacher Charlie laid his hand on the humbled Jonah and stormed hell one final time with rebukes and demands for Satan to release this poor soul.

Nancy had never before witnessed such a demonstrative expression from churchgoers. It left her with mixed emotions. Something else troubled her: the pained expression on Gary's face.

CHAPTER TWENTY-THREE

~

Nancy cradled the sleeping baby in her arms as she sipped the last of her sweet tea. Shouts and laughter from the front yard pleased her. The emotional state of the children was important to her. Nanny Sue dried the dishes and stacked them inside the cupboard.

"Thank you, for a delicious meal. I was starved." Nancy felt somewhat uncomfortable the way Nanny Sue doted on her.

"You're welcome, dear."

"Sorry you couldn't go to church with us."

"I don't like missin' church, but the baby was up most of the night."

"You should have let me take the twins."

"Mr. Taggart wouldn't hear of it. Too much bother for you. Them young'uns can try your patience."

"Does Mr. Taggart miss church often."

"Ever since Mrs. Taggart passed he's hit and miss."

"Before that?"

"At church ever' Sunday with the family."

"Do you think he's angry at God?"

"Don't rightly know. He don't say. How did you like our church?"

"It was different than I'm used to."

"I imagine so. You probably have a beautiful building. Ours ain't much to brag about."

"I'd have to admit the pews were a bit uncomfortable."

They both laughed.

"And Preacher Charlie's sermon?" Nanny Sue asked.

"Interesting."

"That's all? Just interesting? Nobody got saved?"

"Well, yes, a man went forward."

"Who was it?

"I didn't know him. He seemed dreadfully troubled by the sermon. Personally, I found the sermon to be somewhat harsh."

"I wouldn't call Preacher Charlie harsh. He's a might loud at times but not harsh."

"He does know what it takes to convert a moonshiner," a male voice interrupted the conversation.

Nancy turned to see Wesley standing in the doorway. How did he return home without their seeing him? How much of the conversation did he hear? Her face flushed.

"I don't recall seeing you in church, Mr. Taggart. How could you evaluate the sermon?" Nancy retorted.

"No, I wasn't there, but I know Preacher Charlie. And I know Harlan Carrico, he's the one converted this morning. He works for me. I've preached to him for years, but he never had much use for religion before. He's made moonshine in these parts for years, but he stopped by the mine after church to borrow a sledgehammer. He went to bust up his own still. By now he's probably home to share the news with his family, smelling of moonshine I'm sure from busting up the still, but clean as a whitewashed fence and kind as a kitten. Forever changed. Isn't that reason enough to justify Preacher Charlie's style?"

"You're right. I passed judgment where I shouldn't have done so. I'm realizing I know so little about the people of this community. Our cultures are so…so very different."

"How so?" Wesley asked more curious than confrontational.

"Well, take for example the sermon. I'm used to less invasive tactics, a more subtle and intellectual approach."

"That makes sense. Probably a lot of educated parishioners attend your church?"

"Yes."

"So information causes them to evaluate their lives, to reason."

"Of course intellectuals can sometimes be critical of Christianity. Some of my college professors challenged Christianity as a Band-aid to psychosis."

"A crutch for the weak-willed and a support group for the slow of intellect. I sat in some of those same classes myself, Miss York."

For a moment their minds seemed to blend.

"Don't you think Preacher Charlie's style of preaching might contribute to some of the professors' critical evaluations?" Nancy asked.

"I'll confess I've seen some laughable sights, even downright ignorant actions at some church events. The truth is, there are some folks in our community whose only hope is a direct confrontation for their actions by the seething sermons from Preacher Charlie. It's delightful, no matter how unorthodox, to see an addict stirred to freedom by a preacher's challenge with the gospel message of repentance. Some folks respond to a gentler voice of persuasion. Others respond to an emotional appeal. Personally? I feel too few preachers confront the real issues, like liquor and gambling. Too many preachers are like bartenders who lend a sympathetic ear to the symptoms: a marriage on the rocks or a job in jeopardy. The bartender seldom confronts the source of the trouble. He merely keeps it wiped off the counter. Some people need a foot-stomping, finger-pointing, sin-naming sermon. That's just the way it is, especially in this community. Preacher Charlie is that kind of preacher. He deserves a medal for his grit rather than ridicule for his crass approach."

"I didn't mean to ridicule."

"I'm sorry if I insinuated such. I was simply philosophizing."

"What type preacher do you respond to, Mr. Taggart?"

"Give me a finger-pointing John the Baptist. A sin-naming Preacher Charlie."

"But Jesus said 'Let him who is without sin cast the first stone,' and 'Neither do I condemn thee.'"

"True, and it worked for that situation, assuming you're referring to the woman taken in adultery. Then again, Jesus resembled Preacher Charlie when He turned over those tables in the temple and chased out the greedy-guts. That's head-butting confrontation. Don't you agree?"

"Touché." Nancy smiled.

"I understand many would disagree with Pastor Charlie's style."

"Yes, many would be offended, especially from my background."

"Of course, when a counselor confronts he's using professional techniques; a preacher is using appalling tactics. Personally, I like a preacher to challenge me, not cater to me. The latter tends to rock me to sleep."

"What about your children, Mr. Taggart? What kind of sermon do they need? Their emotions can be rather fragile."

Wesley paused. "I'll admit, kids don't always respond to sermons like adults. Some adults get mad and pout. Mostly, kids get scared and confess. If you're worried, I don't think the sermon today did any harm to my children emotionally. It'll keep the fear of God in them, and the fear of God will help keep them on the straight and narrow."

"Perhaps I should be blunt with you then, since you like such. I've been meaning to talk to you about Gary."

"What about Gary?"

"He didn't respond to the sermon today."

"And why should he? He's rather at the innocent age."

"He's the one who set the fire on Coffin Rock Mountain."

Wesley's facial expression stiffened. He glanced toward the sounds coming from the front yard where the children played in the warm afternoon sun. He contemplatively rubbed his chin with his right hand.

"Are you certain of that?"

"Yes. I confronted him, but he denied it. The facts are he was away from the house when the fire started, and when he returned home, he had soot on his shoes and face."

"I am sorry to hear that. I'll deal with Gary at once."

"There is some good news with the bad."

"And that is?

"Gary can talk. When I confronted him, he verbally denied setting the fire. He spoke only one word when he denied my accusation, but he did speak."

Wesley seemed both disappointed and surprised. He briskly exited the room and headed toward the front yard where the children played. Nancy wished she hadn't told him, at least not yet, for she knew it was partially to salvage her ego from being unable to equal Wesley in an argument. Touché back, Mr. Taggart. She had used young Gary as her pawn.

CHAPTER TWENTY-FOUR

~

Wesley took a deep breath. "Gary Eugene, come here please." He called from the bottom of the steps.

Gary cradled his baseball in his glove and walked across the lawn to his father.

"Son, I need to speak with you. Sit down."

They sat on the steps. Gary hugged his glove against his chest.

"Is there anything you need to tell me?" Wesley spoke caringly.

Gary shook his head indicating he had no idea what his dad meant. Wesley gave him ample time to think.

"Anything you may need to confess?"

Gary stared at the ground.

"Let me be more specific. Did you have anything to do with the fire on Coffin Rock Mountain?"

Gary hesitated and then shook his head no.

"You know I love you very much, don't you?"

Gary stared at his father as he shook his head yes.

"You know Miss York cares about you very much?"

Gary stared at him but didn't respond.

"Whether you know it or not, Miss York cares about you. Out of concern about your welfare, she confided in me it was you who started the fire. I'm very disappointed you didn't tell me, and I am more so disappointed that you lied to her. I understand the fire may have been an accident. Unless you tell me the truth here and now, you won't be able to attend school for one week. I won't have you sitting in her classroom pretending you're innocent and that she made up this story. If you confess now, you'll receive your switching, be confined to your room for the rest of the day and resume school tomorrow. Do you understand?"

Gary slowly shook his head yes.

"I'll ask the question only once." Wesley paused. "You will answer with a verbal yes or no, not a headshake, for Miss York also told me you can speak. Did you start the fire?"

Gary tried to speak, but no words would come out. He slowly shook his head yes.

CHAPTER TWENTY-FIVE

～

Wesley recognized his employee from a distance. He hadn't seen him for weeks. Thomas Fugate arose from the stump upon which he sat and strode toward Wesley as he dismounted the black.

"Mornin', Mr. Taggart."

"Thomas."

"I know I haven't been to work none for some time now, but it's the baby. She come a few weeks back."

Wesley detected the foul smell of liquor.

"How's Mrs. Fugate?"

"Fine."

"Then you really have no excuse except celebrating too much, do you?"

"But the baby…"

"Babies are born into the world every day. This is your third or fourth child? I can understand taking a day or two off work, but you have missed weeks without letting me know. Fortunately for us, but unfortunate for you, we've been able to make it without you, and I've decided we'll continue to do so."

"You don't understand, sir. You don't know what it's like having a baby born to this world…"

"I've had five, Thomas. The latest is almost two. I've raised her without a mother for better than a year now. I have only missed one day of work. Do you hear me, Thomas? One day. And that was for my wife's funeral."

Wesley turned and started toward the office.

"You've never had a cursed baby, Mr. Taggart."

Wesley stopped in mid-stride and slowly turned to face Thomas.

"The blue skin?"

"Yes, the cursed blue skin. You don't know what it's like to wonder if you should drown the child in Troublesome Creek to spare it a lifetime of heartache or let it live knowing the hardships it's gonna face."

Wesley placed a hand on Thomas' shoulder. "I'm sorry. I hadn't heard. I thought you had taken to drinking again. Surely you don't believe it's a curse. It's something else, a rare disease, something curable but not a curse. God doesn't do things like that."

"Whether it's a curse from God or not doesn't matter none, the child is still cursed. She'll be shunned, made fun of all her life. People are scared of'em. No man will ever want her. It's a curse, Mr. Taggart. It's the mark of Cain and everywhere she goes she's gonna be an outcast. Just like my other sons."

"I'm sorry. I truly am. I didn't realize…all three children."

"I've gotta have my job back. I'll work hard. I promise. I won't be drinkin' none either. I've learned my lesson. My family needs food, Mr. Taggart."

Thomas fell to his knees at Wesley's feet.

"Please, Mr. Taggart. Please, sir, please, God…Lord God Almighty…please, Jesus…oh God, please hear me…"

"Stop it, Thomas!" Wesley's command echoed across the valley. He slammed his fist into his open palm. He looked out across the distant horizon.

Thomas remained on his knees, his hands cupped in prayer, his body quivering.

Both remained silent.

A gray sparrow darted past and landed in the holly tree beside the doorway to the office shack. Wesley and his wife had dug up the sapling from the hillside and replanted it the first spring he opened their business. Wesley studied the bird as it flittered from limb to limb. A sparrow doesn't fall to the ground that your heavenly Father doesn't see. He breathed in deeply and slowly exhaled.

"Tell Mrs. Fugate I'd like to buy some of that buttermilk she makes and sends with you. In the meantime, draw some water for the black. I'm sure he's thirsty."

CHAPTER TWENTY-SIX

~

Wesley made it home in time for dinner with the family. The children were delighted. Gary had changed his seating and now sat beside him. Joyce took her guarded seat, beside Nancy, at the opposite end of the table. The meal was a pleasant one. The conversation went in several directions but generally came back to activities at school.

"Has Jack been back to school?" Wesley asked.

"No. I've been meaning to ask you about that. I understand he also has a younger sister who's never been to school. I was thinking of paying them a visit to see if I could get the parents to be more involved in their education."

"Joyce, you and Gary take the twins outside for awhile and get them some fresh air." Wesley observed in silence as they slowly gathered themselves from the table and rounded up the twins. They were taking longer than necessary; Wesley cleared his throat and they picked up their pace.

"Make sure the twins keep their shoes on. You know how sensitive they are to catching cold," Nanny Sue said.

Nanny Sue shooed them from the house. Nancy suddenly realized the sensitivity of the subject.

"Not a good idea," Wesley said.

"You don't think the Callahan children should be in school?"

"No, not that. It's a waste of your time to pursue such. The father won't support you."

"I'll convince the mother."

"That's not the way things are done around here. Anyway, Mrs. Callahan is deceased."

"Then I'll convince Mr. Callahan."

"Like I said, that's not a good idea."

"The worst he can do is say no. I've experienced rejection before. My ego isn't that fragile." She laughed. "I won't be crushed. I promise." She crossed her heart.

Wesley didn't smile. Her smile slowly disappeared.

"What I'm trying to tell you is it's not a good idea for you to even go to their home, let alone with a request."

"Why?"

"The father, Hiram Callahan, is...he's different, sometimes difficult. Actually, he's unpredictable. It wouldn't be advisable for you to be there alone, especially if he's been drinking."

"Then what if I take someone with me?"

"Who?"

"Well, I don't know. Maybe Joyce."

"Absolutely not."

"Then you go with me."

"I can't...I don't have the time."

"Don't you care about those children's education?"

"I care, but I can tell you, their father won't work with you."

"Then go with me and let's convince him the children need to be in school. Surely the two of us can convince him. He'll respect your opinion, Mr. Taggart."

"I'm sorry. I can't."

"Can't, or won't?"

Wesley looked at her but didn't answer.

"Then I shall go by myself." With that abrupt statement she stood and stomped from the room.

Wesley pushed his chair from the table, stood and stepped to the fireplace where he retrieved a picture frame from the mantle. He stared at the photograph of his wife. He slowly loosened the back of the frame, removed a piece of paper and read it silently:

Nancy Sue (Brewer) Taggart, daughter of Monroe Thomas Brewer and Nancy Marie (Strong) Brewer; Monroe T. Brewer, son of Isom Andrew Brewer and Mary Anne (Callahan) Brewer; Nancy Marie (Strong) Brewer, daughter of Willie Levi Strong of

Shenandoah County, Virginia, and Mary Louisa (Fugate) Strong of Rockingham, Virginia…

Wesley slipped the paper back inside the picture frame, closed the frame, and held it to his chest. He turned to Nanny Sue.

"Did I ever tell you I tried to discourage her from taking the black the day of the accident?"

"No."

"I always feared the black was too spirited for her, but she loved to ride him. Behind her gentle smile there was a nature as determined as a bear in a beehive." He returned the picture frame to the mantle, walked across the room to the window and looked toward where Nancy sat on the child's swing in the front yard.

"And Miss York's persistent ways remind you of her?"

"Too much so, I'm afraid."

CHAPTER TWENTY-SEVEN

~

Teaching exhausted Nancy, and she always had plenty to do after school. Today she needed to mail a letter to her parents, and Joyce delightfully accompanied her to the post office. Nancy had enjoyed her few moments with Ida Mae but was disappointed there was no mail from Cincinnati, leaving her in a melancholic mood. Joyce didn't seem to notice, as her gaiety showed. As they journeyed side by side along the middle of the railroad tracks, Joyce skipped, landing on each tie and keeping count. Nancy swatted at a fly that seemed attracted to her loose hanging ponytail.

"What was your mother's name?" Nancy interrupted Joyce's counting.

"Nancy Sue."

"Really?"

"Nancy Sue Brewer before she married Daddy."

Joyce resumed her counting.

"So was your mother named after Nanny Sue?"

"Yep. She's also named after Granny Brewer. Granny's name was Nancy Marie. I'm named after Granny, too. Joyce Marie."

"Really?"

"Nanny Sue has the same first name as yours, too, but we always called her Nanny Sue. I like it that you have the same name as Momma and Nanny Sue."

Nancy didn't know how to respond. They walked on in silence, except for their footsteps on the railroad ties and the occasional kicking of gravel. Joyce reached out and took Nancy by the hand. The melancholy seemed to lift.

A dog barked in the distance. The sun turned the sky into a radiant orange as it fell behind Coffin Rock Mountain.

"You going to see the Callahans?" Joyce interrupted the silence.

"Maybe."

"Daddy don't want you to go, does he?"

"I don't think so."

"Want to know why?"

"Yes, I really would."

"Cause Hiram Callahan killed Momma."

Nancy stopped dead in her tracks. She stared down at Joyce. She recalled her conversation with Wesley. He didn't tell her any of the facts. Why? He must certainly despise Hiram Callahan. Then again, he didn't show anger toward him. He actually protected Hiram's reputation from what he had done.

"Well, he didn't actually kill Momma, but he caused it."

"I don't understand, but I don't want you to talk about these things if it bothers you."

"Me and Nanny Sue talk about it sometimes when Daddy ain't around. It helps me to talk. Gary Eugene needs to talk, but he can't. He just runs away. Happened ever since the accident. Gary seen it happen."

Nancy couldn't believe what she was hearing. She wanted to know more, but she dared not ask Joyce to talk about the details of her mother's death.

"Another witness seen it, too. Mr. Deaton. He was on his way to school. Momma had just picked up the mail. She was on the black. Gary was ridin' double behind her. A coal train was coming, so Momma stopped the black to let it pass. Hiram Callahan came flying up behind her on his horse and slapped the black hard on the rear end. The black reared and then took off. Threw Momma and Gary off. Momma landed on the tracks. Gary tried to get her up. The train was coming."

Joyce paused, interrupted by the slight sound of pounding hooves. A horse and rider appeared in the distance.

"Mr. Deaton told the whole thing to the judge. That's why Hiram Callahan was in prison."

Nancy slowly sat down on the track. She said nothing. Joyce sat down beside her.

"You alright, Miss York?"

"Yes, dear. It's just I can't believe how difficult this must be for your father...for Gary...for you, sweetheart."

"I really miss Momma. Daddy can't talk about it none, but he did say she's in heaven. It helps a lot, with the feeling inside that I get, to know Momma's in heaven." Joyce paused and looked in the direction of the quickly approaching rider. "I wonder if she sees us. Right now, Miss York, does she see us sittin' here on this railroad track, you and me, talkin' about her?"

Nancy didn't answer. She embraced Joyce and held her tightly. She felt her tiny body begin to sob. Nancy wiped at her own tears, but they continued to flow.

The horse approached at a gallop. Nancy squinted to see who the rider was. She didn't recognize the gigantic man who slapped the reigns against the horse's sides. He passed them without slowing; the horse kicked cinders onto their clothing.

"That was very rude," Nancy yelled at him.

The man didn't look back.

"That's a very rude man, Joyce. Do you know who he is?"

"Yes, ma'am. That's Hiram Callahan."

CHAPTER TWENTY-EIGHT

~

Some exciting things happened on Gary's seventh birthday: Indian Summer warmed the November air to T-shirt weather, his daddy gave him his first BB gun and his Cherokee blood boiled with adventure. Something else happened, too. His curiosity lured him back to Coffin Rock. No amount of personal persuasion could convince him otherwise, though he tried to reason with himself. After school Gary ran straight home, fetched his gun and headed to the woods. He climbed the same path taken before, cautious not to interrupt another secret meeting. The rock stood deserted; the fire had burned all the vegetation and many of the trees around it. The blood was gone, washed away by rain. Still, it showed signs of recent activity. He lay upon a mossy cushion that carpeted part of the rock, cuddled his BB gun across his chest, closed his eyes and daydreamed of the distant past.

Is this a sacred burial ground of my relatives, the Cherokee? Did an Indian carve the head on the corner of the rock? Is the chin of the carving a landmark for distant travelers? Then again, what about the present? Whose blood did I see covering this rock before? Who were the hooded fellows that met on the rock in a secret meeting? He dozed.

They were on him before he could escape. He knew from their hoods it was the secret group. Their leader stood over him while four others held him down, spread eagle. Gary wanted so very much to know who they were; he wanted much more to be home.

"Whatcha doin' snoopin' round our meetin' place?" the leader asked.

Gary feigned boldness, trying to wrestle free, but he was filled with fear.

"What're we gonna do with'em?" another asked.

"Can't just let'em walk, cause he might tell on us," another chimed in.

"Let me think," the leader shouted above their voices.

Gary tried to distinguish their faces but could only see eyes peering from the red hoods. He prayed silently, for the Lord to forgive him. He didn't mean to lie to Daddy, but he wouldn't believe the truth. He believed Miss York instead. He wanted to go to school. He liked school…he liked learning."

Gary realized how much unlike Jesus he was, for he wasn't quite ready to pray for the Lord to forgive his enemies.

The leader spoke again, his tone less determined.

"Confound you, Gary. You done gone and messed up our secret club. Now we gotta take care of you."

The sky above revealed a perfect blue, not unlike the baby-blue eyes that stared at him from behind one of the hoods. Whose eyes are they? What are they gonna do to me? Gary closed his eyes and gazed beyond the hooded attackers, beyond the visible surroundings, into the heavens mentioned by the writers of Preacher Charlie's Bible. I'll be going there soon, if God will have me. Surely somewhere up there God is looking down at me, like Preacher Charlie said.

Gary wiggled like a worm on a fishhook trying to escape. I'm not going to die a coward. His right hand slid loose. He grabbed for the mask of one of his assailants, but he jumped back, hood still in place. The leader tackled him, pulling his face close Gary smelled his onion breath, but worse, he saw the fiery eyes. Gary wanted to see behind that mask, but he was scared and wished to be home.

"I'm gonna give you one chance," the leader screamed. "You hear me, boy? Just one chance! If you take it, we'll letcha go. If you don't, nobody'll ever know what happen'd to you. You ever see a dog run over by a freight train?"

Gary tried to block the memory of his mother.

"That'll be whatcha look like by the time we get finished with you. Now listen to me real good, son, 'cause it's your one and only chance."

The others slowly loosened their grips.

What are my chances against all of them? I'll just play along and see what happens.

"You gotta swear you'll join us and never identify any of us. We're the Red Strings and we ain't gonna fool around and let no twerp like you mess up our club."

Gary had heard about the Red Strings. They were opposition to the KKK. Daddy had warned him neither was any good. "Anyone who hides his identity behind a mask can't be trusted," Daddy had told him.

Gary studied the situation a long minute. With everything within him screaming to fight back, to run, to tell his daddy, he agreed to the oath instead. With one simple headshake he became one of them; a secret meeting, hood-wearing Red String club member.

They helped him up, patted him on the back and gave him the secret handshake. He awkwardly managed a smile, but he still couldn't see their faces behind their hoods. He wondered what they were thinking.

The trip home seemed the longest he'd ever taken. He found a thousand reasons to stall along the way. Ironically, it felt good being a part of a club, accepted and belonging to a cause. Still, he felt ashamed. At the fork in the road his daddy told him he would someday face, having to choose for himself, without a parent or a teacher there with a switch or a warning, he made the coward's choice.

He'd never before understood what Preacher Charlie meant by "lost in sin." For the first time in his life, he felt like a sinner.

CHAPTER TWENTY-NINE

~

Nancy removed a handful of newspapers from her satchel and stacked them neatly on her desk. She turned to the chalkboard and wrote in bold letters: *Current Events*. She turned to the class and smiled.

"Today we begin a special project studying current events." She drew a double line underneath the two words. "Now, who can tell me what I mean by current events?"

She surveyed the room. No hands were raised.

"Okay, let's break it down into small bites. Shoog, what does current mean?"

Shoog hesitated, then looked around the room for help.

"It has to do with the way the North Fork runs, 'specially in high water time."

Nancy hesitated. She turned to the chalkboard and highlighted the word: *Current*.

"Your answer is correct: the flow of the river, a current. Current is also associated with electricity." She quickly retreated from that statement, for many of the homes didn't yet have electricity. "When we use the two words together, it has a meaning altogether different. Current events are the events and issues of life taking place in our lifetime, right now. So, today we're going to talk about some of the events taking place in the world or that have taken place recently. Anyone interested in what is happening around the world?"

All hands shot up.

"Wonderful! I'll start out with a little summary and then we'll have a discussion. Ready?"

The students seemed eager to learn. She turned again to the chalkboard and wrote the dates: 1950-1957.

"From the mid-century some major events have unfolded around the world: Mr. Churchill has retired as Prime Minister of Great Britain; Mr. Peron has been overthrown as dictator of Argentina. The conflict in Korea has ended…"

A hand rose.

"Yes, Charles."

"My older brother was over there, but he's home now."

"We're grateful he's home. Also, in the past seven years, the Supreme Court has ruled against segregated schools. The Reverend Martin Luther King and a woman by the name of Rosa Parks have championed the civil rights movement by organizing a bus boycott in Montgomery, Alabama…"

"What's a boycott," someone asked. Nancy defined the term.

"What's segregated schools?" another asked.

Nancy cautiously described segregation, ending with an explanation of the Jim Crow mentality that permeated the south.

"Lincoln already give'em their rights," someone rebutted.

"But those rights have been violated time and again," Nancy explained.

"Captain Strong gave'em their rights here in Breathitt right after the Civil War," someone yelled out.

"That fuedin' caused a lot of our white kin to be murdered, though," another accused.

"Wouldn't have had a problem here in the first place if Captain Strong's daddy hadn't brought them slaves from Virginia," another countered.

"The Strongs think they own this county," someone chided from the back of the room.

"One of the Callahans probably shot Captain Strong down in cold blood up on Lick Branch," another defended.

Miss York tapped on her desk with a pencil and held up her hand for order. The room quieted. "We must learn to raise our hands to speak, and when someone else is speaking, we're not to disrupt them."

A hand raised slowly.

"Yes, James."

"My daddy said that what's happening between whites and black people shouldn't affect us none anymore 'cause we don't have no black people livin' 'round here."

"Are you aware that right now in some schools, black children aren't allowed to attend?"

"The only colored skins we don't allow in our school is them blue skins," a student chimed in.

A few heads nodded in agreement.

Nancy realized she had touched on a sensitive subject among the hill folks. She made a mental note of the accusations and realized they held deep-seated emotions. She must research such among this community. Prejudices must be challenged but probably not here and now. She decided to move on to another subject.

"Let's continue with some other events. Doctor Jonas Salk has invented a vaccine that may end the dreaded disease of polio. Further, one of the greatest minds of all time, Dr. Albert Einstein, died last year. His discoveries made it possible to split the atom."

The students seemed unfamiliar with the names and uninterested in their inventions. Nancy surmised they were hopelessly stuck in their small world along the North Fork. She wondered how she could move them into the future, or better still, just bring them into a present worldview.

"On a much less serious note, one year ago here in America, the Mouseketeers debuted on television. How many of you have seen them?" She immediately wished she hadn't asked the question.

No hands went up. Faces expressed embarrassment. She didn't wish to humiliate them for their primitive means, but she couldn't think of an easy out, so she stumbled on.

"Let's talk about one of the most recent events in history. Has anyone heard of Sputnik?"

A few hands rose.

"What do you know about Sputnik, Manuel?"

"It's a plane the Russians have that goes all the way around the world real fast and spies on us, but I don't believe it. I think the Russians just made the whole thing up."

"Really?" Nancy was thrilled with the dialog. If only she could get George to enter into conversation, and of course, Gary.

"That's what I heard down at the post office. We beat'em to Berlin and they're just trying to show off. Not a word to their claims. My daddy says the same thing." Manuel seemed proud of his input.

Nancy glanced at her watch.

"Before we break for lunch, let me share one more important discovery in this decade…the last couple years actually. Two scientists, Frances Crick and James Watson…" she paused while she wrote their names on the chalkboard. "These two men have made one of the greatest discoveries of all time. They've decoded the double-helix structure of what scientists call the DNA. They've found the building blocks that make up the entire human body."

She noticed the disinterest on the students' faces. Why were they not interested in new discoveries? Of course, it could be their hungry stomachs.

"This subject sounds complicated, so I'm going to try and simplify it by comparing it with a set of Legos. How many of you have heard of the toy building blocks called Legos?"

A few hands rose.

"Okay. Does anyone have a set of Legos?"

No one raised a hand. Again, Nancy realized her assumptions were unrealistic for this impoverished community. She noticed Joyce whispering to Gary and forcefully raising his hand for him.

"Okay, Gary has a Lego set. Gary would you tell the other students about your Lego set?"

Gary's face flushed. The students snickered.

"I'm sorry, Gary. I didn't mean…"

Gary stumbled from his seat and dashed out of the building.

CHAPTER THIRTY

~

Rumors in the community were Kelly Combs was seriously ill and getting worse. Some said he acquired the sickness while serving a prison sentence, as if that made it different than other sickness. No matter where he got it, the community had to deal with it: tuberculosis. He was married to Beulah Jane and they had a large family. Folks felt he was basically a good fellow but once ran with the wrong crowd. It got him into trouble with the law. After prison Kelly sought treatment for the sickness, but no remedy worked. This made it hard on his family. He couldn't hold down a job. To make matters worse, his oldest son, Lloyd Todd, was left with lingering physical effects from what the doctor in Jackson diagnosed as meningitis. The Combses squatted in a dilapidated house next to the Taggart property.

Of all the hardships and concerns Nancy encountered, she most feared the contacting of a disease. She cared much for the children's health and started a rigid agenda at school of making the students wash their hands before lunch and after each break. They carried the water from a spring a quarter mile away. At first, volunteers for water detail abounded, but as cold weather settled in, the students cooperated reluctantly; most of their winter clothes were worn bare. They dreaded the task of breaking the ice.

Nancy's project exhausted the supply of lye soap. Without trying to alarm her parents, she wrote requesting a case of soap be sent.

Christmas approached. Nancy looked forward to going home during the break. Letters from home were frequent and expressed concern.

She sat in the parlor preparing for another school day. A pounding on the front door startled her. She rushed to the door to find a student and neighbor, Lloyd Todd, standing there all frantic and scared. Tears streaked his unwashed cheeks. His eyes, puffy and bloodshot, looked as if he'd been up all night.

"Momma needs help real bad." Lloyd wiped his nose on his sleeve.

"What's the matter?" Nancy asked.

"It's the young'un. He's bad off."

Nancy rushed to the Combses' house, past Kelly who stood on the front porch having one of his coughing fits. She didn't bother to knock but burst inside to find Beulah Jane sitting in a rocking chair holding her limp baby, crying and praying for the Lord to spare him. Nancy took the child from her arms. It was burning with fever. She hurried to the kitchen and plunged the infant feet first into the bucket of drinking water. The child whimpered. Beulah remained in the parlor, wailing. Nancy removed the child from the water and dried it with a dishcloth. She cradled the baby in her arms and walked the floor.

That is the way Wesley found her, cradling the infant. Crying. The baby was dead.

Wesley slowly unfolded her arms from the infant. She didn't resist and didn't speak. She simply stared blankly. He laid the child on the kitchen table where he covered its blue body with the damp dishcloth.

Nancy collapsed into his arms, silently weeping.

CHAPTER THIRTY-ONE

~

They slowly walked the cinder pathway home. Wesley removed his jacket and placed it over Nancy's shoulders. It hung to her knees. She pulled it tightly around her chilled body.

"I really embarrassed Gary in class the other day. Did you hear?"

Wesley seemed glad to hear her speaking.

"Joyce briefly mentioned it. The students laughing mostly embarrassed him. He'll be okay."

"They carried their antics into the lunch hour, and it's difficult to keep a rein on twenty-four students spread out over the playground. Still, I must make it up to him some way."

"I'm sure you will."

"I'm beginning to doubt my ability to do anything right here in your community."

"You just did something right, Miss York."

"What? Let a blue skin baby die in my arms?"

"No. Holding a child in your arms to let it die in dignity."

"How many babies die from the blue skin sickness?" Nancy asked.

"The child didn't die from blue skin."

"But its body was blue…"

"The blue skins live into old age. This child died from something else."

"Kelly Combs has tuberculosis, doesn't he? Was that what killed the baby?" she asked.

"Yes, Kelly has TB, but I suspect the child had meningitis."

"Meningitis and not tuberculosis?"

"Probably. The blueness you saw was a purplish rash, the first stages of gangrene. I also noticed red splotches. The child was exposed to tuberculosis. Meningitis is somewhat a cousin to tuberculosis."

"So what is the blue skin disease?"

"It's different than what you just saw on the baby. The blue skin people don't have blotches like the baby did. Their entire body is blue: hands, lips, toes. Folks over at Troublesome Creek mostly have it, and, of course, Hiram Callahan's child close by here has the blue skin. He married a girl from over by Troublesome. He lived there before moving here. They're isolated over on the Troublesome, no road or train, so they don't go to a doctor for the condition to be properly diagnosed. The blue skins don't have symptoms like other sicknesses, and they don't die from it. Their skin is just blue."

"So, it's not really a disease. It's more an abnormality. Then why is it so dreaded?"

"I'm not sure. Perhaps because we fear what we don't understand, so the blue skins are misunderstood by many. They feel inferior, sometimes even freakish. Since people don't understand the condition, they sometimes shun those who have it, and those that have the condition sometimes isolate themselves."

"Is that what Hiram Callahan has done with Sherry Jane?"

"Probably. Then again, some of the mountain folks are prone to think the blue skin is some type of curse. Some parents are ashamed of their offspring and abuse them. Others fear their children will be ill treated and so they hide them to protect them from abuse. Can't say I really blame them. People can be awfully cruel, especially children to children."

"It must be a terrible thing to deal with. How many have this condition?"

"I'm not really sure. I doubt anyone's ever researched enough to document it."

"How long has it been going on?"

"Long before I was born. Folks say it's been going on ever since Martin Fugate moved to Troublesome Creek and married Elizabeth Smith in the early eighteen hundreds. Four of their seven children were blue skins."

"Were the parents blue skins?"

117

"That's uncertain. It doesn't seem to matter. Many of the parents of blue skins look completely normal. It doesn't seem to be hereditary."

"What could cause the disease?"

"I have an idea. I've written a friend of mine at the University of Lexington. He's promised to come over sometime and do some research."

"What exactly do you think is causing it, Wesley...Mr. Taggart?"

"I suspect it to be silver poisoning. I believe there's silver ore in the rocks at Troublesome Creek. Maybe somehow its composition is being absorbed into their water supply, and it's poisoning the unborn children."

"Really? If silver were the culprit, wouldn't the poison affect all the children and be fatal to some?"

"I've thought of that, but I can't come up with any other explanation. Perhaps the silver is in small doses that affects only certain children."

"Perhaps. I think of silver ore as being out west...Nevada, Colorado, California."

"Mostly, but it has been found as close as Virginia and Missouri, both bordering states to Kentucky. Legend has it that silver was found right here in Kentucky, not far from here. I plan on prospecting over on Troublesome Creek soon. I wish somehow I could help solve the problem of the blue skins."

"That would be wonderful. I hope you can solve this horrible malady. How do you know so much about silver?"

"That was my study at the university. I'm a geologist; rocks, soil, minerals. Salt mine. Remember?"

"What a silly question. Sorry. You won't be moving to Troublesome Creek...I mean moving the children...before I move back home to Cincinnati?"

"Not as long as the salt mine holds out."

"Is that a concern, that the mine is being exhausted?"

Wesley hesitated.

"Mr. Taggart, is there a problem with the salt mine?"

They were arriving at the house. Joyce and Gary waited on the steps.

"I think the salt mine is okay."
"I'll pray for your business."
"Thank you, Miss York.

CHAPTER THIRTY-TWO

~

Freshly cut holly and mistletoe adorned the Taggart residence. Anticipation mounted as the Christmas break approached. When snow started falling Monday morning, the Taggart children were elated. By the end of the school day, six inches covered the countryside and the pupils' excitement peaked the Richter scale.

Nancy sat on the parlor sofa reading, distractedly. After starting and stopping the same page three times, she laid aside the book, walked to the window and peered out. This became the routine all evening as she monitored the weather, for there was no letup of the heavy snowfall.

Joyce eased down beside her. "Don't you like snow, Miss York?"

"I do, but I don't want to get snowed in. If we cancel school, the students might fall behind in their studies. I was wondering, does heavy snow ever cause the train service to be canceled? I'm worried I might not get home for Christmas."

"So that's what has you pacing the floor."

Nancy smiled at Joyce and patted her on the hand.

"I think winter is God's gift to children," Joyce said.

"Really?

"There surely can be no other reason for it. For adults it's shoveling, busting ice from the springs and a lot of other things they despise doing. For us, it's a wonderful time of snowball fights, angel making and sleddin'—not to mention school closin'."

"I thought you enjoyed school, Joyce Marie." Nancy smiled.

"I do. I really do, but I like winter, too. I like snow. I especially like snow cream."

"What is snow cream?"

"You've never had snow cream?"

"I can't say that I have, but then again, I don't know what it is so I can't say for certain I haven't had it."

"It's a combination of sugar, canned milk, vanilla flavoring, with just a pinch of salt, all mixed into a huge bowl full of freshly fallen snow. Nanny Sue showed me how to make it. You'll love it! If you add chocolate, it's even better."

"Really?"

"Nanny Sue, can we make Miss York some snow cream?"

Nanny Sue looked up from her knitting. "If'n you bundle up to keep warm. I don't want your daddy gettin' mad at me for neglectin' my duties and lettin' you get sick. You know the penalty for gettin' sick."

"Penalty?" Nancy asked.

"Camphor oil and Vicks smeared all over our bodies," Joyce explained.

"Castor oil. Don't forget the castor oil." Nanny Sue smiled.

"Want to help gather snow for snow cream?" Joyce looked at Nancy and begged. "We can have a snowball, fight, too."

"I didn't really bring clothes for playing in the snow."

"You can wear Momma's clothes," Joyce said.

"No, I couldn't. It wouldn't be right."

"It's okay, Miss York," Nanny Sue said. "The children could use some funnin'. Haven't gotten much of that lately."

Nancy hesitated. "If you think it's okay, Nanny Sue."

"The children need it. Need to get out of the house."

Once bundled up, they passed Nanny Sue's approval and headed outside with a washbowl to retrieve snow. Joyce and Gary heeded Nanny Sue's strict dress code, buttons buttoned all the way to their chins and hats pulled down over their ears, until the romping started, then coats were loosened and hats were left wherever they got knocked off the head.

Nancy felt awkward but surprised Mrs. Taggart's clothes fit her so comfortably. They were nice. Store bought.

A snowball hit her on the back. She scooped a handful of snow and spun around to throw it. To her surprise, Wesley stood there. He appeared startled.

"Oh, I'm sorry, Miss York. I thought you were…" He didn't finish his sentence.

Nancy thought she knew what he almost said. She sensed his pain. Embarrassment spread across her face. She wanted to run away. He walked toward her.

"I didn't expect you to come home so soon. I'm sorry about the clothes…Nanny Sue said…no, Nanny Sue isn't to blame for my decision." She felt ashamed she would try to blame Nanny Sue for her decision.

"It's okay, Miss York. I'm okay with it. Clothes are meant to be worn. I would already have given them away to someone, but I haven't gotten around to it."

He avoided eye contact. She thought she saw a trace of a tear. She wished she could skip this awkward moment fraught with emotion.

"Come help us, Daddy." Joyce struggled with the washbasin. Wesley tromped to her rescue.

Nancy awkwardly joined in with the rest of the snow gathering and the making of snow cream. Once the last of the snow cream was downed and the dishes put away, they gathered in the parlor. Joyce and Gary played a game of Chinese Checkers. The twins played with a jack-in-the-box. Nanny Sue rocked the baby. Wesley sat opposite the room from Nancy, studying what looked to be a map. Nancy, still uncomfortable about being caught in Mrs. Taggart's clothing, buried her face in a book, staring blankly at the pages. She wanted to retreat to her room, but it was too early.

"Tell Miss York your Christmas story, Daddy," Joyce requested.

"Mr. Taggart is busy, sweetheart," Nancy protested.

"Daddy's story is a short one. Please, Daddy."

Wesley folded the paper and laid it aside. He cleared his throat and began the story. The story line was basic, mostly following the Scripture of the gospels' narrative. Nancy wondered why Joyce was so insistent Wesley recite a story all knew so well.

"And the shepherds came to the cave and found the babe wrapped in swaddling clothes and lying in a manger. It was winter. The snow fell softly. God chose wintertime to give His gifts to children: snow cream and the Savior. For I'm sure we can biblically

122

prove Christ was born during the winter season. Want to know how?" Wesley used expression and feeling when he asked the question.

"How, Daddy?" Joyce squealed.

Nancy jumped in surprise at Joyce's outburst.

"Because the swaddling clothes prove it was wintertime. For can you imagine the children's Christmas lines otherwise…"

"Can I tell it, Daddy, please?" Joyce interrupted.

"Go ahead, Miss Taggart," Wesley feigned disappointment.

Joyce stepped to the middle of the room, cleared her voice, and continued the story as if performing onstage at a Christmas play.

"It had to be winter or else the Bible would have to say the shepherds came and found baby Jesus, lying in a manger, stark naked, for the summer night was too hot and sticky for swaddling clothes. See, Miss York, it had to be winter, 'cause of the swaddling clothes."

Wesley started laughing. Joyce ran to him and threw herself into his arms.

He hugged her and laughed and laughed.

Swaddling clothes and snow cream, especially for kids. It was good to see Wesley laughing; this was the first time she had seen him laugh since she'd arrived in the community.

Gary sat by himself, observing. He smiled but mostly watched.

CHAPTER THIRTY-THREE

~

Morning dawned with a thick blanket of snow; gray skies continued to dump snow like feathers shaken from a downy pillow. Nancy groggily entered the kitchen to find Wesley at the kitchen table sipping coffee. She was surprised he hadn't left for work. Nanny Sue hovered over a pot on the wood stove, stirring its contents. Nancy could smell the simmering oatmeal. It was one of her favorite dishes from the hands of Nanny Sue, who glanced up as she entered the room.

"Morning, miss."

"Good morning, Nanny Sue. Mr. Taggart."

Wesley lowered his coffee cup and smiled at her. "Miss York."

His work shoes sat on the opened oven door; his coat hung from the back of a chair pushed near the stove, steam rising from the shoulders and water dripping onto the floor. His dark hair clung to his head, glistening. Nancy felt embarrassed to have slept so late. She should have been up monitoring the situation, determining if school should be closed. She wondered what Wesley thought about her sleeping so late.

"I'm sure you've already decided to cancel school," Wesley said.

"Why, yes, of course. Does it usually snow this much?" She rubbed the back of her neck.

"We get our share, but this is a rare one. Already measured eighteen inches. And there's no let up in sight. Looks like the Christmas break is starting early."

He seemed to be talking louder than usual; the words pounded in her head. She didn't respond.

"Are you okay, Miss York?"

Nancy felt tightness in her neck; her head throbbed. She started to sit in the chair opposite Wesley. Why was he staring at her? Why was he speaking so loudly? She felt dizzy.

"Miss York? Nancy? Are you okay? Get a wet wash cloth, Nanny Sue."

His command echoed in her head. Please, don't yell. The room spun. She saw him rush toward her. She felt her legs give way.

She woke in a strange room with a pounding in her head. The pain became more intense when she moved, forcing her to lie still. The light around the curtains seemed piercingly bright. She squinted at her surroundings: an unfamiliar picture hung on the wall, a washbowl sat at the foot of the bed, a man's fedora hung on a high bedpost. From the opposite side of the room the legs of a chair scraped across the hardwood floor.

"Ouch!" Her voice echoed in her head.

"Nancy." A male voice whispered.

She thought she recognized the voice, and she tried to turn and see who was there. Excruciating pain shot through her entire body. She heard the echo of footsteps coming nearer. She tried to raise herself up; her body felt weighted.

"Nancy, lie still, dear. Can you hear me?"

"Yeeesss…" The word seemed so terribly long.

"Nancy, dear, I'm here for you."

"Is that you…?" Her eyes closed and she didn't finish the sentence.

Her eyes blinked open. She tried to remember where she was and how she got there. She faintly recalled someone had spoken her name and dear. It sounded like her father. How could that be? She sensed someone in the room.

"Daddy, are you there?"

"It's me, Miss York. Nanny Sue. How you feelin'?"

"Terrible. What's happened to me?"

"You're mighty sick, child. Doctor Lewis says meningitis."

"Meningitis? Like the Combses' baby?"

"Yes."

"Will I be okay?"

"We think the worst has passed. Thankin' the good Lord."

"Where am I?"

"You're still at the Taggarts' place, upstairs in Mr. Taggart's room. You needed the quiet of this room, child."

"I thought I heard my daddy's voice. Was I dreaming?"

"No, dear. Your daddy's here. Downstairs resting. He's been up all night, by your bedside. I'll fetch'em for you."

"Thank you, Nanny Sue. How did he know?"

"Mr. Taggart went to Jackson and phoned him. He came the next day on the train."

"How long have I been sick?"

"'Bout a week. Mr. Taggart knew right away what it was. He got Doc Lewis here and called your daddy the first day you started ailin'."

"What day of the week is it, Nanny Sue?

"Tuesday."

"Tuesday? What date?"

"Christmas Eve, dear."

Nancy sighed. "I like Christmas Eve. It's one of my favorite…" She closed her eyes.

Someone knocked lightly on the door.

"Come in," Nanny Sue said.

The squeaky hinges created an eerie mood as the door to the huge bedroom slowly opened. Nancy tried to focus on the figure standing in the doorway. She heard the footsteps coming toward her. She reached out. The figure clasped her hand. A voice, slow and faltering and ever so tenderly, but pleadingly, called to her.

"Miss…York…please…don'…"

It was Gary. He was talking, slowly and with much difficulty, but he had spoken a few words.

"Please don't worry, Gary. I'll be okay in a few days."

He crumpled beside the bed and tried to say more. No words came. Only sniffles.

Nancy tried to raise herself in the bed to comfort him, but she couldn't. The pain was too severe, and she felt too weak. She closed her eyes and reached out and patted Gary on the shoulder.

More footsteps.

She opened her eyes and noticed another figure in the doorway. She squinted.

It was Wesley.

CHAPTER THIRTY-FOUR

~

Their plan worked. They transported Nancy by train to Jackson and then by car to the newly established hospital on the university campus in Lexington. Nancy's father wanted to get her home, but he settled for this halfway point. It offered her the best of care with the least distance of travel. Wesley accompanied them to Jackson. Her mother joined them at Lexington. Both junctions were full of emotion: one departing, one reuniting.

Charles York subtly pressed for his daughter's resignation from her teaching position. Nancy vehemently refused, then begged him to understand. She won. Mr. Deaton agreed to substitute until she returned. No dates were established.

They stayed at the hospital for two weeks. Nancy's system responded positively to the penicillin. The doctor released her to stay in a motel for another week. If all went well, he'd release her to go home to Cincinnati.

Nancy lay propped up in bed reading a letter from Wesley. Her mother sat across the room in a recliner, also reading.

"Gary's not talking again!" she read aloud. She paused from the letter and laid it in her lap. "I'm so sorry to hear that. He actually spoke a few words at my bedside but then went silent as if his mouth wouldn't work."

"What's wrong with the child?" her mother asked.

"He was traumatized when he saw his mother killed in an accident."

"That's so sad, dear. Was it a car wreck?"

"No. She was thrown from a horse."

"Like a steeple chase, or something? I've heard that's a dangerous sport."

The door to the room opened and Charles entered carrying a bag of food and a stack of papers. Snow covered the shoulders of his tweed overcoat.

"Snowing again?" Nancy was relieved to not have to explain the details of Nancy Taggart's death.

"Lightly. The weatherman says it's little to no accumulation."

The aroma of burgers filled the room. Nancy felt her stomach growl.

"Hungry, Nancy?" he asked.

"Starved."

"What took so long, Charles?"

"I stopped at the Lexington Public Library, dear, like Nancy requested."

"And?"

"Interesting. It's at Gratz Park, built the turn of the century with Carnegie funds. Unique building. Like Wesley said, it has a Kentucky Room. The room is full of information about Kentucky, and yes, it has information on the history of bloody Breathitt."

"Thank you, Daddy."

"Bloody Breathitt?" Doris asked. "You didn't say anything…"

"That was a long time ago, Mother. It's much safer now."

"I think you'll find this particular manuscript especially interesting. The librarian was kind enough to let me check it out. She gave me a temporary library card."

He handed Nancy a saddle-stitched, letter-sized booklet.

She studied the title: *They Came To Save Us*, by W. E. Taggart. She thumbed through the pages. There were no pictures. She didn't try to hide her wonder at the author's name: W. E. Taggart. "Could it be Wesley Eugene? Did Wesley write this?"

"Got my attention. That's why I checked it out."

She read the author biography. A smile broke out on her face.

"You can read it later, dear, after dinner," her mother said.

"Why not during dinner, Mother, please?" Nancy reached for the hamburger her mother had unwrapped for her. "This is unbelievable, Daddy."

"What's unbelievable?" her mother asked.

"This booklet is written by Wesley Taggart. He must have written it while he was attending the university here." Nancy took a bite of the burger, opened the book at random and began to read to herself:

The North Fork flowed into the Middle Fork near Troublesome Creek. Together they joined the South Fork just before forming the Kentucky River. The river was our lifeline; ironically, it became our demise. The fertile soil along its bottomland grew healthy crops for our families, and the waterway carried our timber to the marketplace. However, all the food grown on those bottoms never made it to the dinner table, for floods were frequent and devastating. The corn grown on those bottomlands, and the plenteous fresh streams that fed the river, served conveniently for making whiskey: too accessible for the poor and too plenteous for the greedy.

Booze was no foreigner to my family. It wrecked the lives of many relatives. We buried them in the various cemeteries scattered throughout our county. I'm told a freight train ran over and killed my great-grandpa, Sheridan Taggart, as he laid on the tracks passed out from liquor. Liquor contributed to the poor health and early death of Grandpa Taggart, who died before I was born. My great uncle on my mother's side, Captain William Strong, was a demon, partly contributed to the devil's influence, but mostly to liquor. A captain in the Union Army during the Civil War, he failed to relinquish his duties after the war. Along with a following of assassins and bushwhackers, he wrestled control over Breathitt County. Hiding behind the hypocritical cloak of the "protector of the freed Negroes," he assumed powers not allotted to laity, controlled politics by ambush and intimidation, captured the courthouse in Jackson just to have his way and acted as judge, jury and executioner on more than one occasion. He earned the hatred of many a widow; rightly so.

"Captain Strong must have been the man the children were referring to in our current events studies," Nancy said.

"Who is Captain Strong, dear," her mother asked.

"One of my students' relatives from the Civil War, Mother."

"How interesting," her father said.

Nancy continued to read from the booklet, aloud:

> But what goes around comes around, for Ed Callahan finally bested Captain Strong for control of Breathitt County. Uncle Bill, as some called him, decided to call it quits, but the younger Callahan, motivated by hostility from the past, refused Captain Strong a peaceful retirement. "To live by the sword is to die by the same," a famous person once said. It certainly was true for Uncle Bill.

> With his young grandson, Carl, riding double behind him on a mule, Captain Strong rode down Lick Branch to the local store. He never made it home. The feuds he fed in the past fueled an enmity that remained relentless until Captain Strong writhed in his own blood. A volley of bullets riddled his aged body; he crumpled to the ground, where his assassins fired point blank into his body. In horror, his grandson witnessed the violent fate. What a price!

> The dirt path onto which Captain Strong fell ran through the area of my childhood; I played often on the hillside where the ambushers had hidden. I walked a hundred times over the soil that lapped up the blood spilt a half century prior.

> Hid away in those surrounding hills, distilled moonshine dripped into jugs, then into the bloodstream of individuals and finally into the bloodlines of generations. It remained in my family. Daddy died way too young, but not before he sired a

house full of young'uns. My mother succumbed to typhoid when I was ten. The orphanage became our only option.

At first I resented my plight, jerked by the roots from my family and native surroundings. I tried to keep the family together, but the social workers said "No." I viewed myself as a caring person, trying to keep the siblings together, but no one seemed to care for me, not even God. I felt abandoned and forgotten and angry.

In trouble often at the orphanage, I spent my days isolated in my room of self-pity. The patient personnel never gave up on me. They kept unlocked from the outside the door I had shut tight from within myself. Over time the staff helped me to see the virtuous quality of compassion I possessed for my siblings was working against me; compassion, no matter how righteous, when turned inward, becomes self-pity and ultimately becomes self-destructive. They recognized in me something I couldn't see in myself, and they never gave up on me.

With time I accepted my circumstances and regained my will to live, not only for myself but also for others. I began to volunteer for responsibilities not my own. Gifted with a more than average intellect, I wanted to give back, so I tutored others in the orphanage.

The director of the orphanage saw to it that I enter the university—the orphanage's first. I am forever indebted to the director and his staff.

After my first year of college, I married. The next month Uncle Sam called on me. Two years later I returned home to see my one-year-old daughter for the first time. I finished college and decided to go back to my roots, back to my people—back to try and make a difference for others.

With two children and a dream, we're going back to Breathitt County. I realize to make a

difference in that part of the country, it will be a slow
and arduous task, for it is a troublesome land, but
with my education, Nancy Sue's loving support and
by God's grace, I am committed.

Nancy lay the manuscript aside. She wiped at a tear streaking
her cheek.

"Are you okay, dear," her father asked.

"Yes. I'm beginning to see things clearer: the rage that
simmers just below the surface of some whose roots are tied to
generations of violence, the traditions that hold them fast to their
native land and the resentment some feel toward outsiders whose
motives are to rescue them."

She thought again of her students; she reflected upon their
pitifully proud faces. She thought of Joyce and Gary and the twins
and the motherless baby. She thought of Nanny Sue. She needed to
get well and go back. She thought of Wesley and the argument at
the dinner table and the poetical manner in which he defended his
community, as if he'd rehearsed the argument a thousand times. She
realized he had: within himself. She knew she had to get well; for
she knew she had to go back. This time it would be different; they
would no longer be a project to her. She missed them. She longed to
see them.

CHAPTER THIRTY-FIVE

~

Clouds hung heavy. The air smelled of hickory smoke that drifted lazily from the flue in the middle of the ridgeline. The melting snow around the smokestack revealed the crudely hewn, moss-covered hickory shake roof. Wesley approached the cabin cautiously. He dismounted and wrapped the reins loosely around the fencepost outside the yard; the black pranced nervously from the snarling dog that guarded the porch.

"Easy boy," Wesley said calmingly.

The sudden neighing of the black goaded the dog. He lunged toward Wesley, who whacked him across the nose with the suede glove he held in his right hand. The dog yelped and scampered behind the cabin, sending snow flying into Wesley's face.

The aged boards creaked with each ascending step. The doorknob squeaked; Wesley paused as the door opened slowly, remaining slightly ajar.

He was halfway up the steps. "It's Wesley Taggart."

The door flew open and Thomas Fugate stepped onto the porch in his stocking feet. "Howdy, Mr. Taggart."

"Hello, Mr. Fugate."

"Don't call me that. Call me Tom."

"Then you call me Wesley."

"But you're my boss, Mr. Taggart."

"I'm also your neighbor, Thomas. It sure is a long way over here to the Troublesome."

"That's why I stay at the mine weekdays and only come home weekends. It's just way too far. When we startin' back up at the mine?"

"As soon as the weather breaks. I figure next week. Sure was a deep snow."

"Most snow I seen since nineteen fifty. 'Bout twenty-one inches that November as I recollect."

"That was the year and month my Gary was born."

"How's he doing, talkin' and all?"

"Not too good. He's spoken but a few words since the accident. I'm not giving up hope, though."

"Thank the Lord fer hope."

"Yes. How's your little one?"

"Oh my goodness, Mr. Taggart, I'm sorry to leave you standing out in the cold. Come on in the house and set yourself down awhile."

"Thank you, Thomas."

Wesley stomped the snow from his boots, removed his hat and ducked his head to pass through the doorway. The dimly lit room made it difficult for him to see, so he surveyed the sounds of the cabin as his eyes adjusted: someone rocked in a chair by the stove, giggles emanated from the far corner. He tried hard to make out the faces in the dim lighting.

"Mr. Taggart, this is my wife, Emma Lee, and my two sons. He pointed to the corner where two lads played with what looked like homemade wooden horses and riders. "Clyde be seven, 'bout the same age as yours. Jimmy be five. And 'course my littlest one, Mary Lou."

"Howdy, Mr. Taggart." Emma was still rocking.

"Mrs. Fugate." Wesley nodded toward the rocking chair. His eyes slowly adjusted to the lighting. The cabin seemed unusually small. The rocker sat to the left, next to the small cast iron wood-burning stove in the center of the room. Pushed up to the right wall was a disheveled cot with a wooden stand at its head. A larger cooking stove stood at the back wall of the cabin, a free-standing cabinet crowded the wall right of the stove and a single door off to the left and back of the room led to what he assumed was their only bedroom. A wooden table with mismatched chairs sat beyond the cast iron stove, toward the right and next to the single window covered with homemade curtains of feed-sack material.

"Take off your coat." Thomas grabbed a chair from the kitchen table and carried it to Wesley who removed his coat and hung it across the back of the chair.

"Thank you." Wesley sat down.

Thomas rearranged the covers on the cot and sat on its edge. The two boys moved from the corner closer to their mother, each clutching a toy. Even in the dim lighting Wesley noticed the dull blue hue of their skin, compared to the skin color of their mother.

"The boys are a mite bashful," Thomas said. "Mr. Taggart's my boss, boys. Wanna say hello to'em?"

They didn't speak. Clyde hung his head and fiddled with his toy; Jimmy stared at Wesley.

"Say hello, boys," Emma coaxed them. They still didn't speak.

"Enjoy being off school, Clyde?" Wesley asked the oldest.

"Clyde ain't in school just yet. Thought we'd send him next year, though," Emma said.

"That'd be good. My son really likes school."

"Hungry, Mr. Taggart?" Thomas asked.

"I couldn't impose upon you, Thomas...or Mrs. Fugate..."

"It'd be a pleasure, Mr. Taggart," Emma said, "'specially after what all you done fer our family."

"Your husband is a hard worker, Mrs. Fugate."

"I know he is. I know what you done fer him...and us."

Emma rose from the rocking chair and handed the baby to Thomas. "I'll make a bite to eat."

The two boys followed her closely to the kitchen area.

"Wanna hold 'er, Mr. Taggart?" Thomas reached the child toward Wesley.

Wesley cradled the infant in his arms. The sharp smell of a urine-soaked diaper, unlike what he was accustomed, brought a renewed appreciation for the caring attention Nanny Sue gave to his family. He peered into the face of the infant. Her skin was a bluish hue, not unlike the color of a child's lips and hands after eating a handful of mulberries. The bluish color was more pronounced than he had assumed. He thought of his own toddler, her skin light and smooth.

"Ever seen a blue skin before?" Thomas asked.

"Yes, but I never held one so close." He glanced toward the two boys, playing with their small wooden toys. They moved closer to Emma.

"Our third." Emma poured milk from a container into a glass.

"Sorry." Wesley wished he could recall his response. "I mean..."

"No, it's alright, Mr. Taggart. Ain't normal, no way you look at it. It ain't normal a'tall. Somethin' really wrong," Emma said.

Except for the clatter from the kitchen area, the room grew awkwardly silent.

"The blue skin children is one of the reasons I'm here," Wesley said. "I have a hunch about what's causing the skin discoloration, and I'd like to check it out. I'm thinking..." The neighing of the black disrupted his thoughts.

Emma entered the room carrying a glass and small plate. The boys retreated to the corner and resumed their play with their toys.

"It's not much, Mr. Taggart." She set them on the small stand and moved the stand to where Wesley sat.

"It's plenty, Mrs Fugate."

"Hope you like buttermilk."

"I love buttermilk and...do you mind if I crumble the cornbread into the milk?"

"Not a'tall. That's just the way Tom likes his buttermilk. I'll get you a spoon."

"I didn't realize I'd be the only one eating..." Wesley said.

"We already had somethin'," Thomas said.

"Well...how kind. Thank you very much. I am hungry."

"You was going to tell me your ideas about the blue skin," Thomas said.

"Yes." Wesley paused and spooned a mouthful of soaking cornbread. He wiped his lips with the back of his hand. "Do you have any silver plates or cups you use to eat and drink from?"

"No, don't think we do. Emma?"

"No."

"Mrs. Fugate, did you have any pure silverware you may have used before the children were born?"

"No. Why do you ask that?"

"I think the blue skin is the result of silver poisoning. Over consumption of silver can cause a blue discoloration of the skin. I think your children, along with others here along the Troublesome, have somehow become contaminated by silver. So, if you aren't using silver for food consumption, then the children are consuming silver some other way, maybe through the drinking water."

"But they're born blue, Mr. Taggart, before they eat or drink a drop. What about that?"

"I've given that a lot of thought. For the unborn, it would have to come from the mother ingesting silver."

Wesley became suddenly aware of Emma's disquiet.

"Of course, no one is to blame because no one had any way of knowing and it's only a theory of mine, no proof yet. I think there's silver in the rocks here on Troublesome Creek. Somehow it's being distilled into the drinking water."

"But not every young'un has it, not even in the same family," Emma argued.

"True, Mrs. Fugate, but some of the children may be more susceptible. Of course, this is only a theory, and I'd like to either prove or disprove it. That's why I'm here. I want to prospect your property, check it for silver. If we find silver, we can try and prevent the children from ingesting it. Maybe we can prevent other children from being exposed. Further, if I find silver, I'd like to form a partnership with you and any locals who want to participate. It would make a great living for your family. Of course, everyone would have to work for free until we make a sizable strike."

"But I depend on my income from the salt mine…"

"You'd still work at the salt mine while I do some exploration here. When I find indications of silver, I'll procure…obtain finances to hire a crew right here on the Troublesome."

"That'd be wonderful, Mr. Taggart, if we found silver, not just to cure the blue skin children, but to help us with living and all," Emma said.

"How long you think it'll take?" Thomas asked.

"I'd like to take some water samples back home with me. I can do some preliminary tests. Do you have a well or…?"

"A spring. Little ways up the creek."

"Do you mind showing me?

"Not a'tall. Let me get my boots and coat."

"Sure. Oh, I also brought some groceries. They're in the saddlebags. Figured you folks were snowed in. Even brought some candy for the boys."

"The boys will surely like that," Emma said.

"I'll pay you back, Mr. Taggart," Thomas said.

"You don't need…"

"Yes, Mr. Taggart," Emma spoke up. "Tom always pays his bills. He's a fine husband."

"Okay. When you get back to work. Maybe next paycheck."

"That'd be kind. Thank you, Mr. Taggart," Thomas said.

Wesley put on his jacket and stepped to the door. He turned to Emma. "Thank you for lunch, Mrs. Fugate. You make delicious cornbread and the buttermilk topped it off."

"You're mighty welcome. It's a pleasure to meet you, Mr. Taggart. Tom talks mighty highly of you. Come back again and visit. Maybe we'll have time so I'll be able to fix up a spread."

"I look forward to it. I'd sure love to hear that Clyde and Jimmy are in school this fall."

Emma didn't answer.

Wesley opened the door and stepped onto the porch. Snow was falling; a good inch of white covered the back of the black. A gust of wind tossed his hat onto the steps. He bent down to retrieve it. That was when he saw the tracks in the freshly fallen snow. They were the tracks of large boots. Has someone been eavesdropping on our conversation? Who? Why?

CHAPTER THIRTY-SIX

~

Nancy stepped out of her father's car and onto the sidewalk in front of their home. She slowly turned in a circle, taking in the view of the neighborhood. She breathed deeply and sighed.

Fluffy snowflakes accumulated quickly on top of her father's new Edsel; she scooped a handful of the snow and tossed it at her father as he approached the trunk to retrieve the luggage. He ducked; she laughed.

"It's good to have you home, Nancy."

"I'm glad to be home, Daddy."

"Hurry, dear, you mustn't catch a chill." Her mother exited the car.

Nancy held her face skyward and let snowflakes collect.

"Nancy, dear," her mother called firmly to her from the front steps.

"Coming, Mother."

The postman rendezvoused with her as she started for the house.

"Miss York! How are you? Heard you'd been ill."

"I'm feeling much better, Mr. Turner. Thank you for asking."

"Good to see you. Are you home to stay?"

"I'm hoping to return to my work soon."

"You take care."

"Thanks."

"Oh my, I'm about to forget my work. Here's a letter from down in Kentucky. Probably from some friends you made down there."

Up there, she said to herself, smiling as she recalled her first conversation with Ida Mae Deaton. The Appalachians are up.

"Thank you, Mr. Turner. Is your family well?"

"The wife is a little under the weather."

Nancy scanned the return address:

The Taggart Family

Copeland, KY

Her heart raced. She started up the steps but realized she'd ended her conversation with Mr. Turner abruptly. She turned back to him. "I'll say a prayer."

"Thank you. So we'll see you in church Sunday?"

"Hopefully."

She turned back toward the house. That's when she saw Aaron standing at the top of the steps, tall and handsome, his athletic build imposing. His face beamed.

"Hello, Nancy."

"Aaron. What a surprise!"

He descended the steps, offered his arm and escorted her to the porch.

"I didn't expect...how did you get into the house...how are you?"

"One question at a time, please."

"Sorry. I didn't expect to see you, at least here, at the house."

"I've been looking after the place since your parents were away."

"Thank you. That's so kind."

"How are you feeling?"

"Much better, thanks. It's good to be home. I so look forward to sleeping in my own bed. Do you realize it's been four months?"

"Four months and a week. I've missed you, Nancy."

"Is that why you wrote so often?"

He laughed. "I've been busy, you know, with grad work and all. But I haven't received any mail from you, either."

"Busy also. Working long days and trying to get writing in."

"How's the project coming?"

"I've filled a few notebooks. Got a lot of typing ahead of me. That's the one thing I've really missed: my typewriter. And, of course, you...and my family."

"Glad you're home. I really didn't think you should have gone in the first place. I felt you were putting your career on hold all along. It's behind you now. Time to go on to other things."

She didn't answer. He gave her a quizzical look.

"What?" she asked with a smirk.

"Surely you aren't going back down there."

"Up there."

"Whatever. I can't imagine you going back there after all you've been through."

"I want to go back."

"Why? All you've gotten out of this is a few months behind on grad work and a sickness that could have killed you."

"But it didn't."

"Surely you aren't serious about going back."

"They need me."

"Who are they?"

"The children…the community…friends I've made."

He stared down into her eyes.

"Why are you looking at me that way?" She averted his gaze.

"I need you, Nancy."

His statement surprised her. She looked up at him. He reached for her hands. She acquiesced. He held her hands firmly. "I need you, Nancy."

She clumsily held his hands, while memories of their life since childhood flashed by. She suddenly remembered the envelope now crumpled in her hand. She wondered what it contained. Her heart yearned to read its contents.

CHAPTER THIRTY-SEVEN

~

Wesley loosened the reins and let the black gallop. He seemed eager to be headed home; they were already chasing the faint hue of the western sun. Wesley squinted as snowflakes blurred his vision. The freshly fallen snow now covered the trail, but the black sensed the worn path that snaked along Troublesome Creek.

Whose tracks were on the steps? Why didn't they make their presence known? Were they eavesdropping? Why?

The trail took a sharp left at the junction of the Troublesome and the North Fork. High Rock loomed to the right. It seemed much larger in winter, unobstructed by foliage. Wesley swam often at the rock as a youth. Bravery and cowardice teetered as the local boys mustered courage to leap from the rock into the North Fork swimming hole. He once camped at the base of High Rock while a social worker and a sheriff's deputy scouted the community looking for him. A caring neighbor revealed his hideout. He smiled as he considered his impetuous youthfulness.

The black's vapory breath escaped in rhythmic blasts. The snow melted as it dropped onto the black's heated body. Wesley gathered the reigns; the black slowed his pace. Got to let him cool.

He saw the puff of smoke the instant he felt the thud on the right side of his head; he knew immediately. His body jerked sideways as if tethered; he grabbed for the saddle horn. The black lunged at the crack of the rifle. The reigns slipped from Wesley's grip as the black bolted into full gallop. Wesley squeezed the stirrups to the black's sides, trying to balance himself. He needed to escape the attacker's sights; he needed to stay in the saddle.

The rifle cracked again and the bullet grazed the saddle. Was the gunman shooting at the black? Wesley leaned forward, trying to retrieve the reigns. His head spun. Warmth soaked his collar and seeped inside his coat. The rifle cracked again. And again. The black didn't slow. Wesley held tightly to the saddle horn. He fought the temptation of sleep.

The slowed pace of the black stirred his consciousness. Wesley winced at the throbbing in his head that kept pace with the trotting of the black. He removed a glove and felt the indentation of the wound. Not good. The flow of blood seems to have stopped. Good.

He felt tired. If only I can stop the black and lay down for a few minutes. He closed his eyes. Visions of his wife focused; her pleasant smile beckoned. Perhaps it's my time. The thought of home, his children and Nanny Sue motivated him. I must keep going. He thought of Nancy York and how much she meant to his family and what a difference she'd made in their community. He wished he'd told her the same instead of challenging her motives. How is she doing? Did my letter to her arrive?

Darkness settled in. The black kept going, now down to a steady walk. The moon rose slowly, its light reflecting off the snow like a giant lantern in the sky. The black paused at a creek to drink; his heavy breathing concerned Wesley. He let him drink for a moment and whistled him onward. He didn't want him to ingest too much of the cold water. Wesley thought he heard voices. The black neighed. Then there was silence.

CHAPTER THIRTY-EIGHT

~

Hyde Park had been Nancy's only home. Her father inherited the family residence from a spinster relative, Aunt Berry. From childhood Nancy thrilled in riding her bike in this exclusively residential neighborhood. With its wide streets, beautiful homes and manicured lawns it was one of the most picturesque suburbs of Cincinnati. She and Aaron were childhood sweethearts. They had spent many a summer afternoon splashing water on each other from the Kilgour Fountain located at the city square. Charles Kilgour, a real estate developer in the area, had donated the fountain to the community of Hyde Park.

Nancy had to admit she enjoyed being home. While her mother prepared dinner she lounged in the parlor opposite Aaron. Doris had insisted Aaron stay for dinner. He made sure Nancy approved before he accepted the invitation. That seemed kind. It was good catching up on old times. They had lived all their lives but blocks apart, attended grade school and junior high together and departed ways only because Nancy's father insisted she attend St. Mary's all-girl high school. Aaron went to Purcell High. They came together again in college.

Nancy respected Aaron. He came from a good family, was always her academic competition and was now a medical student at the Cincinnati campus. Awaiting dinner, he delighted her with news of recent events at the university: retiring professors, remaining professors and newcomers. She missed the university. She planned to return for graduate work but not until she finished her assignment in the Cumberlands. She sensed Aaron's concern and frustration that she'd postponed graduate work.

145

A call from the kitchen brought her father from his upstairs study. The table setting exemplified a prodigal's feast; her mother seemed proud. They found their usual places and bowed for grace.

"Humbly we thank thee, Father, for this occasion, both the meal and the attendance of those at this table. Truly you have smiled upon us again. Thank you for bringing our dear Nancy home. Thank you for our kind friend Aaron. I thank you for my sweet wife. Bless our time together as we break bread again as a family. In thy holy name, Jesus, we pray. Amen."

"I've been worried so about you, dear." Her mother dished roast beef onto Nancy's plate.

"I'm fine mother. Thank you." She retrieved her plate.

"I never should have consented to you going to that troublesome place."

"You didn't, Mother, if I recall correctly." Nancy smiled.

"I did, too, my dear."

"Doris just drug her feet a little," her father piped in.

"Roast beef, Aaron?" Her mother reached for his plate.

"Yes, please."

"Of course, things aren't as safe here as they used to be. I still can't believe what happened to Mrs. Pugh, stabbed with a knife in her own home." Doris piled Aaron's plate high with beef.

"Yes, that was terrible," Nancy said.

"To think a jury would let the man who confessed to the horrendous murder go free. I guess there's no safe place anymore. There you are, Aaron." She handed Aaron's plate back to him.

"How's school, Aaron?" Her father passed the dish of dinner rolls to him.

"Coming along, Mr. York. Semester finals were a little rough, but that's to be expected. I look forward to my practicum."

"I'm sure," Charles said. "What particular field are you considering?"

"Hematology."

"Which is?"

"The study of blood, organs that produce blood and diseases related to blood."

"A worthy profession," Charles said.

"It has its skeletons."

"Oh," Charles said.

"Ancient Egyptian means of drawing blood."

"You mean bloodletting?"

Charles and Aaron laughed. Their conversation continued regarding the advancement of the medical field of hematology.

The meal ended. Doris retreated to the kitchen to serve dessert.

"Aaron, could silver in a person's bloodstream cause the body to turn blue?" Nancy interrupted the conversation abruptly.

"It could, and it has. Why do you ask?"

"I've heard of some people in the mountains whose skin is a blue color. Someone suggested to me it could be caused by silver ingestion."

"I've heard of circus freaks whose body is blue from purposefully ingesting silver, but it's dangerous. Have you seen any of these blue folks?"

"No. I've just heard about them."

"Interesting," Aaron said.

Doris returned from the kitchen and served tea and cake. The men continued their conversation, which eventually got around to sports and manager Birdie Tebbetts' Cincinnati Redlegs. Many were concerned about the future of the aging Crosley Field, formerly Redland Field. Some were still upset over the name change after local businessman Powell Crosley purchased the team in 1934. Speculation was the new ownership had its eyes on a World Series championship and a new ballpark.

Nancy eased from the table and followed her mother into the kitchen. She could still hear the engaging conversation of her father with Aaron. Her dad really liked him. She liked Aaron. Then she remembered the unread letter.

CHAPTER THIRTY-NINE

~

Wesley hadn't been in a church building so huge since attending student chapel at the university. The grandeur of the arched, stained glass windows captivated his imagination. Biblical figures, larger than life, hovered over the audience: Noah exiting the ark; Moses holding the commandments aloft; young David strumming a harp. Each of the figures reminded him of a particular story from the Holy Scriptures and of the fragility of humanity. Each transmitted an aura of immortality, which was something Wesley struggled to comprehend but accepted.

An imposing pipe organ struck up the bridal procession. Wesley's wondering thoughts refocused. The resounding notes, each with certain duration and pitch, proclaimed the imminent message: here comes the bride. Five bridesmaids sauntered along the lengthy aisle, stopping at the piece of tape marking their spot near the deep varnished, wooden altar that ran the width of the sanctuary. The flower girl eventually cleared the gauntlet of familiar encouragers and, seemingly relieved, turned and looked toward the back of the sanctuary. The crescendo from the silver coated pipes vibrated the soul as it ricocheted off the vaulted ceiling. The audience rose, cued by the mother of the bride who stood and turned to see her husband and daughter, arm in arm, standing in the vestibule. The couple stepped slowly to the doorway, flanked by two young tuxedoed men holding the doors open.

Wesley couldn't see the expression of her veiled face. He could only imagine: naive, pure and excited. He'd only known her for a few months, but that was sufficient time for him to know there was a certain attraction to her. What a difference she'd made to his aching heart. What delight she'd brought to his troubled home!

His gaze followed her every movement as she glided along the aisle: step, pause, step, pause to the rhythm of the bridal march. Her father laboriously mimicked her delicate steps. Popping flashbulbs gave a strobe effect along the candle lit aisle, illuminating her white, silky garment. Wesley was sure he caught a glimpse of her smile. She stopped short of the altar; the organ music slowly subsided.

A momentary hush enveloped the sanctuary, quickly chased away by sniffles from the front pew and the changing positions of the photographers.

"Who gives this woman to be married to this man?"

"Her mother and I."

Her father lifted the veil and kissed her lightly on the cheek. Her father stepped back, but she fell into his arms and embraced him vigorously, then wiped away a tear from beneath her veiled face. Her father hesitantly stepped aside and took his place beside his wife.

Wesley felt ashamed that he wasn't happy for the groom. He ached inside as if his future was being ripped from his bosom. Why did he long to hold her in his arms, to claim her for himself, to be the one to say I do? He realized from that moment on that would never be. Did he love her? If so, his giving her up to another she chose over him was the greatest test of his love for her. True love paid the ultimate cost when called upon to do so. For Nancy's sake, he wanted to be happy for the groom.

"If there be anyone who has reason to believe these two should not be joined together, let him speak now or forever hold his peace."

Wesley wanted to speak. He wanted to object. He wanted to explain that he, too, loved this woman. He felt himself gasping. His mouth felt dry. Words wouldn't come, no matter how hard he tried to form them.

"Since there be no one…"

"Do you…?"

"I do!"

Tears coursed his cheeks; perspiration beaded his brow. Someone dabbed his face gently with a cool cloth.

"Do you…?"

Wesley felt himself fading from the scene. Or was the scene fading from him? He couldn't tell. He liked the coolness of something moist on his brow. Someone was speaking to him. Someone called his name.

"Wesley! Wesley, do you hear me?"

CHAPTER FORTY

~

The light seemed intensely bright. Perhaps it was the flashbulbs of the photographers. But there was no popping; the light was constant.

Where am I? Wesley squinted to survey his surroundings. Things seemed somewhat familiar.

"Wesley, can you hear me?"

A man's voice. Whose voice was it? He couldn't tell. He turned his face toward the voice.

"Ouch!"

"Easy, sir."

It was a woman's voice. Whose?

"Wesley, it's Doc Lewis. Can you hear me?" The man spoke again.

"Yes."

"Good! Glad you're finally awake."

"What happened to me? Where am I?"

"You're in my office. Family got you here a few days ago. You've been shot."

"Shot?"

"Bullet grazed your head. Ruined your hat. Left you with a nasty cut and concussion. We've mostly been concerned about the concussion and fever. Fortunately for you the fever broke a few minutes ago."

Wesley winced as he reached to touch his head.

"Easy, Mr. Taggart."

It was the woman's voice again. He tried to focus on the blurry white figure by his bedside.

"I'm sorry, but I don't recognize you. Miss …?"

"Brenda Sue. Bobby Lawson's daughter from over Howard's Creek. I'm Dr. Lewis' nurse."

"She's been caring for you night and day. You'll need to buy her lunch when you're up and about."

"Thank you, Miss Lawson."

"Just doing my job."

Wesley closed his eyes. "I'm sorry. I feel so tired."

"No, it's best to rest," She replaced the damp cloth across his forehead.

"Thank you."

"I have another patient to check on. I'll be back in a few minutes. Miss Lawson will attend to you."

Wesley heard the door open and close. He heard the rattle of utensils and the sound of water from a faucet. He traced the sounds of her steps as the nurse returned to his bedside and swapped out the cloth from his forehead.

"I need to change the bandage, Mr. Taggart."

"Okay."

She began to slowly unwrap the bandage from his head.

Did the doctor shave my head? That must be ugly? How deep is the wound? He remembered the wedding. How can that be? I'm here in the doctor's office. Was I even at a wedding? No. I was visiting Tom Fugate. His family. Was the wedding a dream?

"You've been awful restless for the past hour or so. Any pain?"

"Only when I move my head."

"That's normal."

"Was I talking in my sleep?"

"You were mumbling some."

"About what?"

"I couldn't rightly tell. You seemed troubled. Anything you'd like to talk about?"

"My family, are they okay?"

"They're all fine. Spent the weekend in town. Nanny Sue brought them. Went home yesterday evening. Didn't want to miss any more school."

"School's back in session?"

152

"A couple weeks now."

"Mr. Deaton teaching?"

"He was."

"He's not now?"

"Not since the new teacher arrived, a young lady teacher."

"Miss York?"

"If that's the one who took sick. She's back. Don't rightly know her name. They arrived Sunday evening on the train."

"They?"

"A young man escorted her. Saw them at the White Flash having a sandwich. Nice looking couple. Oh, I almost forgot, when you feel up to it, Sheriff Watkins wants to speak with you about the shooting."

Wesley didn't respond.

CHAPTER FORTY-ONE

~

The nurse attended to the gentle tap on the door.

"You've got company, Mr. Taggart.," Brenda Sue said. "I'll just take advantage of this visit and look after a couple things. Be back shortly."

Wesley tried to focus on the tall man standing at the foot of his bed.

"Hello, Mr. Taggart. I'm Aaron Baldwin. I just left your house…got to meet your lovely family. Nancy asked me to stop by and say hello for her."

"How nice of you…of Miss York…of Nancy. Sorry I can't sit up. They say I have a nasty concussion."

"I've heard. Your daughter Joyce filled me in on the details. They all seem encouraged by the doctor's report."

"Nancy, will she still be staying at my house?"

"Yes. She's eager to get back into the classroom."

"My nurse said she saw you and Nancy at the White Flash today…"

"That's mostly why I'm here. Nancy didn't realize you were in town…here in the doctor's clinic, or else she would have insisted on seeing you. Once we arrived at Copeland and she found out you were ill, it was too late to come visit…and, of course, she has to teach tomorrow."

"I understand. So, will you be spending the night and returning back to Copeland tomorrow."

"Actually I only have a few minutes and I'll catch the departing train to Lexington, then on to Cincinnati."

"Cincinnati?"

154

"That's where I live."

"How do you know Nancy?"

"We've been lifelong friends. We grew up together in Hyde Park, a suburb of Cincinnati."

"Not staying in Copeland, Mr. Baldwin?"

"Oh no. I'm due in class...college tomorrow."

"A professor?"

"Student. Graduate work."

"How kind of you to stop by."

"Nancy insisted."

"Is she well?"

"Very well. The doctor released her with a clean bill of health."

"That's wonderful."

"Yes, it is. Wish I could stay longer, but I have to catch the train."

"Will you be returning soon to Copeland ...to see...be with Nancy?"

"I can't say for sure. We'll see. Nice to meet you. Sorry it's under these circumstances. Please let Miss York know I stopped by."

With those departing words he was gone.

Please let Miss York know I stopped by. "Please let Miss York know...." Wesley repeated the words. "Miss York." She's still Miss Nancy York.

CHAPTER FORTY-TWO

~

Sheriff Sam Watkins didn't bother to knock. Wesley looked up and there he stood, looming over him, broad and tall. He held his hat in his left hand and cupped his right hand on the forty-five that hung low at his waist. He had tight-fistedly ruled the county for the past eight years. Crime had calmed under his leadership.

"Evening, Mr. Taggart."

"Sheriff Watkins. Please call me Wesley."

"Okay. Mind if I sit for a chat? That is, if you're feelin' up to it."

"Feeling much better. What's on your mind?"

"Been wondering about this shootin'. Did you happen to get a look at the shooter?"

"No. It happened suddenly...no warning...no sight of who fired the shot."

"Sounds suspicious, but don't you think it could have been a stray bullet?"

"I don't think so. It was more like four or five shots. One hit me, another my saddle. Sure glad my horse didn't get hit."

"I was wonderin' what were you doin' over at the Troublesome anyway?"

"I went to see Tom Fugate. Employee of mine."

"Is that Dan's boy?"

"Could be. I don't know many of the folks over there."

"Probably Dan's boy. About thirty?"

"Yes. Has a wife and three children."

"I'm purty sure that's Dan's boy. Anyway, who knew you was going to the Troublesome?"

"My family. I told the Deatons when I stopped in to check on our mail."

"What was the nature of your visit with Tom?"

"I'm planning on some prospecting on the Troublesome. I think there might be some silver in those hills."

Sheriff Watkins laughed.

"What?"

"You ain't bought into the John Swift silver legend, have you?"

Wesley didn't laugh.

"Have you?" Watkins pressed for an answer.

"No, Sheriff. I'm a geologist by training, not a fable chaser. I have reason to believe there's silver over there. If that's true, it'll be a mighty blessing to those poor folks living along the creek."

"I'd say. Maybe someone doesn't want you to find the silver... if there is any, I mean. That'd be motive enough for murder. Who all you told about your silver assumptions?"

"Tom Fugate mostly, since he lives there and works for me. Made some comments to friends. No one else, especially no one on the Troublesome."

"The shootin's probably not about the silver. Probably just one of them cantankerous Troublesome blue fellas. They carry a mighty big chip."

"Or maybe it was just some stray bullets, Sheriff, like you said," Wesley said matter-of-factly. "No cause for them to shoot me."

Sheriff Watkins seemed to give Wesley's last statement some thought before he continued. He covered a lot of ground with his questions. Wesley had met him only occasionally, but was now impressed by his thoroughness. The sheriff left no unturned rocks, even picked up some to examine closer.

"I've gotta hunch," the sheriff concluded. "You aware Hiram Callahan is out of prison?"

"Yes, and I'd have to admit that concerns me. Wouldn't he know he'd be a suspect if he shot me?"

"Typical psychopathic behavior. Uninhibited impulses. Pleasure in their criminal acts. No sense of guilt or shame. A godless conscience...or none at all. Never learn from past crimes. Never think they'll get caught 'cause they think they're smarter than everybody else. That man's been in prison twice already and he'll more'n likely be back in again. Callahan probably done it. He's the kind. Born criminal."

"I wouldn't say a criminal is just born that way, Sheriff."

"Really?"

"Maybe it has something to do with the way a person's brought up...you know, hardened by circumstances, by the harshness of the land...the type of parenting under which they're molded, you know, domineering and such."

"You're talking about half the people in this county. Most of them ain't criminals. Callahan has a criminal mind and I'd put nothin' past'em. Born that way."

"That's your field, Sheriff, not mine. Why would he want to shoot me? I never did anything against Hiram Callahan...even though I'd have to confess I was tempted. Bill Deaton's the one who testified against him. I didn't even contest his parole. Why would he shoot me?"

"Hate. That man is eaten up of hate. And revenge."

"But he's the one that killed...caused my wife to be killed... like I said, I never testified against him."

"He's got other reasons to hate you."

"What?"

"You were the one who won the hand of the girl he was sweet on. That alone was enough for him to hate you, and he spent time in the pen for a crime involving your family...your wife. That's enough to make him seek revenge, and he's taking it out on you."

"Can you prove that?"

"He was seen up on Troublesome a day before the attack on you. I know that for a fact. Of course, nobody'll testify against'em. His deceased wife is kin to most on the Troublesome, you know. The rest won't risk their own family's safety."

"So how you going to prove anything?"

"I'm not, or at least probably won't be able to. Wish I could. That's not really why I'm here."

"Then why are you here, Sheriff?"

"To warn you. To warn you to be careful and to make sure you take care of that family of yours. Watch out for them. It's no tellin' what Hiram Callahan might do to quench his thirst for revenge. Watch your back and don't let your family venture too far from your sights. Give serious consideration about venturing over at the Troublesome and leaving your family unattended."

Wesley didn't answer.

"Be seeing you. You get well and get home as soon as you can. And take my advice and stay away from the Troublesome."

CHAPTER FORTY-THREE

~

Nancy slogged through a mixture of snow and mud; a quick thaw had left the trail a quagmire, nearly impassable. The soles of her boots were caked with mud, and she tired of cleaning them. She had followed the directions Joyce reluctantly gave her, but she was now concerned either she'd written them down incorrectly or she'd taken a wrong turn along the way.

She rehearsed the directions: Follow the train tracks to John Little's Branch; cross the branch on the wooden swinging bridge and follow the path to the right fork; cross the right fork at the log bridge and follow the path until it comes to the house; the trail ends at the house.

The last house she passed was about half an hour ago; the trail had continued, but narrowed. The winter sun, barely visible through the haze developing in the sky, dropped below the southern tree line; darkness descended quickly. Shadows obscured the worn path. Reluctantly, she realized her decision was a mistake; she had to turn back. Now. At that exact moment she smelled smoke. Can that smell be from the Callahans' chimney? Just around this bend. I'll check around this one more bend. She followed the faint outline of the path, occasionally stumbling over a protruding rock. Her shoes felt like weights; her clothes, soaked from perspiration, clung to her skin from underneath her unbuttoned winter coat. She brushed back matted hair from her forehead. Stubbornness had dwindled to survival.

Her intentions were admirable: talk Mr. Callahan into sending Jack and his younger sister to school. Jack needed restoration from his expulsion by Mr. Deaton. After all, Mr. Deaton wasn't really the teacher when he sent Jack packing; she was. She assumed Mr. Deaton thought he was doing her a favor, but it wasn't a favor she needed at the expense of a child's education. She wanted him back in school. The younger sister could certainly not attend without her older brother escorting her through these obscure backwoods. Nancy felt terrible the younger child had never attended school. She was a blue child, but a child nonetheless who needed to be in school.

A movement in the trees startled her. She peered into the darkness engulfing her, trying to identify the varying shapes and sizes. Another movement! Something swooshed past her head so closely she felt the wind it created. Perhaps an owl, but they don't bite. Or do they? Looking skyward she saw only a faint hint of any constellation. The clouds were gathering instead of diminishing. Towering trees spread their limbs like intertwining fingers, forming a canopy above her pathway, but she didn't feel protected, rather swallowed up. She pulled her coat hood over her head.

I must turn back. Turn back to what? It's half an hour of traveling in daylight back to the nearest house. It's pitch black. Follow the trail; surely it'll lead to someone's house.

The smell of smoke intensified. She continued down the path, reluctantly, carefully. The trail broke forth into a small clearing. She stopped; her senses intensified. The aroma of the smoke carried a hint of dinner, drawing attention to her gnawing stomach. She heard rushing water splashing against creek stones. She saw the shadowed form of a small house. Was this Callahan's residence?

"Lord, help me," she whispered as she stepped cautiously into the clearing.

The log shack sat on leaning stilts jutting from the creek bank. Nancy approached cautiously; more than once she'd come too suddenly upon an overzealous watchdog. Adrenaline kicked in; her body suddenly felt cold.

Nancy pondered how to begin the conversation with Mr. Callahan. She questioned if the children would be receptive. Was Jack too bitter to return to school? Her plan had seemed so right and simple before. Now she wondered.

Is that someone standing in the shadows on the front porch? She stopped dead still, struggling to calm her escalating heartbeat. Her breathing came in wheezy pants. She strained into the darkness, trying to identify what seemed to be a large individual. The figure remained motionless. Friend or foe? Is this the right cabin? Should I call out?

A flash of light exploded in the darkness and illuminated a face: male, stubble covered. Hiram Callahan. Steely eyes reflected the light from the glowing match. She gasped faintly. Did he hear me? He held the flaming matchstick to a cigarette that hung loosely between his lips. Puffs of smoke formed a ghostly mirage about his countenance. Nancy remained transfixed. Can he see me? Why are no sounds coming from the cabin? Where are the children? Was that a devilish grin?

He flipped the burning match onto the ground where it flickered for a moment in the mud, then smoldered. Darkness again.

Nancy wanted to turn and run back down the path, to take her chances against the darkness, but she seemed unable to will her feet to move. She felt trapped. Afraid. Alone. Vulnerable.

CHAPTER FORTY-FOUR

~

Nanny Sue laid the child into the crib. He whimpered, but she didn't seem to notice. She tiptoed across the wooden floor, flipped the light switch off, gently pulled the door shut, and joined the other children in the living room. The twins played on the floor; Joyce and Gary stood at the window, their faces cupped against the rain-streaked glass, staring into the darkness.

A lightning flash illuminated the front yard and the sheets of driving rain that pelted the windowpane; a simultaneous crack of thunder shook the house. The children's bodies jerked at the explosive jolt. The twins, noticeably frightened, hugged tightly, their faces pressed against each other, making it impossible to identify them from their dusty blond curly hair, showing signs of a much needed haircut.

She walked across the room to where Joyce and Gary stood looking out the window and placed her hands on their shoulders. "It's gonna be alright, children. Don't usually get storms like this in wintertime. Strange how the good Lord's nature sometimes acts."

"Where could she be?" Joyce wiped her eyes.

"Not sure, child, but she'll be coming along soon. Probably stopped off at a neighbor's place to get out of the rain."

"I shouldn't have let her go, especially alone. It's my fault. I should have gone with her," Joyce said. "She's probably lost and will never be found."

"I wouldn't have allowed it, child. That would just have made two of you soaked like drowned rats instead of one. Your daddy disapproved of you going."

"I wish Daddy was home."

"Your daddy's got to get well before he comes home. Hopefully in a day or two."

Another lightning bolt lit up the valley.

"Look! Somebody's coming!" Joyce exclaimed.

"Maybe her," Nanny Sue said matter-of-factly.

"Or Daddy!"

Gary ran to the front door and swung it open just as the thunder jolted the house again. He leaped back, placing his hands over his ears.

The lightning silhouetted Kelly Combs as he ascended the steps; he stopped at the doorway, dripping wet and shivering.

"Come on in, Kelly." Nanny Sue waved her hand. "You're gonna catch pneumonia in this weather."

Kelly stepped inside the door, pulled a handkerchief from his hip pocket and muffled a cough.

"What's wrong to bring you out on a night like this?" Nanny Sue asked.

"Wife sent me to warn you. We got troubles, Nanny Sue. The river's risin' faster'n I've ever seen it 'cept the thirty-seven flood. We know Wesley ain't here, so we thought I better let you know things ain't lookin' good."

"I think it'll slow down, Kelly, soon's it stops rainin'. And the thirty-seven didn't flood this property. That's why Wesley bought it, cause it sets on higher ground."

"I got my doubts this one won't get higher than the thirty-seven. Ground's already saturated from the melted snow. Waters got no place to go 'cept up."

"Sure you ain't panickin'?"

"The creek's already in our yard, and it's only been a couple hours since the downpour started. Ain't never seen it rain so hard in all my days. Best be thinkin' 'bout goin' to higher ground anyway just in case. We're headin' to momma's old place over at Big Branch. Y'all are welcome to join us."

"I think we'll be okay since our house sits a might higher'n yours. We're even with the tracks and they were built up for just this reason. The thirty-seven didn't cover the tracks here. We got ourselves another problem."

"What's that?"

"Teacher's gone missing."

"Miss York? When?"

"Took off right after school today to visit with Hiram Callahan."

"Lord God Almighty, help us, sweet Jesus," Kelly momentarily bowed his head. "Why'd she do a fool thing like that for anyway?"

Kelly tried to stifle a cough, but it burst from his mouth. His body bent over and convulsed with each anguished expulsion of the windpipe.

"You okay?" Nanny Sue placed a hand on his shoulder.

Kelly straightened as the coughing subsided. "Sorry. I'm a bit winded from running here. What about the teacher?"

"She wanted to try and get the Callahan children in school."

The hacking started again. One of the twins began to cry. Joyce rushed to his rescue.

"You better get home and change into some dry clothes or you'll catch pneumonia."

"I'm okay but what you plannin' on doing about Miss York? Can't send nobody out in a rain like this. Anyways, them creeks over there at Callahan's place are already flooded for sure. No way she can get back now…even if she's okay."

The room grew silent except for the baby's whimpering and the pelting rain against the windowpanes.

"Ssssh." Joyce tried to comfort the baby.

"Sorry Wesley ain't here." Kelly muffled his cough.

"Joyce and I was just talking how we sure wished he was here. He'd know best what to do."

"How's he doing?"

"Doc Lewis wants to keep him a few days for observation. He's been really bad…wound got infected, I think."

"Wish I could help out with Miss York, but I gotta get the family to higher ground. Makes me feel mighty bad leavin' y'all here without Wesley."

"We'll be okay. Your family needs you right now. You run along and take care of Beulah Jane and them young'uns."

They stood in the doorway and watched Kelly slosh across the rain soaked yard, the lightning causing a strobe effect revealing his gaunt frame hunched against the rain and shielding his head with his hands as if he could protect himself against the fierce lightning flashes.

The intensity of the rain had come without warning. They didn't have the convenience of an up-to-date weather report, though they had The Old Farmer's Almanac, but it gave only generalities, not specifics: when to plant and harvest, when to fish and when to expect dog days and Indian Summer. They weren't prepared for this, nor could they be.

Wesley wasn't home. Miss York was missing.

Nanny Sue didn't attempt to make the children go to bed. They watched the clock as the hands struck midnight. From the corner of the living room the Motorola squawked out flashflood warnings by counties and towns. As the water raised higher, and the rain kept coming, the announcer's conversation turned into concern. His team remained on the job airing reports they received from shortwave radio users. The town of Hazard was under water. Areas around Jackson were being evacuated. Nanny Sue frowned. Her community was in between. Kelly Combs might be right.

The lightning flashed again. The lights flickered and went out. Total blackness.

The screaming of the twins pierced the darkness.

"It's gonna be alright, young'uns. Don't you be afraid." Nanny Sue spoke calmly and felt her way across the room. "Joyce, get the candles from the pantry."

Nanny Sue's ears followed the sounds of Joyce making her way through the darkness, giving out instructions.

"Third shelf from the bottom," she called out. "Matches are on the shelf above the stove."

Joyce returned with two flaming candles.

"Thank you, dear. Just place them on the mantle."

Nanny Sue cradled the twins, humming softly until they calmed and fell asleep in her arms. She laid them feet to feet on the couch, covered them with their matching blankets and turned her attention to gathering up their toys from the middle of the floor.

Joyce sat in Wesley's overstuffed chair by the fireplace, thumbing the pages of a textbook. She dozed and the book fell onto her lap, startling her awake. She placed the book on a stand and curled up in the chair. Gary lay on the floor, next to the door, his head resting on his baseball glove. Nanny Sue covered him with a throw from the back of the couch.

Throughout the night Nanny Sue paced the house, stopping only to attend to the children and peer out into the darkness, wondering. The children remained asleep, on the couch, the chair and the floor. She gently rearranged their blankets and lovingly replaced Gary's ball glove with a pillow for his head. She glanced often at the clock. Where was Miss York? "Help her, dear Jesus, help her." Will tomorrow bring sunshine? How's Wesley doing? Worried to death about us, I'm sure.

Darkness fled the dawn of another red-streaked sky—more rain. Nanny Sue donned a shawl, stepped outside and walked the length of the wraparound porch observing the devastation. Daylight revealed a sea of churning, murky water across the valley. As far as she could see, the community was under siege of the raging current. In the blackness of the night, the stealthy flood waters had crept up the banks like a cat stalking a blue jay: deliberately and relentlessly.

A commotion ensued across the river. She recognized Langley Davis, by his beaver hat and overcoat, standing in his boat and shoving off the bank into the raging current. Looked like a coil of rope draped from his shoulder. What does that fool man think he's doing? That's when she saw the house, bobbing and twirling in the current. Surely he ain't gonna try and catch that house. A rocking chair swayed on the front porch of the house; a rooster perched on the roofline, scurrying from end to end. The house swayed back and forth in the powerful current, like a bobber being jerked by a catfish.

"Gonna hook me a whale," he yelled across the river to Nanny Sue.

"Whatcha gonna do with your whale, Jonah?" she called back.

Surprisingly the voices carried across the sea of water.

"I'm gonna ride it to Nineveh 'n back."

"Better watch out or that whale might take you some place worse than Nineveh."

Nanny Sue smiled to herself. She wondered how she could carry on a conversation so frivolous in such a serious time as this. "That man's half crazy," she said aloud.

He managed to circle the house with his boat, encasing it with his rope, then he paddled furiously toward the shore, where he leaped from the boat and hurriedly tied the end of the rope to a tree. The line immediately grew taut and the house slowly swung toward the shore.

"Gotcha," Langley yelled jubilantly, like an angler snagging a trout.

The rope snapped, the house floated onward, bobbing, spinning and picking up speed as it caught the swifter current. Its top caught the swinging bridge and snapped a main wire. Part of the bridge tumbled into the water and was carried downstream.

Langley kicked the ground and snarled like a mad dog.

Nanny Sue laughed. "Crazy ole coot."

The commotion brought Joyce and Gary charging onto the porch. They stopped dead in their tracks, the looks on their faces revealing their disbelief.

"Bad, huh?" Nanny Sue said.

They stood in silence for a long while, observing their surroundings.

From across the river a truck approached in the distance and pulled onto the side of the road near the damaged bridge. Two men exited and pulled a boat from the bed of the truck and dragged it to the water's edge.

"What are they doing?" Joyce asked.

Nanny Sue didn't answer.

The two men stepped into the boat, pushed off the bank and were immediately swept downstream by the raging current. The men paddled hard, dodging floating trees, sodden animals and partially submerged logs. They finally landed the boat a quarter mile downstream from where they put in. Nanny Sue breathed a sigh of relief.

"Why would they do such a fool thing?" Joyce questioned.

"The bridge is out."

"They shouldn't have attempted to cross the river unless it was a matter of life and death," Joyce protested.

They observed in silence as the two men pulled the boat ashore and went separate ways. One walked the tracks toward their house. Nanny Sue and Joyce stared toward him, while Gary hurried down the steps, stomped through the water in the front yard and sprinted toward the tracks.

"Gary, where you going?" Joyce yelled after him.

He rushed toward the approaching man. He didn't stop until he leaped into the man's outstretched arms.

"It must be Daddy," Joyce exclaimed.

"Just wait here, child," Nanny Sue ordered.

"Daddy must be better, Nanny Sue."

"Thank the good Lord, dear."

"I will, Nanny Sue. Every day I will."

Joyce stood at the top of the steps waiting. "Hello, Daddy."

"Hello, Joyce. Nanny Sue."

Wesley ascended the steps slowly, Gary holding his hand. Joyce embraced his waist, burying her head in his stomach. Crying.

"That was a foolish thing to do," Nanny Sue scolded Wesley.

"Had to get here. Trains aren't running, so I thumbed a ride to Haddix and paid Charlie Watkins to bring me the rest of the way. He wanted to check on his folks so it worked out. I figured the swinging bridge might be out so we brought a boat along. Got a little concerned there for a minute."

"You weren't the only one who got concerned!" Nanny Sue exclaimed.

"We saw it all, Daddy. You scared us half to death. 'Course we didn't know it was you at first. Gary realized it the moment you started up the tracks."

Gary looked up at his daddy and smiled. Wesley ruffled Gary's full head of hair.

"Glad you're home, Wesley."

"Missed you, Daddy." Joyce hugged him again.

"The twins still asleep?" Wesley asked.

"Been up most of the night. I didn't have the heart to make 'em go to bed at a decent hour. This whole thing has been troublin' to us all."

"I understand. I hear Miss York is back from Cincinnati. How's she feeling?"

Nanny Sue didn't answer. She stared across the water.

"Is something wrong, Nanny Sue?"

"Yes, she's back."

"She's in trouble, Daddy."

"Trouble? What kind of trouble?"

"She went to visit Hiram Callahan last night, you know, to try and get him to let the children come to school. She hasn't returned." Nanny Sue said.

"It's my fault, Daddy. I shouldn't have told her how to get there."

"It's not your fault, sweetheart," Nanny Sue said. "She was bound and determined to speak with Hiram Callahan about his kids. She should have listened to your daddy, but she has a mind of her own."

Wesley didn't respond. He slowly opened the door and walked inside the house.

CHAPTER FORTY-FIVE

~

Charles York steered his Edsel onto the dealership driveway. He was one of the few customers to purchase Ford's latest experiment, designed to replace the intermediate line vacated by the company's upgrade of their Lincoln model. He glanced at the advertisement blazoned across the dealership window: The same *Air of Elegance*, the same *Look of Superb Ability*. He liked his new car, which he'd chosen over Chevrolet's *Sweet, Smooth and Sassy* model. He heard rumors Bing Crosby and Frank Sinatra would do a live *Edsel Show* on CBS-TV. The rumor had been enough to sway him away from Chevrolet. Such a possible endorsement spoke volumes to him of the future of the Edsel Company. He was delighted to be on the cutting edge of progress.

He braked and maneuvered the car alongside the curb. As the service supervisor approached, he rolled down the window.

"Morning, sir." The attendant smiled.

"Good morning. Beautiful day, isn't it?"

"Every day is beautiful when you're this side of the grass. How's she running, sir?"

"Great. I'm just here for an oil change."

"Name?"

"Charles York."

"Yes, sir, Mr. York. Got you down. First one's on us. Leave your keys in the ignition and feel free to enjoy some hot coffee in our customer waiting area."

Charles appreciated the customer-oriented service he received. He glanced at the supervisor's name tag.

"Thank you, Robert. How long do you think it'll be?"

"Forty-five minutes at the most."

Charles reached across to the passenger seat and retrieved his *Cincinnati Enquirer*, a longstanding morning newspaper recently purchased by the E. W. Scripts Company. He exited the car and made his way to the waiting area, scanning the news as he walked. That was when he noticed the headlines: Eastern Kentucky Flooding. After reading the first paragraph of the article, he slowly sat down, stunned: both Jackson and Hazard were reported flooded.

Is Nancy okay? How can I get in touch with her? Has Doris heard? I must call home. Doris will be frantic. He raced to a pay phone, inserted a coin and quickly dialed his home number. No answer. He retrieved his coin and tried again. The same. His mind raced.

He ran to the service area to find his car being elevated on the hydraulic lift.

"I have to go," he yelled to the mechanic.

"We just got started." The supervisor left his desk and walked toward Charles. "Is something wrong?"

He held the paper open toward the supervisor. "My daughter, Nancy, she's there."

"Where?"

"Eastern Kentucky. Where the floods are. I have to go. Now!"

The supervisor looked toward the mechanic and nodded his approval. The mechanic turned a lever to lower the lift.

"Sorry, Mr. York. Hope everything's okay. We'll reschedule. Just give us a call."

"Thank you."

The lift lowered and Charles jumped into the car, engaged the starter and squealed tires as he jerked the lever into reverse. The Edsel bounced as he raced over a speed bump and turned onto the street toward home. Is Nancy okay? Has Doris heard? Is she okay? She always answers the phone. Why did she not answer? Has someone already told her about the flooding? Her emotions aren't strong.

He didn't hear the clanging bell, notice the flashing light or see the oncoming train. Suddenly everything went blank.

CHAPTER FORTY-SIX

~

Nancy sat on a broken Nehi soda crate, which lay upside down on the ground, her knees locked in her arms and pulled to her chin. Her torn and stained skirt clung to her body. Red mud caked her coat, which draped unevenly across her shoulders and hung to the ground. With eyes bloodshot and swollen, she stared into the flames of a fire that spewed steam from rain sodden logs. Her long, dark hair plastered her head and hung limply in a matted mess.

Why? That was the question she kept asking herself. Why did I not think to bring an umbrella? Why did I not listen to others who warned me about the dangers of this strange land? Why does the stomach hurt when you're hungry? Why do I not realize the impetuous spirit sometimes traverses the border of stupidity? Why did I, a total stranger, think I could make a difference in the lives of the two young Callahans? Why does the smoke of burning logs smell stronger than the smell of the log itself?

She dabbed with a damp handkerchief at a long scratch across her forehead and deep into her right cheekbone. Blood stained the cloth.

A few feet away the flooded river raged relentlessly. She shivered. Pulling her coat tighter around her body, she felt the penetrating stare of Hiram Callahan; he sat on the opposite side of the campfire.

Only yesterday she'd taught her class in a warm, dry classroom. That seemed like a long time ago. The past twelve hours seemed like an endless nightmare, terrifying, of which there seemed no end in sight.

Who knew she was here? Nanny Sue and the kids knew. They'd be in no situation to help her. It pained her to have been so close to Wesley as she passed through Jackson but not realizing he was in Doctor Lewis' clinic she had not stopped to see him. Was he doing okay? Had Aaron been able to see him? Aaron was so kind to escort her back to these mountains; especially knowing she cared for another.

Hiram continued to stare at her but didn't speak.

She wanted to go home, home to the Taggarts' place. She longed to sit with them at the dinner table. She yearned for civil communication.

The dismal sky showed no hints of change. Her emotions felt the same: dull, colorless. She felt trapped.

Exhausted, she dozed; she dreamed of Wesley. Something startled her awake.

CHAPTER FORTY-SEVEN

~

Charles York couldn't remember how it happened; he suddenly found himself wedged on the floorboard of his car. He tried to free himself; he couldn't. His right arm seemed pinned behind his back. Excruciating pain shot through his head when he moved. He heard the rumble of what seemed to be an engine; the ground vibrated. Is that a train? Inaudible voices called to him. He tried again to move; the pain seemed unbearable. He closed his eyes and lay still.

Sirens! Was he dreaming? More voices!

He saw Doris's face, frightened. "It's okay, dear," he whispered.

Nancy came alongside and placed her arms comfortingly around her mother. Doris calmed.

"Thank you, sweetheart," he mouthed to her.

She smiled.

"I love you, Daddy."

He smiled back and sighed. Silence.

CHAPTER FORTY-EIGHT

~

Nanny Sue was reliving a twenty-year-old tragedy. She had been forty years old when the thirty-seven flood had swept through this community. She stood on the porch drying her hands on her apron, observing. Life seems to come in cycles.

The rains had stopped. The murky floodwaters crested but remained constant. As far as she could see, most of the community was under water. She worried about Wesley, still weak from the gunshot wound, but working nonstop helping neighbors retrieve furniture and finding temporary shelter for them. The Taggarts' wraparound porch looked like a refugee camp. She walked the length of the porch, speaking to the neighbors, checking on the children. Joyce entertained the twins. Gary remained to himself, sitting on the railroad tracks, staring across the floodwaters. Neighbors could do little but wait.

She was grateful to Wesley. He treated her like blood kin. Though sometimes on the quiet side, keeping you wondering what he really thought, he was such a caring man. Tragedy always brought his inner qualities to the surface. Nanny Sue observed as he refilled coffee cups. In between serving coffee, he found ways to stay busy: rearrange the furniture on the porch to make more space, toss a stick into the water to watch Giggs retrieve it, wipe Giggs' soaked fur, speak to the children. He made a couple trips to the kitchen doing women's work. She suspected the busyness was a positive diversion for him; still, she was concerned.

Nanny Sue walked to where he gathered dishes. "Worried about her, Wesley?"

"She's got to be frightened to death, Nanny Sue."

"Miss York's a right tough girl coming here in the first place. She's probably doing fine out there, probably worrying 'bout all of us."

"You really think so?"

"I do. I really do. She was right brave going to the Callahans' by herself. She probably realized the storm was coming and had time to seek shelter before the flood; neighbors would've taken her in. They'll watch after her."

"It's the not knowing part that troubles me. More than that, not being able to get to her cuts me deeper than I can express. What must she be thinking by now? Thinking we don't care?"

"She's thinking just like we are, thinking we're all trapped. Knowing we're all in the same situation, hopeless to change our predetermined destiny. Learnin' to trust the good Lord. Realizin' when God sneezes, the earth shudders. Can't alter providence; you learn to accept it. You know that as well as anyone."

"Faith isn't effortless, Nanny Sue. I feel like I've got to do something to help her. Doesn't God expect nothing less than our best effort? I can't stand just waiting."

"The cross wasn't effortless, but it was a lot of waitin'. He just hung their waitin'. Waitin' on the Father's will to be done. Waitin' on the tale to be finished. Jesus done the best thing He could've done for us by just waitin'. Maybe you need to learn to wait without frettin'. If God don't see her, Wesley, ain't nobody can find her."

"You're right, but it's still hard to just sit here and do nothing."

Wesley ceased challenging Nanny Sue's theology. He gently massaged his brow.

"I'd best wash the dishes," he said.

"That's not what I mean by waitin'," she scolded him. "I'll wash the dishes and you rest yourself. You're not well yet, Wesley."

CHAPTER FORTY-NINE

~

The meeting hadn't gone well with Hiram Callahan; she'd failed in her task. The children wouldn't be in school. Jack rejected her extended olive branch; Hiram refused to let Sherry Jane attend without Jack.

She had tried different approaches. She threatened Hiram with truancy laws regarding keeping Sherry Jane home from school.

"No government agent's gonna tell me what's best for my child, so Sherry Jane ain't comin' to your school. First off, this community don't really care 'bout no Callahan. Second, no blue child will be accepted by the other students."

"I'll watch over Sherry Jane," she said.

"Can you change the color of 'er skin, Miss York? Can you keep the other young'uns from thinkin' she's freakish, from laughin' when they're at recess, calling her names, refusing to accept 'er in their circles. Can you promise to be by 'er side every hour of the school day?"

Nancy had no answer. Mentally she'd just given up her mission when the sky burst asunder, hammering the shack mercilessly. The water came in torrents. She didn't want to stay but graciously accepted Callahan's invitation. The water rose rapidly; the cabin groaned and swayed. They'd fled the premises just as the wooden pillars gave way. The shack tumbled into the raging creek and disappeared into the darkness.

Hiram aggressively coached them through the night onto higher ground, rushing through openings made visible by violent lightning flashes, demanding they not stop to rest. Branches slashed Nancy's face; briars tore her clothing. He finally slowed, searching.

They huddled under a small overhang of rock until dawn. At first light they realized they were stranded; completely surrounded by water; hungry, wet and cold, but alive.

Hiram Callahan had saved their lives.

A sudden ruckus at the water's edge stirred Nancy from her thoughts. She stood and looked toward the Callahan family standing knee deep in the water. Jack, twenty feet from the shoreline, swam furiously against the current. Hiram was shouting commands. Nancy's heart sank.

CHAPTER FIFTY

~

Wesley realized immediately something was wrong. Gary stood on the tracks, frantically pointing toward the floodwaters. His face appeared ashen white, his lips moved, as if trying to speak, but no words came forth.

Wesley looked in the direction Gary pointed. A small house, or what was left of a house, drifted toward them, spinning with the current. He recognized it immediately: the Callahans' cabin.

He glanced at Gary, still staring and pointing frantically at the floating house. Wesley suddenly realized Gary also recognized the cabin. Wesley had taken Gary and Joyce to deliver a Christmas basket to the Callahan family. Hiram was in jail at the time, leaving the family destitute. They found Mary Emily Callahan sick of consumption. She died that spring. Wesley paid for her casket. They clothed her in the dress his family had given her for Christmas.

Mrs. Callahan's untimely death was the primary reason Hiram Callahan received early parole. That was also why Wesley hadn't objected to the parole.

Wesley ran to Gary, knelt and wrapped his arms around his trembling body. He's assumed the worst had happened to Miss York.

"It's okay, son. It's okay. Miss York's okay."

Gary's sobs slowly subsided.

"It's only a house, Gary Eugene. Ain't nobody in it. Miss York's going to be okay." Wesley tried to comfort him with words, but he doubted in his own heart.

Gary shook his head in disagreement, desperation apparent in his eyes. Wesley loosened his embrace of Gary. Gary walked in the direction of the drifting house. First he walked, then trotted and finally began to run full speed. Wesley stared after him, silent.

Nanny Sue stood beside Wesley, a hand resting on his shoulder. Joyce stared after her brother.

"That child's bluer than those young'uns over on the Troublesome. Their skin's blue on the outside, but that boy's soul is blue on the inside. It's a troublesome blue, Mr. Taggart. Ain't no medicine can cure that kind of trouble."

"Ain't you going after him, Daddy?"

"Aren't."

"What?" Joyce asked.

"Aren't you going after him. Not ain't."

"Sorry. Please, Daddy, aren't you going after him?"

"I will, sweetheart, but I need to give him space."

The small house drifted close to the bank. Bennie Strong and Jess Bush waded into the water and wrestled the small house ashore. Bennie climbed inside. Wesley watched. A crowd gathered, pointing and offering opinions.

Bennie reappeared from the house. "All's clear. Ain't nobody inside."

The crowd cheered.

"You might wanna take a look at this though, Wesley."

Bennie held a satchel over his head.

"Full of books and papers. Initials NRY on the outside." Bennie tossed the satchel to Wesley.

Wesley knew immediately. He pulled Gary close to him.; Gary pulled away and ran along the tracks.

CHAPTER FIFTY-ONE

~

"It's a boat, Miss York," Sherry Jane yelled. "We're gonna be saved."

Nancy rushed to the water's edge. Sherry Jane ran to her, clapping with glee. Hiram barked orders to Jack who struggled against the fierce current, fighting his way toward a partially submerged dinghy wedged against a tree trunk and rock. The water rushed sadistically around the barrier, pushing, crushing and threatening any moment to capsize the weather-beaten boat.

Jack swam closer; the water pushed harder.

"Stay to the right of it and swim beyond it," Hiram yelled, "then swim back with the current. Don't let it trap you, son."

"Is that safe, Mr. Callahan?"

He turned and stared at Nancy but didn't answer. She tried to read his steely eyes.

"That's it, boy. A little farther and swim back with the current."

"Mr. Callahan, shouldn't you be helping him? He's just a boy!"

"Hush up, woman!"

Nancy stepped into the water.

Sherry Jane grabbed Nancy by the skirt and pulled her back. "No, Miss York. Don't rile'em."

Nancy hesitated.

"Now!" Hiram yelled. "Go with the current."

Jack turned to his left; the current swept him under. He surfaced ten feet from the boat, beating the water violently.

Too far away. Nancy fought to remain silent.

"Swim harder, boy! Harder!"

The current tossed Jack, brutally, past the boat. A branch snagged his shirt. The current pulled him under.

Sherry Jane screamed.

Jack surfaced with his hand clasped around the branch. He fought back, slowly pulling himself toward the boat, going under water to pull, surfacing to breathe.

Nancy held her breath. Help him, Jesus. Please, Lord.

"Put a foot into the boat, boy. Pull yourself in. That's it, son. You're a Callahan. Ain't no cowards in the Callahan clan. That's it, boy. Climb aboard 'er!"

Hiram slammed his fist into his open palm. "You did it, boy, you did it. He did it, girls. See that boy. Taught'em to swim. Now get 'er loose and bring'er in, boy."

Jack worked the boat free of the tree and paddled with his hands to bring it to shore. Hiram flipped the boat bottom side up, dumping the water.

"Welcome to my ark, ladies." Hiram pushed the boat back into the water.

With Jack holding the end of the boat, Nancy and Sherry Jane climbed aboard. Hiram found a pole and joined them. Jack shoved the boat out into the current before jumping onboard. Hiram pushed hard with the pole against the riverbank and the boat slipped away from shore, the top of the gunnels riding precariously close to the water's surface.

The boat drifted with the current, while Hiram steered with the makeshift tiller. Nancy noticed Jack in the bow, silent, shivering. She slipped her coat off her shoulders and placed it around him. The boat listed starboard; water rushed over the side.

"Easy, miss," Hiram snapped.

"Sorry."

They drifted downstream in silence, except for the slapping of the current and the occasional scraping of the pole against the boat.

"Who's that?" Sherry Jane pointed in the direction of the train tracks. "Is that the Taggart boy?"

Nancy looked in the direction Sherry Jane pointed. Gary stood on the tracks, waving.

CHAPTER FIFTY-TWO

~

Somberness permeated the crowd. All of the men had volunteered to help.

"If Miss York is alive, we must find her," Wesley said. "It's her satchel. It's the Callahans' cabin. Something has definitely happened to her. We'll walk the tracks, looking for signs. We'll carry a boat to John Little's Branch, put in there and try to make it over to the Callahans' place."

The men nodded their approval of the plan.

"What about little Gary?" Jess asked.

"We'll find him along the way. He'll be sitting on the track up by the school, I suppose. Doubt he'll go much further."

Joyce didn't like the way her daddy said "If Miss York's alive, we must find her." The emphasis seemed to be on "if" rather than "is alive." She watched as they filed off the porch and followed them part of the way down to the tracks. Four of the men carried the boat; the others walked ahead in silence. Their silence troubled her.

CHAPTER FIFTY-THREE

~

It was Sherry Jane's idea. Her daddy hesitated but acquiesced. In the dialog, Nancy saw a side of him she hadn't before. Perhaps he wasn't an impossible nut to crack after all, given some time. Sherry Jane persuaded him to reconsider his first impression: they'd let Gary come on board. Perhaps it was Sherry Jane who could persuade him to change his mind about school.

"Need a ride, Gary?" Nancy called out.

Gary ran to the water's edge, relief showing on his face. Hiram steered the boat to shore; Jack leaped over the bow and held the boat steady while Gary climbed aboard. He lunged into Nancy's outstretched arms. She pulled him to the seat between herself and Sherry Jane and snuggled him. His rigid body relaxed.

Jack stepped back into the boat and took his seat in the bow. Hiram pushed hard against the pole and the boat slipped back into the current.

"Love your coat, Jackie," Sherry Jane teased her brother.

Jack jerked the coat off his shoulders and turned to hand it to Nancy. The boat shifted.

"Cut it out, you two," Hiram barked.

"You wear it, Jack. You're soaking wet. I'm afraid you're going to catch cold," Nancy said.

"Just teasin', Jack. Sorry," Sherry Jane said.

They floated on in silence.

"Know what I'm thinking?" Nancy asked. "I'm thinking of a hot cup of coffee, a fireplace and some dry clothes."

"Lost all our clothes," Sherry Jane said.

"We'll get you some more clothes, Sherry Jane." Nancy placed a hand on the child's knee.

"Don't cotton to charity, Miss York," Hiram barked.

"Not charity, Mr. Callahan. Neighborly duty. Remember the good Samaritan?"

"We Callahans can make do on our own."

"You call this makin' do?" Jack shouted at his dad. "We got nothin' now. Lost our house and we're ridin' in a borrowed boat."

"Watch your tongue, boy. Don't go sassin' your old man. I've done right by you all these years."

"'Cept when you was in the pen."

"Stop it, Jack," Sherry Jane yelled.

"Please, Mr. Callahan, can we just talk about something else?" Nancy broke into the conversation.

"Like what?" Hiram barked.

"Like I want to thank you for saving my life."

"Nothin' anyone else wouldn't have done."

"It was a kind and neighborly act. Just like the good Samaritan in the Bible."

"Don't go tryin' to stick religion down my throat, miss."

"Just making an observation, Mr. Callahan, not pushing my faith on you. That was brave of you, Jack, retrieving the boat."

"Thank you," Jack mumbled.

They drifted in silence. Nancy gazed across the blanket of water that covered the valley. If the community wasn't under siege, the scene would be awesome; a vast lake stretching from one mountain base to another, birds soaring overhead, a sunbeam piercing the gray sky. Quiet. It's a quiet that almost speaks to you.

"Look out!" Jack yelled.

Too late. The bow of the boat topped a log, which lurked just beneath the surface. The boat tilted starboard as it slipped onto the log; water topped the gunnels and the boat flipped, sending its passengers into the cold, murky water.

CHAPTER FIFTY-FOUR

~

Wesley found the scenario incredulous. They had walked the distance to John Little's Branch. No sign of Gary, nor of life anywhere. Surely Gary had stayed on the tracks, but how could they have missed him? Where was he? The child could be incorrigible at times, always trying to run from his problems. Anger flushed Wesley's face, then doubt and concern. The scene before them revealed the devastation of the flash flood. Not a house in sight in any direction on either side of the river. The houses were either gone or under water. The conjunction of two creeks was too much for the North Fork's riverbanks to handle.

"Sorry, Wesley, but we'd be fools to try and cross here in this boat till the water reccdes some," Bennie said matter-of-factly. "Ain't no place to land 'er."

"You're right, Bennie."

"Done all we can do, Wesley," Jeff added. "Ain't nobody survived lest they got to high ground fast, and that'd take a might bit of luck. We might as well go home and wait it out."

Wesley didn't answer.

"Sorry 'bout Gary Eugene. Can't imagine where that boy went off to," Bennie added.

"We'd better check the schoolhouse. He might have stopped there," Wesley said. "We can leave the boat and ride it back later, when the water goes down some. It's too heavy to carry all the way back home and there's no need to endanger anyone's life for nothing by putting it in the water."

Except for the crunch of their brogans on the gravel, all was silent. All were somber.

187

A mockingbird called from the distance. Wesley looked in its direction. Nature has won again. How appropriate! A mockingbird. "God has sneezed again." He recalled Nanny Sue's words.

"What was that?" Bennie asked.

"Just thinking out loud, Bennie."

Wesley wanted to thank the men for trying, but words seemed pointless:

Thank you for being willing to risk your lives on a mission that was doomed from the start.

You're welcome, Wesley. And thank you for leading us in this gallant effort to rescue those whom we knew were doomed from the start.

You're welcome, men. We did our neighborly duty; we can be proud of ourselves for that. Congratulations, men! Job well done!

Pat, pat! Clap, clap!

Silence seemed more appropriate. Still, was he becoming cynical? Where did such thoughts come from? He didn't know what to think. This was a position he wasn't accustomed to assuming. His body ached, but there was no particular spot. Not like a toothache, or a headache. It was a body ache…a dreary aching of mind…a heart ache. I dare not be so thin-skinned. He thought of his wife; he tried to imagine her expressions when Gary was born. Oh how she loved her first boy. He tried to picture his beautiful Nancy Sue as she and Gary walked together along the tracks, his little hand cupped inside hers. His imagination pictured little Gary clearly: smiling, happy. He attempted to recall his wife's face, young and vibrant. A mental image appeared: unclear, foggy. He tried harder to focus. He could only picture her as a photograph, in black and white, like the one that sat on his mantel. She was fading…distant…as if it was another life, another world. He didn't like that feeling. Gary had seemed to move on with his life, becoming quite attached to Miss York. Now, how strange both Gary and his wife could both be gone, and so suddenly. His thoughts wandered to Nancy York. Her image appeared clear in his mind, her face bright and colorful. A dagger of shame pierced him. He consciously blinked, endeavoring to stop his wandering thoughts.

He glanced up the hillside at the weatherboard schoolhouse. The building would have made a good shelter from the storm, but it seemed deserted. Perhaps no one felt at liberty to encroach on its purpose.

"Think he's there?" Jeff asked.

"Maybe. Gary?" Wesley called out.

No answer.

"Gary, are you in there?"

"I'll check on'em, Wesley," Bennie said.

Bennie scrambled up the hillside directly below the schoolhouse. The men sat on the tracks and waited. They watched as he forced open the door. They heard his footsteps echo across the hardwood floor of the classroom. The footsteps stopped. They waited.

Each of the men had their own mental picture of that classroom: a picture etched on their minds from eight years of enduring long hours of instruction from Mr. Deaton. Inside the single room sat worn, wooden desks with their initials carved in some inconspicuous place, or at least they thought so at the time they carved them. They received stripes as proof it was their carving; stripes worn with honor. Some of their initials were carved alongside another set of initials of their sweetheart and encased inside a heart. For some that person was now their wife; for others it was now the wife of their neighbor.

The footsteps echoed again, but all knew, it was the footsteps of one. Bennie reappeared, alone. The hinges squeaked as he closed the door.

"Sorry, Wesley. No sign of'em here," Bennie called down to them from the portico.

Wesley closed his eyes and bowed his head.

CHAPTER FIFTY-FIVE

~

Nancy could wait no longer; she hurried from the house to the railroad tracks and headed in the direction of the schoolhouse. That's when she saw them; she hesitated. They trudged along the tracks in no particular order. Wesley walked in the lead, alone, head bowed.

She waved, but he didn't respond. He must be so distraught, not finding Gary. She waved again. A couple of the men waved back, but not Wesley.

"Mr. Taggart, it's me, Nancy!" She cupped her hands and yelled to him.

Wesley stopped. She saw his long, incredulous stare. He seemed not to move. The others stopped beside him. Some patted him on the back. He continued to look toward her.

Hesitantly at first, then more assuredly, he walked toward her. She ran to him. Both stopped a step away from each other. The others encircled them, weary but euphoric.

"Hello, Mr. Taggart."

"Hello, Miss York. I'm glad you're safe."

"Thank you for searching for me. All of you." She raised her voice. "Thank you all for searching for me… for us. The Callahan family is safe, too. A cheer erupted from the men.

"I'm so very happy to see you, Miss York."

"Then how about a smile, Mr. Taggart?"

"I'm sorry. I hoped it didn't show. I am very happy, Miss York, for you and for the Callahan family, but Gary's still missing. We searched from here to the school and beyond but never found him."

"Oh, Wesley, please forgive me. I'm so sorry. It's dreadful of me. I should have…"

"What?" Wesley asked.

"Gary's safe. He's with us!"

He clasped her hands. "With you? Really?"

"Yes! Really!"

Applause erupted from the men.

Wesley remained silent. Tears coursed his cheeks.

Nancy pulled him close. His rigid frame awkwardly accepted her embrace. He lowered his head onto her shoulder. The others offered congratulatory pats and a word of gratitude to the Lord as they walked past the couple to greet their own awaiting families.

"He's safe, Wesley. We're all safe. God is good, Wesley, good to all of us this day," Nancy spoke softly to him.

She could feel his body trembling as he tried to subdue sobs that emanated from deep within.

She saw them before Joyce spoke. They slipped closely behind Wesley.

"Gary's here, Daddy."

Nancy released Wesley and he turned to see Joyce and Gary standing a few feet away. Smiling.

"Gary!"

Wesley bent down onto one knee and Gary ran to him and leaped into his outstretched arms.

"You got to hear the story, Daddy." Joyce pushed her fingers through Gary's wet hair. "Mr. Callahan saved them from the water that tore down his house and then Jack Callahan swum into the raging water and got them a run-away boat. Then they picked up Gary, but the boat overturned. Mr. Callahan grabbed onto the boat and they all held onto the sides and the boat floated right down the river to our house. 'Course they looked liked drowned rats when the men pulled them out of the water and they were shivering like they'd been in an icebox all day. Oh, Daddy, it's so good to see you and I'm so happy I could just cry."

"It's alright to cry sometimes, dear, especially after all we've been through today." Wesley wiped at a tear with his coat sleeve.

Joyce grabbed her daddy around the neck and hugged him tightly. Wesley held her and Gary with one arm and extended his free hand to Nancy, who took it gently into both of her hands and knelt beside them, holding his hand against her moist cheek.

"I must thank Hiram," Wesley said. He scanned the crowd.

"He's already left," Nancy said. "I expressed my gratitude."

The distant rumble of a train interrupted the conversation. They heard the two long blasts of the whistle, followed by a short and a sustained blast as the train passed the whistle post rounding the curve about a quarter mile out of Copeland.

"Sounds like a passenger train," Wesley said. "That means the tracks are open to Jackson. That's got to be Tom Morris pulling that whistle lever."

"How can you tell, Daddy," Joyce asked.

"Just can, dear. Like any musician worth his salt, Tom has a certain touch with the lever of that steam trumpet."

The group hug subsided as Wesley slowly rose to his feet. "Glad they could get through. Good sign. I'm glad it's not as bad as the thirty-seven flood."

They stood together by the tracks, arm in arm, and watched the looming passenger train round the curve and chug toward the station, hissing and puffing. Gary pressed his hands to his ears as the sustained whistle continued to blow intermittently, sounding one long and final warning as it neared the public crossing. The brakes screeched an ear piercing sound, metal abrading metal, and the train ground to a halt in a cloud of steam. A lone passenger disembarked and walked rapidly in their direction. He carried one small piece of luggage, which he carried lightly.

"All aboard," echoed across the flooded valley. No one boarded.

Two short bursts of steam rushed though the whistle. The engine groaned against the weight of its passenger cars, and slowly, but steadily, the train rumbled forward.

It rumbled toward them. They waved as the train passed. Wesley gave the engineer a thumbs-up.

"Is that Mr. Morris, Daddy?" Joyce asked.

"Yes. Good man."

"You sure know a lot about trains," Joyce said.

"Maybe when the waters recede we can take another train trip, maybe go to Lexington."

"I'd like that, Daddy. Can we see the college you went to?"

"I'm sure."

Nancy knelt beside Gary and gave him a slight kiss on the cheek. He blushed and then awkwardly clasped his arms around her neck.

"Wonder who that is that got off the train." Joyce said.

Their attention quickly turned to the lone traveler approaching them.

"He walks like Aaron Baldwin," Nancy said.

"Your friend who stopped in to see me at Doc Lewis' clinic?"

"Yes. We were childhood friends."

"It was very kind of him to stop by and check on me."

"He's a kind person," Nancy said, lifting her hand to shield her eyes from the sun. "It is Aaron. I wonder why he's come back so soon."

"He probably heard about the flood. Perhaps your parents asked him to check on your condition."

"Perhaps. I can't imagine Daddy not coming if he was that concerned."

CHAPTER FIFTY-SIX

~

Except for the rhythmic ticking of the clock, the room remained quiet. Nancy had barely spoken since the news of her father's death. Occasionally voices from those lounging on the porch filtered into the house, but they were subdued. Reverent.

Nancy sat beside Aaron on the couch, her head resting against his shoulder. Wesley stood across the room from them, staring out the window. Nanny Sue stood sentry by the door. She'd put the twins to bed. Joyce and Gary remained outside with the displaced neighbors who had set up housekeeping on the veranda; the tragedy of the flood was overshadowed by the recent rescue. Ironically, the flood seemed a reprieve from the mundane of winter, opium for the spirits bedraggled by the habitual daily toil. When the news from Cincinnati filtered through the crowd, their celebration abruptly subsided.

Wesley reflected on the scene before him. His heart ached for the displaced families. Though his home was spared, he knew how they felt. Some of the women cooked on the open flames of a campfire blazing along the tracks. Others kept guard as the children entertained themselves with a game of tag, making sure they remained away from the raging river's edge. Men lounged on the steps, whittling and waiting for supper.

The Callahans had left shortly after being rescued from the current. They headed to a relative's place over on the Troublesome. Callahan had spurned the concerns of neighbors that the passage might be impossible. Wesley wished he'd been able to thank him for the rescue. He wondered how Tom Fugate's family was doing. Did the waters flood them out? Did they have enough food?

Wesley stepped from the window and eased into a chair opposite Nancy and Aaron. He wished he could think of something comforting to say to Nancy.

"How can this be?" Nancy broke the silence. "I just can't believe he's gone. He was so healthy. Why my daddy? He was so kind and gentle and understanding."

No one answered. Aaron shifted his position on the couch and gently touched Nancy's trembling hands resting in her lap.

"What will Mother do without him? How is she, Aaron?"

"I can't really say for sure. Everything was so sudden. My mom and dad are with her and will stay with her until you arrive... and longer if necessary. The doctor gave her a mild sedative. She was resting when I left."

"Mother won't be able to make it without him. I know that. She's a good mother and she was good to Daddy, but Mother depended on him for everything. What will she do without him?"

"It'll work out somehow," Aaron said. "Maybe you should try and get some rest for now. We have a long day ahead of us. I have tickets for the morning train. You'll have to be up early tomorrow."

Aaron's gentle mannerism impressed Wesley.

"I'm not sleepy." Nancy shifted her position on the couch.

Nanny Sue had slipped away to the kitchen. She returned with a steaming cup.

"Drink this, dear. It'll help some."

"Thank you, Nanny Sue," she whispered.

"Sassafras tea, dear. I hope you like it."

"I'm sure, Nanny Sue. Anything you make is good."

She gently touched the cup to her lips and sipped its contents, cradling the cup with both hands, trying to keep it steady.

"It's good, Nanny Sue."

"Glad you like it."

The room fell silent again. Nancy studied the contents of the teacup. Aaron toyed with a loose button on his corduroy jacket. Nanny Sue left for the kitchen.

Wesley observed the scene. He'd been here before, in this same living room, staring into a cup of tea. Staring into the face of death. Drinking the dregs of reality. He longed to offer comfort. How? What can I say or do that will console her when she's lost her

195

dearest friend? He knew the feeling well, the long, lonely journey to the end of the world, with seemingly no strength to come back.

Nancy sat the cup clumsily onto the coffee table. She retrieved a handkerchief from her sweater pocket and dabbed her eyes. She suddenly looked up at Wesley. She stared at him, as if time was suspended. He felt awkward.

"Why would God do this to me? Why would a loving God do this? Why could I not be there for him when Daddy needed me most?"

He'd heard the question not too many months before; it was his own. Some meaningful friends had ineptly answered the question for him. He eventually stopped asking why. Not because he found the answer. Rather, because he tired from trying to figure it out.

He thought of a recent Psalm he read. Perhaps that could offer comfort. While contemplating on the Psalm of David, he'd settled in his heart that God was good, and that God walked with mankind in the valley of death. He still wondered why God allowed tragedy. Perhaps he would never know the answer to that question, so how could he explain the scripture to her.

Nancy continued to stare at him. Does she want me to offer words of comfort? His thoughts seemed too hollow for such heartbreak.

He wanted to hold her in his arms, to tell her he understood, but propriety restrained him.

"Why, Wesley?" she pleaded.

"Perhaps we shouldn't ask why God did this, Nancy, but rather why does God allow things like this to happen to us."

He didn't want her to become angry toward God; still, he didn't want to sound judgmental regarding her grief. Should he have remained silent? His statement seemed so shallow when compared to the authors of Holy Scripture.

It was all there in her eyes: his own fears and questions, the pain no pill can diminish, the light of life dimming, the flower of youth withering, the soaring spirit plummeting into the quagmire of despair.

He wanted to reverse time, to stop the inevitable. He longed to make her smile again, to give her reason to hope. The winter of life, with its howling winds and frigid temperatures, had just shut down the passage to her being. Only time could bring back the warmth of spring and the life that followed. Time had been his friend; it would be Nancy's friend also. He knew how long time could linger; it wasn't to be rushed. Nancy would have to wait. He would have to wait for her.

CHAPTER FIFTY-SEVEN

~

"I'm sorry, under the circumstances, but I need to talk to you about another subject, Wesley. So I'm glad for this opportunity," Aaron said after Nancy retired to bed.

"I need to apologize to you for a promise I failed to keep."

"Which is?"

"When you visited me in the hospital, I promised to let Nancy know. Only today did I have the opportunity…"

"With what you and this community have gone through, there's no need for such an apology."

"Thank you for understanding. Excuse me for interrupting your train of thought. What's the other subject?"

Here we go. It's about Nancy. She's become too attached to my family…and me. I'm too old for her. I'm taking advantage of her youth. She deserves better than I have to offer.

"It's about Gary."

Wesley blinked. Gary? What does he know about Gary?

"I hope he isn't in trouble again." Wesley feigned a smile. He wished he hadn't jumped to such conclusions about Aaron.

"No, not that at all. When Nancy was home, she told me about his speech condition. I've shared with my colleagues at the university, fellow students and professors, and they're quite interested. I have some questions that might…no promises…but hopefully, might help us diagnosis his situation properly, and with the right treatment, he may be able to talk again."

"That would be wonderful, Aaron."

"Do you mind answering some pointed questions?"

"Not at all."

"When exactly did he stop speaking?"

"Right after the accident that killed his mother...my wife. We assumed the trauma caused it."

"Nancy says he did speak when she challenged him on a... what was it...a fire he may have caused?"

"Yes, but it was only a single word. Then again, during Nancy's sickness, he spoke. It was only a few words and somewhat jumbled up and not with clarity."

"You've never had him diagnosed by anyone other than the family doctor, right?"

"That's right. Doc Lewis."

"Your wife fell from a horse...and was struck by a train?"

Wesley hesitated.

"I'm sorry. I know this must be very difficult for you."

"No, I'm okay with your questions. Ask anything you need to know. It's just that it was much more than falling from a horse. If it was that simple, I probably...I'm sorry. I don't mean to ramble so."

"It must have been...still is very difficult for you..."

"Yes, but if you can help Gary, I'll be so grateful. Ask whatever is necessary."

"Did Gary show any signs of speech loss before the accident?"

"None."

"After the accident, did Gary show any physical signs of injury...specifically head trauma?"

"Yes, he had a bad bump on the back of his head."

"Which side?"

"Left."

"There was no x-ray of the injury?"

"No. Just visual observation. That was a few days after the accident...after the funeral...we realized something was wrong."

"So his inability to speak was simultaneous with the accident?"

"Yes."

"This is what I...we think may have happened. The injury caused bleeding and swelling in the area of Gary's brain that controls speech. Depending on the severity, we think the condition may be reversible. We would need to do a battery of tests."

Wesley didn't respond.

"Do you disapprove?"

"No. Why do you ask?"

"You seem distant...non-responsive...I know how parents sometimes feel about doctors experimenting on their children..."

"No, it's not that at all. I was just wondering if I've been negligent in getting proper help for Gary up to this time."

"Not at all. Don't go there. You were right with your assumption it was emotional trauma. Doctor Lewis affirmed that. Only those trained in the field of neurology could properly diagnose this. It may still not be the case. His may be a psychological response to a very traumatic experience. With the blow to the head, I'm leaning toward aphasia?"

"What's that?"

"Aphasia is the partial or total inability to speak due to damage to the brain caused by an injury or disease."

"How could you tell in Gary's case?"

"Tests."

"How do you correct it if it is aphasia?"

"Depending upon the severity, for Gary, if it was the accident...perhaps surgery to correct any abnormality such as scar tissue or blood clots...but considering Gary has spoken a few words since the accident, maybe speech therapy would reverse the condition. Concisely, he will simply have to learn to talk again."

"Could this be possible?"

"I think so."

"How would I get the process started?"

"The university doctors could do an evaluation. I would be delighted to introduce you to them. You could go from there."

"I'd be so grateful."

"I'm sure cost is a factor. You'd be welcome to stay at our place during the evaluation process. There are various types of payment options. Plus, the hospital has a wonderful humanitarian program which this area would qualify for."

Wesley didn't respond.

"I hope I wasn't offensive in my assumptions you need financial assistance, Wesley. I apologize."

"Not that, Aaron, though finances will have to be worked out. I was just wondering if the university might also be interested in taking on a much broader project?"

"What might that be?"

"The blue skins. Find out what's causing the children over at Troublesome Creek to be born with blue skin."

CHAPTER FIFTY-EIGHT

~

Spring. Summer. Fall. Winter. One complemented the other, each with its pleasantries. Winter was usually too long and too cold in the Cumberland Plateau, and it always left room for the uncertain. The one thing predictable about winter in the Cumberland was its unpredictability.

The winter of fifty-seven predictably had its unpredicted events: a January flood that inundated the community. On a less serious note, someone kept up a random theft of chickens. Most everyone blamed Sigel behind his back; out of pity no one challenged him. Both the flood and the missing chickens were constant conversation pieces. Nancy didn't care to talk about either; the accidental death of her father consumed her. She blamed herself for his death.

Though the accident left mostly questions, the police report shed some light on the cause of the accident. A newspaper in the car carried the news of the flood. Nancy filled in the blanks.

If only she could have known, her decision of coming to the mountains would have been different. In retrospect, she would have stayed home, enjoying the swing on the front porch in the spring and fall, and in the winter evenings, she would have relaxed with a book by the fireplace. She generally sat across the room from her father, who sat in his favorite chair near the bronze and porcelain floor lamp inherited from his mother. She had no way of knowing it would end this way. Now it is too late to turn back the clock.

"If only I could have known." She repeated the phrase softly, pitifully.

Those were the words that haunted her: night and day. She repeated them to Nanny Sue, to Wesley, to herself. She wrote the words in lengthy rambling letters to Aaron. She scribbled them in the margins of her notebooks. She even let the words slip out while shopping at the Copeland store.

"God don't prepare the road for us, child," Ida Mae told her. "He tries to prepare us for whatever road we're called to travel. We can't pick the road we travel, hard as we try. The one we pick seems never to turn out like we planned. Yours is a bumpy and potholed road, but I think you're up to the journey, Miss York. One day at a time, dear, that's what you got to do. You can make it one day at a time."

The days got worse, not better. The excitement of her career had turned to endurance. She ceased writing. And reading. After a day of survival in the classroom, she escaped to her room at the Taggart boarding house and slept until dinner. After dinner she excused herself to her room, complaining of a headache, or a dozen other excuses. She tried to journal; she couldn't get beyond the first sentence. At night she struggled to fall asleep, then slept fitfully. She skipped meals and napped instead.

Wesley expressed his concern. She told him she was fine, just tired. She realized he wanted to help; still, with her independent spirit, she rebuffed what she perceived as overtures of pity. He eventually stopped attempts to console her and instead busied himself at the salt mine.

She felt he abandoned her in her time of great need.

Aaron wrote often. She looked forward to his letters, always filled with current events surrounding the university. The news seemed a diversion. Aaron also promised to visit during Easter break. Nancy held to the promise as a purpose to keep going.

Her mother wrote weekly, always the same. When are you coming home? She dreaded the letters. She slipped into greater guilt. And anger. Finally little emotion at all: complete depression. The long winter wore on.

CHAPTER FIFTY-NINE

~

Gary frowned at the unusually folded paper slipped inside his reader: it formed a crude star. He unfolded the paper and realized it was a note from the secret club. He scanned its contents:

> The club meets Friday night at eight, after dark, on the rock. Everybody has to be there. Don't nobody be late les you want to pay for it with your hide. Don't tell nobody bout this meeting.
>
> The leader

Some things troubled Gary about the club. One, he was the only member who didn't wear a hood. Why should he since they all knew who he was ever since they forced him to join or else suffer the consequences. Further, the others refused to take their hoods off in his presence. Finally, the way the letter demanded he be there sounded more like a threat than a club. He knew his father wouldn't let him go out that late at night, but the leader demanded he come to the meeting. He was in a quandary as to what he should do.

He waited until all the lights were out before he slipped from under his sheet, still fully dressed except for his shoes. He cautiously opened his bedroom window and slipped into the darkness. The moon remained hidden behind the distant mountains, but the stars twinkled like Christmas lights on the backdrop of a black, velvety canopy. The stars seemed so close he felt he could reach out and pick one, yet so spectacular he wanted to applaud them instead. Though the night was chilly, spring was in the air.

He sneaked out the front gate, closed it gently but cringed as the squeaky hinges seemed amplified in the darkness. The dew soaked through his socks so he hastened onto the tracks and pulled them off and stuck them inside his pocket; splintery crossties pricked his feet as he walked a good distance before he paused to slip his wet feet into his shoes.

The climb to Coffin Rock was more difficult in the darkness. The sounds and shadows of the night frightened him as he made his way along the path. He smelled the smoke and saw the glow of the fire long before he reached the rock. The others were already there; the leader seemed annoyed he was late, like they'd waited on him, even though he'd missed the last two meetings. Gary climbed onto the rock and sat at the edge.

The usual stuff took place: pledges, rituals and the sharing of a cigarette. The smoking had started out with corn silks, but over the months had grown into full-fledged cigarettes they sneaked from their daddies' packs, or butts they found dropped along the railroad track. Gary's daddy didn't smoke, and he felt guilty for accepting a drag from the others', but he found it difficult to refuse their offer. 'Bouts of coughing and a strange sensation in his stomach dulled his conscience.

"I think we should start bringin' girls to our meetin'," the leader proclaimed.

The announcement surprised Gary. Why would they want to have girls at their meeting? He knew his sister wouldn't come.

"Ain't never done that before," someone reminded the leader.

"I thank we've been missin' out some by not lettin' girls in our club," the leader argued. "We could double our numbers."

"What if'n they don't wanna come? Whatta we do? Make 'em?" another asked.

"They'll wanna," the leader insisted.

Gary was confused. Why do we want girls? Why would girls want to come to a secret meeting of hooded boys? Something within told him this was wrong. He couldn't figure out what the leader was up to, but whatever it was, he didn't like it. His right foot hurt. He unlaced his shoe and slipped it off. A blister had formed and burst. He missed the end of the conversation about asking girls to join the club.

"Pay attention, Gary," the leader said.

Gary pulled his sock from his pocket and put it on his foot, then slipped the shoe back on. That helped with the pain.

"Next on our list is the blue skins." The leader stared at Gary. "We ought to make a new rule that no blue skin is allowed in our club."

"I'm for that," someone agreed.

Others applauded.

Gary tied his shoelace. They won't want the Callahan girl in our club. She was about his age, but he'd never ask her to join a silly boys' club. She was kind to him the day they rode together in the boat. Nothing like her daddy. Her blue skin didn't bother him as they sat close together next to Miss York. Why did some in the community treat them badly, like they'd done something wrong? It wasn't their fault they were born with blue skin.

His wandering thoughts caused him to hear only parts of the third item on the evening agenda: the blood sacrifice. He wanted to raise his hand and ask what the leader meant by blood sacrifice, but he knew he couldn't speak, and he was tired of their daunting laughter when he tried.

"Next meetin' is Saturday morning, a week from tomorrow, day before Easter," the leader said. "Meetin' dismissed!"

A cheer rose from the group.

Gary left the meeting wondering about the announced blood sacrifice and how it might involve the blue skins and if the two were related. He didn't want the club to suspect his disloyalty. He waved good-bye nonchalantly and left for home. Reflectively retracing his steps, he slowly walked the tracks, kicking up gravel and blaming himself for getting into this whole mess. Coffin Rock had caused him nothing but harm. First it was the fire, now it was girls at the meeting and some kind of blood sacrifice, but worst of all was the hate for the blue skins.

The moon rose from its slumber just as he approached his house. He paused to watch it illuminate the countryside; he prayed for God to clear his mixed up mind. He prayed he could someday talk again, to express himself, to tell the leader of the club he disagreed with his decisions. He wanted to tell Miss York he didn't start the fire upon the mountain. Mostly he wanted to tell her he was sorry about her father's death and he knew how she must feel.

He slowly opened the squeaky gate, halfway hoping it awakened his daddy so he could talk to him about all the thoughts going through his mind. He couldn't talk to his daddy, or to anyone. He was unable to talk. Lately some of the older children were calling him retarded. Was he?

He stopped to remove his shoes. He took the sock off his blistered foot and reached inside his pocket to retrieve the other sock. It was missing. How would he explain that to Nanny Sue?

CHAPTER SIXTY

~

Wesley figured it would eventually happen, for Hiram Callahan was a bitter man; further, he was a mean man, especially when tanked with liquor. Time spent in the penitentiary set poorly with him. His activities the past few months showed little if any rehabilitation evident from his incarceration. His parole was obviously an act of compassion so he could care for his children upon the death of their mother. Wesley knew of no one from the community who objected to the release on those grounds, even though they might not have agreed it was a good decision for the community's sake. The Callahan children needing a caregiver seemed to override their personal concerns. Still, Hiram loathed the community, saying they accused him falsely. He seemed to hate the community almost as much as he reviled the law that had restrained him, for the community had failed to stand beside him. During the trial, with frequent outbursts, he'd vowed revenge on both the law and the community. Still, Wesley had hoped the camaraderie created by the flood would soften Callahan's resolve for vengeance; it had not. Wesley certainly didn't expect Callahan's vengeance to be released on Good Friday.

The tranquil night exploded with thundering firepower. Hiram Callahan's revenge had begun. Wesley leaped out of bed and rushed downstairs to the front door facing the railroad tracks and the direction from which the shots were fired. The multiple gunshots aroused the entire Taggart household.

"It's him, Daddy," Joyce whispered, kneeling beside Wesley at the front door. "It's Hiram Callahan, ain't it?"

"Isn't it," Wesley corrected her.

"Sorry, Daddy. I'm scared."

"It'll be okay, sweetheart. He's probably drunk. I don't think he intends to harm anyone."

Wesley glanced at Gary standing beside him. Frightened.

"Keep your head down, son. You don't need to be afraid. They're just passing through the community."

Wesley's gut feeling had been correct. He'd expressed his concerns to Sheriff Watkins who reciprocated his feelings. Though Wesley cared about the Callahan children, he felt it was not in the best interest of the children or the community to parole Callahan just because his wife passed. Hiram had been a poor father when his wife was alive; he would be poorer still with her gone. Wesley felt Hiram's alignment with the county's hooligans would also create an unwholesome environment for his son, Jack, not to mention the ghastly surroundings for the little girl. Wesley had expressed the same in a letter to the parole board who had solicited concerns. Wesley didn't appear at Hiram's parole hearing but allowed the parole board to make their decision as they felt best for the family. Now the community would have to deal with the parole board's decision, but deal with it on their own.

Wesley crouched as he slipped across the room and retrieved his .12 gauge shotgun from the gun closet. He loaded shells into the chamber and retraced his steps to the front door. Squatting motionless, he peeked through a slit in the white sheer curtains that covered the front door window. He cautioned for silence by touching his hand gently over Nancy's gaped lips. A dozen more shots rang out. Wesley assumed the intended targets: a glass insulator atop a railroad line pole that shattered into a hundred pieces, the metal sign that signaled the railroad crossing, a beer bottle tossed into the air. Baying dogs joined the ruckus, ready for the kill. No shots hit their house, at least not yet.

Wesley knew Hiram, though an angry man, was a happy man tonight; he was happy because of the crazed havoc he was creating in this turncoat community that had applauded his prison sentence. He was having the last laugh; best to allow him to enjoy it. The more reticent the community, the less likely the skirmish would explode into a full-scale battle.

All went momentarily silent.

"Wesley Taggart," a voice echoed in the darkness.

It was Hiram Callahan. Wesley felt his pulse quicken.

"You come out here, Taggart, and lets you and me have it out once and for all. You know I didn't kill your wife, but you let 'em pin it on me."

Wesley remained silent. Joyce clasped her arms around his neck. Wesley could feel her body trembling. Wesley reached out to Gary and pulled his rigid body closer.

"I know you're in there, Taggart. You come on out now and face me man to man, lest you're afraid to face me man to man. Ain't got Sheriff Watkins to hide behind now, Taggart. How does it feel?"

Another shot exploded the silence. Joyce's body jerked. Wesley cradled her head against his chest. Gary's body grew more rigid.

"Guess you're showing your true color, Taggart. You're yellar and your self-righteous attitude stinks worse 'an skunk carrion."

Wesley fought back the urge to charge into the darkness. He closed his eyes and breathed slow and deep, allowing his breath to escape slowly.

Laughter from Callahan's companions reverberated throughout the darkened valley.

"It's okay," Wesley whispered, "they're satisfied now." He breathed a sigh of relief and brushed his fingers through Joyce's hair. She relaxed her grip around his neck. Gary pulled away from them and stared out the window.

Wesley stood from his crouched position. He opened the door slowly; the cool night air rushed inside the house. He peered into the darkness. The shadowy figures of the Callahan outlaws meandered down the tracks, their laughing, accusations and obscenities slowly drifting into obscurity.

"We could use a fire," Wesley said to no one particularly. Though they were gone, he knew the night wouldn't return to normalcy. "How about some peanut butter fudge?"

"I'll make it." Nanny Sue had stood stealthily in the hallway, cradling the baby, the twins holding onto her night robe, observing the scene.

"I'll help," Joyce exclaimed. "Can I start the fire?"

"We'll do it together," Nanny Sue answered. They left for the kitchen.

Gary remained motionless at the window. Wesley stepped to him and knelt beside him on the linoleum in the semi-darkness. He gently placed an arm around his shoulders and spoke kindly but firmly.

"Son, life will have plenty enough conflicts without hankering for a fight of your own making. Fight outcomes aren't always predictable even when you're in the right, and most all fights usually leave some wounds and lasting grievances."

Gary scemed to resent the lecture. Wesley regretted his lack of action disappointed his son. Evidently Gary wanted to see valor; he seemed to interpret inactivity and restraint as cowardice. Gary continued to stare out the window.

Wesley interrupted the silence. "Some fights can be avoided by waiting them out, others by talking it out and some by just ignoring them altogether, because they aren't worth the bother of a fight."

Gary turned and looked at his daddy. Wesley sensed his silent words by the expression on his face. "But they were shooting at us, Daddy. You didn't stand up to them."

Weslcy wished Gary could express himself; he had to guess at his true feelings. He hoped hc could help Gary understand the importance of self-control in the face of the adversary.

"Never forget, a fight is serious business, so always pick your fights. Don't be too proud to turn the other cheek if it can prevent a fight. Don't fight out of anger or out of being afraid someone will brand you a coward. Fight only because it's the right thing to do, after all other means of peace have been exhausted. Then, after all options for peace have been exhausted, fight with everything within you, till your enemy says, 'I give.' Then help him up, dust him off and if he will, shake his hand and treat him to an Orange Crush and a bag of Planters Peanuts."

Wesley realized he was challenging the carnal spirit. He recognized some things were hard for men and boys to accept, and their human nature fought against it, no matter who the instructor. Turn the other cheek, Jesus had taught, but Peter didn't buy it. He bought a sword instead. The sage of the Old Testament had penned:

"... he that is slow to anger is better than the mighty..." It sometimes surprised Wesley how well he remembered scriptures learned while in the orphanage. Thoughts of the orphanage resurrected mixed emotions. There he had learned both to fight and to accept circumstances.

Wesley wondered if the previous examples he set before Gary exemplified his sermonizing. He pondered his past dealings with Hiram; had he been a good role model for Gary, or was Gary living out emotions he'd instilled, specifically towards Hiram? Even so, Wesley hoped Gary would heed his advice now, but he knew too well that humans often lashed out first and learned later, defaulting to the carnal nature. Revenge allowed anger to roam unbridled, unleashing havoc as it journeyed. Ira furor brevis est (anger is a brief madness), his friends in France had taught him.

For Gary's sake he wanted to run after Hiram and chase him from the community; still, for Gary's sake he wanted to manifest a spirit of compassion. Further, he didn't want his son to perceive him as a coward. Nor did he want Callahan to feel at liberty to terrorize their community and especially his family. Wesley knew the right choice was sometimes the most difficult choice. Nor did the decision please everyone.

Wesley suddenly realized Nancy stood nearby listening. He wondered what Nancy thought about his actions tonight. He couldn't tell from the expression on her face in the dim lighting, and she remained silent. Her silence left him pondering.

CHAPTER SIXTY-ONE

~

Someone rapped on the front door. The door opened almost immediately, and a set of footsteps could be heard stepping across the linoleum floor. Wesley, Nancy and Nanny Sue sat at the kitchen table wondering.

"Thank you, son," a male voice said.

The steps continued toward the kitchen. Sheriff Sam Watkins stuck his head inside the doorway. Wesley stood to greet him.

"Sheriff."

"Wesley. Gary let me in. Ladies."

"Morning, Sheriff." Nanny Sue's face showed little welcome.

"Good morning," Nancy said.

"Have you met our school teacher, Miss Nancy York?" Wesley asked.

"Don't believe I have. It's a pleasure, ma'am."

"Care to join us for some coffee, Sheriff?" Wesley offered the sheriff a chair at the table.

Nanny Sue poured a cup of coffee and handed it to the sheriff.

"Thank you, Nanny Sue."

Nanny Sue didn't respond.

"Heard you had a wild Friday night, Wesley," Sheriff Watkins said matter-of-factly.

"An understatement, Sheriff."

"It was unbelievably frightening for the children. Have you arrested them?" Nancy asked.

"No."

"Going to?"

"Probably not."

213

"Sheriff Watkins! They could have killed someone. Hiram Callahan threatened Wesley. Tell him, Wesley," Nancy insisted.

"It was pretty bad, Sheriff," Wesley concurred.

"Hear me out, Wesley, Miss York, before you jump to conclusions. I talked to Callahan and he had reasons to do what he did. Child's gone missing."

"Oh, no! Which one?" Nancy asked awkwardly.

"The little girl."

"Sherry Jane," Nancy whispered.

"Not sure if Callahan got drunk before or after she was gone, but either way, she's missing. He sobered up enough overnight to tell me the same after I spoke with him this morning. Thought you folks might've seen the girl. I heard Miss York wanted her in school. Have you seen her, Miss York?"

"Now hold on, Sheriff Watkins." Wesley's voice rose slightly. "That sounds somewhat like an accusation. Not fair after we've been accosted by Hiram and his thugs. You're interrogating the wrong person."

"I'm doing an investigation, Wesley. Questions are a part of an investigation, not an accusation."

"I understand your need to investigate, but you don't need to waste time here with such questions. We haven't seen nor heard from the Callahan children since the flood."

Gary's sudden appearance in the doorway interrupted the conversation.

"Need to talk to you, Gary, about one wet sock and another missing sock," Nanny Sue said.

Gary looked stunned.

Wesley studied his face. Did he hear our conversation? Something's wrong. A missing sock wouldn't cause that kind of apprehension. Gary knows something.

"Gary, have you seen Sherry Jane, the Callahan girl?" Wesley abruptly asked.

Gary shook his head no.

"She's missing. Sheriff Watkins is trying to locate her."

"Wouldn't know where she is, would you, son? Hear any of the other children discussing anything about her?" Sheriff Watkins piped in.

Gary hesitated before shaking his head "no" then quickly exited the room. They heard the front door open and shut before Wesley spoke up.

"Sheriff, maybe I should apologize. Gary knows something."

"How can you tell?"

"I'm not sure. I just can."

Nancy didn't comment; she simply stared at Wesley, puzzlement showing on her face.

"Let's give him a head start, then we can follow," Sheriff Watkins said. "Still wondering why you didn't retaliate last night when Callahan came through the community making a ruckus."

"Can't rightly say, Sheriff. I was wondering about something myself."

"What's that?"

"How did you find out about the ruckus so quickly?"

"I'm the sheriff, Taggart. I've got ways. Got eyes in the back of my head and a nose like a bloodhound."

CHAPTER SIXTY-TWO

~

Tears streamed down Gary's cheeks. He wanted to pray for Sherry Jane but hesitated. *I'm a sinner and God ain't gonna listen to no sinner like me. I've all but sold my soul to the devil by joining the secret club and participating in their sins.* It was all coming clear to him...the refusal to allow blue skins into the club...the talk of blood sacrifice...the blood he'd seen on the rock the first time he visited. Blurry-eyed, he ran as fast as he could up the hill, all the time wondering if he was too late.

Will they really sacrifice a human? A child? Surely not! On up the hill he scurried, darting bushes and jumping rotted logs strewn along the path. He gasped for air but pressed on to the turn-off for Coffin Rock.

His anger boiled. *I have to do something to stop them!*

Then he saw them; simultaneously, they saw him. They were all there, in their ritualistic circle. A mass of blood and the remains of a sacrifice grotesquely adorned the center of the rock.

"You...kill...I...hate...for...this," he stuttered and then charged into the pack.

The club members scrambled for safety as Gary swung at them with his fists and kicked and bit like a cornered raccoon. Someone knocked him off the rock, but he grabbed a stick and scampered back up, all the while stuttering incoherently. The first swing of the stick, a crashing blow, hit the leader on the side of his head, knocking his hood half off. The second sent a couple flying off the rock.

"Why...do...this?" He continued to swing the stick, glancing blows left and right at whoever was nearest him. The club members

216

leaped from the rock one by one, leaving Gary standing alone, like the king of the mountain. His body shook uncontrollably. He began to cry.

"So you been pretendin' you can't speak," the leader said.

Gary wiped at the tears.

The club members regrouped and came at him from all sides and wrestled him to the ground. He struggled and clawed and bit, like a mad dog fighting for its life. They subdued him. He stopped his futile struggle and lay on his back, stretched spread eagle by his captors, feeling helpless.

He looked heavenward, beyond the hooded faces, beyond the fluffy clouds, beyond the deep blue of the sky. He envisioned the face of Jesus hanging on the cross with the Roman soldiers mocking Him. His bruised and bloodied face looked so pitiful, just like Preacher Charlie had painted in his sermons. Gary wanted to tell Jesus how sorry he was for lying and for not telling his daddy about the secret club, but he couldn't get the words to come out right. He could think them but he couldn't speak them in order.

"My...fault...sorry...," he whimpered.

Further struggle proved useless; they held him tightly to the rock. The leader stood directly over him, clutching a thick stick knotted on the end. He slapped the stick in his open palm as he glared down at Gary, who closed his eyes and waited.

I deserve to die. I should've told someone what they've been up to, but I was too chicken. I could've stopped all this. The slap of the stick against flesh stopped. Gary's heart pounded in his ears. He could hear their breathing and his own.

"What in tarnation's gotten into you, Gary? You plum done gone crazier than a loon," the leader yelled.

"You...crazy... killed...innocent...girl."

"Whatcha talkin' about, Gary?" the leader asked.

"Blue...skin...killed...Sherry...Jane."

"We ain't killed nobody."

"Sacrifice...killed." Gary struggled to look toward the carcass.

The club members began to laugh.

"We ain't kill't nobody, Gary! That's just a chicken."

217

"So I found my chicken thieves," a strange voice surprised all of them.

Sheriff Watkins and Wesley Taggart stood within earshot, surveying the scene.

"Line up and take them silly hoods off your heads before I jerk your ears off with them," the sheriff barked. "You boys got some explainin' to do, to me first, and then to your daddies."

Wesley stepped quickly toward Gary. The boys released their grip on him.

Gary leaped to his feet and fell into his father's embrace. He sensed his father weeping. He'd never before seen his father cry. For some reason it felt good. He began to cry also. Strangely, he felt happy.

CHAPTER SIXTY-THREE

Nancy could tell something wonderful had happened. Wesley's face beamed; Gary's face reflected a sheepish grin. Still, Wesley didn't speak, he simply stood there, smiling.

"What?" Nancy asked.

Wesley tried but couldn't speak, overwhelmed with joy.

"What is it, Daddy?" Joyce shouted in anticipation.

"Aaron was right." Wesley's voice cracked with emotion.

"Right about what?" Nancy asked.

"Gary's condition. It must have been the blow to the head... pressure...something that caused a temporary aphasia. He can speak...up on the mountain...out of desperation he started speaking... not real good, but he spoke enough for us to figure out what he was saying. You've heard him speak, Miss York; now I've heard him. He's going to be okay...be able to speak normal...I believe it with all my heart." Wesley awkwardly wiped tears from his eyes.

"It's a miracle, Daddy. Another Easter miracle," Joyce said gleefully. "Let me hear you, Gary. Say something."

"Not so fast, sweetheart," Wesley cautioned. "It may take some special tutoring...like Miss York's friend explained. We now know he can speak...it's just a matter of time...and work on his part."

"I'm so thrilled!" Tears welled-up in Nancy's eyes.

"Can you work with him, Miss York? I mean...I'll pay you for it," Wesley said.

"Yes. Absolutely. I can't take money for it, but I'll gladly work with him. I'll have to seek out some direction on how...what to do. I'll ask Aaron. He can get us information from the university."

"That will be wonderful." Wesley looked down at Gary, who smiled his approval.

"Speaking of Aaron, I forget to tell you. He's arriving today and will be taking me home for the Easter break. I need to check on Mother."

"That's good," Wesley said. "I'm sure your mother will be thrilled to see you. And, of course, Aaron will be thrilled."

The room grew awkwardly quiet.

Is Wesley disappointed I'm leaving? Why doesn't he say so? He doesn't even act like he cares or that he'll miss me.

"Excuse me. I best pack."

CHAPTER SIXTY-FOUR

~

Nancy held the picture frame in her hand, staring at the photograph of Mrs. Taggart. She looks so beautiful: large eyes perfectly set with a gentleness accentuated by long eyelashes; flawless shaped lips with a hint of a smile; long wavy hair swept back from her forehead and flowing across her shoulders. What was the color of her eyes? Her hair? How tall was she? What did her voice sound like? Nancy stared at the black and white photograph.

Strangely, Nancy felt Mrs. Taggart looking back at her with a surreal gaze that challenged Nancy's right to be standing in the room she'd decorated, to enjoy the affection of her children and the attention of her husband. Nancy felt awkward.

A door opened. She quickly placed the frame on the mantle and turned to face Wesley. He, too, seemed to stare at her but didn't speak.

"I was admiring the beautiful portrait of Mrs. Taggart."

"She was beautiful."

"You must miss her terribly."

"Every day."

Nancy didn't respond.

"I thought that by now the pain would have dulled, that the loneliness would have eased, but it hasn't. Lately it seems to have intensified. Death is so dreadful. I know how much you must miss your father. I'm so sorry for your loss."

"Yes. I miss him. I dread going back to Cincinnati, afraid of the pain it will cause me. Then I feel ashamed I think only of myself. Life must be terrible for my mother right now. I don't know what I can do to help her."

221

"Your presence will comfort her."

"I don't see how."

"Your presence in this house has comforted us, Miss York, and no matter where life may take you, we'll always be grateful for the joy you brought to this house."

Wesley's words, though she assumed were intended to be helpful, stabbed her in the heart. She didn't want life to take her anywhere else. She wanted to be here, in this house, with Wesley and his children and Nanny Sue. Wesley had opened the window of his soul and gave her leave to exit. He didn't even say he'd miss her. She could only assume there was no room in his heart for love for another; his heart still belonged to Mrs. Taggart. He still called her Miss York.

"I must be going," she said abruptly. "I shouldn't take advantage of Aaron's patience."

She picked up her suitcase and walked out of the house, leaving Wesley standing by the mantle, staring at the portrait of his wife.

CHAPTER SIXTY-FIVE

~

Nancy seemed to hesitate in boarding the train; Aaron nudged her up the metal steps and into the passenger car where she took her seat. Wesley, Joyce and Gary watched through the passenger windows. They waved to Nancy and Aaron as the huge steel engine strained against the load of the passenger cars. The rhythmic three beat cylinders of the black and silver 5000 series locomotive momentarily vibrated the atmosphere. The train hissed a long sigh as the steel wheels started rotating, ever so slowly, then faster and faster with a cadenced clatter as each wheel clanked at the connecting joints of the metal tracks. The Taggart family continued to wave as the train glided along the tracks that floated deftly on a sea of crushed stones; they stared longingly after it as it disappeared around the bend of the North Fork, leaving a cloud of smoke dissipating in the breeze. They stood silently until the train became but a distant rumble.

"Let's go home," Wesley said.

"How long before Miss York returns?" Joyce asked.

"After the Easter break, dear."

Wesley wondered if she would ever return, especially after she read the note he'd slipped into her purse. If she did return, could their relationship ever be the same?

CHAPTER SIXTY-SIX

~

They exited the train at Jackson. Since the Copeland swinging bridge hadn't been replaced after the flood, Aaron had left his car parked at the Jackson station and had taken the train from Jackson to Copeland. Nancy hadn't seen his car. She seemed impressed but distracted. He placed her luggage in the trunk, then offered to buy her a soda. She declined. She spoke little as the car sped along the blacktopped surface toward Cincinnati. The tires hummed a repeated medley, a bit off key, but consistent. The intermittent white lines flashed by hypnotically. Aaron's recently purchased car made the trip much more convenient than the passenger train that had first brought her to the Cumberland. While Aaron fiddled with the radio dial, trying to clear the static as they drifted in and out of the range of local stations, Nancy stared silently out the window as they passed the rolling horse farms as they neared Paris. Aaron stopped the dial as the resonant voice of Elvis Presley filled the car. He hummed along.

I saw you crying in the chapel...

Nancy subtly wiped at a tear that trickled down her cheek.

You ain't nothing but a hound dog...

The lyrics caused a mood swing for which Nancy was appreciative. Aaron tapped rhythmically on the steering wheel.

Another mansion loomed in the distance. A long gated driveway, with flowering trees lining the length of the lane, led to a white columned porch that spanned the entire front of the large stately house. Majestic horses grazed in the wooden fenced pastures surrounding the estate. A man dressed in denim jeans, a plaid shirt

224

and a baseball cap waved to them as he led a mare along a path, followed by her gangly foal.

They stopped for lunch in Frankfort. Aaron shared the local history of times gone by in this capitol city and insisted they stroll the historic cemetery high on a bluff overlooking the Kentucky River. Huge cliffs rose from the water's edge, and water far below flowed deep through the palisades along its journey to Carrolton, where it empted into the Ohio. Leisurely walking through the cemetery they paused at the grave monument of Daniel and Rebecca Boone. Aaron read from the headstone: "Daniel Boone's grave; Born seventeen thirty-four; died eighteen twenty; entered Eastern Kentucky seventeen sixty-seven."

Nancy tried to enjoy the moment, but her mind wandered in a hundred directions: the civilizing of this formidable land, the kindness of Aaron, her mother's emotional state, her students back at Copeland, the blue skin children, Joyce and Gary, graduate work and more. Her thoughts, no matter how far-reaching, always returned to Wesley. Already she missed him and wondered what he was doing. She wondered if he missed her, or if he was too busy to care. Of late he seemed quite preoccupied with his business.

"Flat boats loaded with the locals' wares made their way from here all the way down to New Orleans," Aaron interrupted her thoughts. "The river actually flows northwest to the Ohio where it then runs southwest into the Mississippi."

Aaron is so kind, intelligent and handsome. Why do I not love him for more than a dear friend?

"I have to show you the self-supporting stairway in the old capitol building."

It's not fair to Aaron for me to think of Wesley when he's entertaining me. I abuse his kindness.

"Did you know the old capitol building is the only pro-Union state capitol that was occupied by the Confederates?"

Still, Wesley has made no overtures of his affection for me. We had our moments, but he's made no commitments to me. Then again, have I given him the opportunity? I always challenge him on so many issues.

"Nancy?"

"Oh, I'm sorry, Aaron. What did you say?"

"I was just rambling about Kentucky history. The Confederates planned to form a Confederate government in Kentucky and probably would have had not they been defeated at the Battle of Perryville. Both Jefferson Davis and Abraham Lincoln were from Kentucky, you know."

What is Wesley doing now? Does he miss me as much as I miss him? Does he miss me at all? I haven't been an easy person to be around the past couple months. He must be glad to be shed of such a moody person as I've been.

"You did know that, Nancy, about Lincoln and Davis?"

"Oh no!"

"What?" Aaron seemed somewhat frightened by Nancy's outburst.

"I forgot to pay Mr. Taggart for my room and board for the month."

"I paid it for you."

"No, Aaron. I can't let you."

"It was my delight, Nancy. I don't get to do things for you with you being away, so this was my opportunity to do some little something for you."

Nancy fumbled through her purse.

"I'm not going to let you do this, Aaron."

"It done, Nancy. Don't steal my blessing."

A folded piece of paper fell from her purse. Nancy bent down to retrieve it, but Aaron swept it up and handed it to her. For a brief moment their gaze met. She couldn't miss seeing the tenderness in his sky blue eyes, nor the love that yearned for her affection. Neither spoke.

She slowly unfolded the paper and glanced at its contents.

"Dear Miss York," it began.

She clumsily refolded the paper and returned it to her purse.

CHAPTER SIXTY-SEVEN

The black settled into a steady canter. Wesley held the reigns loosely. His pulse quickened as he approached the rock where the ambush had occurred. He sensed the black, too, seemed apprehensive. He instinctively glanced from left to right. Surely no one will be waiting to shoot me again. Who shot me? Why?

The preliminary tests he ran on the ore and water samples from the Troublesome had been disappointing: no indication of silver on the Fugate property. Though his tests didn't eliminate all possibilities of minerals, Wesley was very doubtful precious metals existed. He knew there was plenty of coal on the property, but he'd never relished the idea of being responsible for underground coalmines. Further, some additional research helped make his decision; he would not be partnering with the families on the Troublesome. The good news was the winter flood had miraculously opened up a new vein at his salt mine and secured his business indefinitely, though he knew he had to modernize the equipment to stay up with competition. He remembered Nancy had told him she'd pray for his business and he believed her prayers had been answered. He felt less like God had abandoned him; conversely, he felt faith returning. Further, he'd applied for a small business loan and it was just a matter of time before the finances would be released. He'd purchase the much-needed equipment.

How far have Nancy and Aaron gone along the journey to Cincinnati? He calculated they'd be as far as Paris, Kentucky, but he'd never ridden the route by car, so he was unsure. Did she find the note? Did she read it? I shouldn't have slipped it into her purse. That was an invasion of her privacy. I needed to share my feelings. It's unfair to keep her guessing. Was I too presumptuous.

The Fugate house lay just ahead. Wanting to soften the blow to them, he'd decided to deliver the news personally. Plus, he had some groceries to give them. Tom had been sick off and on since after the flood; Wesley was concerned.

The black jerked. Wesley tightened the reigns and bent low. A rabbit darted across the path.

"Easy boy, just a bunny."

He guided the black east along the Troublesome. The awe of spring lined the creek with an array of colored blossoms: pink, red and white dogwood; purple-red eastern redbud with its large clusters; bright pink crabapple; stunning white cherry. All these gave brilliant colors to the background of green foliage that climbed from the water's edge to the top of the hills paralleling the Troublesome. Wesley stopped and let the black slurp from the clear flowing creek. He spooked at his reflection and shook his halter violently. Wesley laughed and patted the black's neck.

A male red-winged blackbird, easily identified by the scarlet and yellow patches on its wings, soared the curvature of the creek. It disappeared in the dense undergrowth. Wesley listened as it called out for a mate: conk-la-ree…conk-la-ree…conk-la-ree. A female responded with a few short chit sounds followed by a longer high-pitched call.

Has Nancy found the note? What does she think? Was I too abrupt?

CHAPTER SIXTY-EIGHT

~

"Afternoon, Thomas."

Tom Fugate sat in a rocking chair on the front porch; a faded quilt—a tear revealed the inner cotton batting—draped across his shoulders. His unshaven face showed patches of gray. The Fugate children, playing in the yard, scurried to the steps as Wesley stepped down from the black. Their blue skin tone seemed more pronounced in the sunlight. Since he'd already met the Fugate children on his recent visit, he was surprised at their timidity. Wesley speculated about the phenomenon of the blue skin and how it affected the children emotionally.

"Afternoon, Mr. Taggart. What brings you over this direction?"

"Wanting to check on you. Sorry you've been sick."

The children scattered back into the yard as Wesley ascended the steps.

"Me too, Mr. Taggart."

Tom extended his hand; his feeble grip shocked Wesley. The blanket fell from his shoulders and revealed a frail body. He was one of Wesley's hardest workers, but the sickness had left him stooped and pathetic. The emaciated body left Wesley speechless.

Tom muffled a cough with the back of his hand and repositioned the blanket over his shoulders.

"Wife thinks it's TB. 'Course we can't be sure. Probably just an infection or something less serious."

"Been to the doctor?"

"Thinkin' about it."

Wesley didn't dare ask regarding his reason for putting off seeing a doctor, for that was obvious among many of the mountain folks and would be too hurtful to his pride. A doctor visit was too expensive.

"Granny Combs' been givin' me some herbs. Seems to be helpin' some."

"Could you use an advance in pay?"

"Couldn't ask for that."

"You've worked hard for me, Thomas. It's the least I could do for you."

"Well, maybe I could have a couple days' advance. I appreciate it, Mr. Taggart. Wife'll be mighty grateful, too."

"Is Emma home?"

"No, she's out gathering some early greens. She knows I like 'em a lot. Be back any minute. though."

"Nanny Sue sent her some groceries. Wouldn't let me come over to the Troublesome without promising to drop them off to Emma."

"Emma'll be happy to hear that. I ain't been able to get out of the holler fer weeks now. Runnin' a little low on vittles so Nanny Sue's kindness will be a great help."

"I'm glad Nanny Sue thought of it."

"Tell 'er thanks fer us."

"I'll do that for sure."

"Real glad you dropped by 'cause there's somethin' I need to talk to you about, Mr. Taggart."

Thomas hesitated.

"I know how much you wanted to mine the Troublesome… and how kind you've been to me and my family and all…but somethin's come up and I needed to ask you about it."

Tom rearranged the blanket across his shoulders. The movement triggered a coughing spasm. He seemed to lose his train of thought. He hesitated.

"What's that, Thomas, that you needed to talk about?"

"Been offered a bit of money fer the property, enough so I could move farther up the Troublesome and have some money left over. Or I could move over closer to work. Emma says she'd like that, me working closer to home."

Wesley was surprised but certainly not disappointed. He tried to show neither emotion. He hesitated in commenting.

"I know I all but signed an agreement to let you mine the property, Mr. Taggart, but the offer is mighty temptin'."

"Mind if I ask how much?"

"Not a'tall. Three hundred per acre and I can keep or sell the house. Another five thousand fer the house if I wanna sell it."

"How many acres?"

"We got fifty."

Wesley mentally calculated the profit to Thomas. The offer is enormous. Someone desperately wants this property. What for?

"Might surprise you who wants to buy it."

"Really?"

"Sheriff Watkins."

Wesley was surprised, but again he tried not to show it. He surmised it was for the coal. The coal itself would bring multiple times that much money, not to mention the timber.

"Did he say what he wanted to do with the land?"

"No, but he's also made a similar offer to my neighbor. Makes me feel mighty bad to go back on my word to you, Mr. Taggart."

"No, Thomas, don't feel badly at all. You've got to do what is best for your family. Selling the property to Sheriff Watkins is the best deal: the right deal. In fact, after hearing what he's offered, I wouldn't hear of going ahead with my previous proposal to you. This is wonderful news not only for you, but also for your neighbor. When does the sheriff want to make the purchase?"

Thomas slowly maneuvered his position in the rocking chair and pulled a folded piece of paper from his hip pocket. He deliberately unfolded the paper and handed it to Wesley.

Wesley read the contents. The document was a simple sales contract. The Wechsler and Wechsler Law Office in Jackson properly prepared it. It conveyed all the Fugates' real estate assets to the buyer: Sheriff Watkins. All it needed was Thomas and Emma Fugate's signatures.

"How did Sheriff Watkins say he'd pay you for the property? Get a loan or …"

"Cash. That's what really surprised me, Mr. Taggart. He had a wad of money that would finance an army. Said he'd been saving all his life and it was time to make some investin'."

"Do it, Thomas."

"You sure, Mr. Taggart."

"Absolutely."

"You won't be disappointed at me fer goin' back on my word?"

"Not in the least. I'll be extremely happy for you. In fact, I would be happy to go to Jackson for you and make the transaction. You can assign me as your power of attorney and I'll make the transaction this week and bring your money to you before week's end."

"That's awfully kind of you, Mr. Taggart. I'd feel better 'bout you makin' the deal fer me 'cause me and Emma can't read a lick. We was just trustin' Sheriff Watkins was tellin' us right. 'Course we can sign our names."

"I'm delighted to be of help."

"Thank you. By the way, you ever find out who took that shot at you?"

"I've got an idea."

"Good. Gonna tell Sheriff Watkins when you see'em?"

"I don't think so, Thomas. I think I'm just going to let a dead dog lie. No need to get his fleas stirred up, or they might bite me again."

CHAPTER SIXTY-NINE

~

Wesley made the transaction in the conference room of the Wechsler and Wechsler Law Office. Jim Wechsler II handled the closing. They knew each other from the university at Lexington. Wesley signed the documents as power of attorney for Thomas and Emma Fugate; Jim dutifully examined each document and placed it in a folder. Wesley occasionally glanced at Sheriff Watkins, who hovered over a stack of money resting on the table. The sheriff seemed anxious to complete the deal.

"Tom's sick, you say?" Sheriff Watkins feigned concern.

"Feeling somewhat better."

"Wasn't sure he was gonna sell to me. People get mighty attached to their land, I thought I made'em a fair offer."

"He's pleased with the deal. What are you going to do with the land? Retire there someday?"

"Maybe, 'course I might do a little prospecting. You think there might be coal on that land?"

"Actually there's quite a vein of coal all along the Troublesome."

"You don't say?"

"I'm really thrilled you found the little Callahan girl, Sheriff." Wesley purposefully changed the subject.

"Just doin' my sworn duty to uphold law and order, Mr. Taggart."

"What actually happened to her?"

"Older brother, Jack, snuck her away to some relatives, over at the Troublesome, actually. Said their pappy was drunk and Jack was scared he'd hurt 'er."

"Hiram Callahan is unpredictable."

"All I need is the twenty thousand dollars cash and we're finished, gentlemen," Jim interrupted the conversation. "Per your contract, Sheriff, the Fugates have until the end of the summer to vacate the house."

Sheriff Watkins slid the money across the table to Jim, who deliberately counted it into stacks of one thousand dollars each.

"It's all there, Jim."

"Just a formality, Sheriff." Jim continued counting.

"Jim, Tom Fugate wants you to place the money in a bank account I set up for him at First National, minus two hundred dollars I'm to deliver to him," Wesley said.

"Surprised you didn't try and buy that property yourself, Mr. Taggart, bein' you're a geologist and all," the sheriff said.

"I considered it."

"Why didn't you?"

"For starters, I don't have twenty thousand dollars in cash."

They all laughed.

"Then maybe I could hire you to do some prospecting for me, check out the possibilities of coal." The sheriff somewhat puffed out his chest. "I even heard rumors there might be some silver."

"How kind of you to consider me, Sheriff. I'm afraid I'll have to decline since I've opened up another vein of salt at my own mine. Should keep me busy for another ten years or so."

"Suit yourself. Offer's still on the table, though."

"With a closing this quick I take it you didn't do a complete title search on the property, Jim," Wesley noted.

"I offered, but Sheriff Watkins only wanted to pay for a quick claim title."

"Fugates lived on that property as far back as I can remember, Mr. Taggart. Land ain't changed hands from them in a hundred years. No need to spend the extra money and time for nothin'," Sheriff Watkins explained. "You sure you didn't want that land, Mr. Taggart?"

"I'm sure, Sheriff. You go ahead and enjoy your land."

"I plan on doing just that, Mr. Taggart, all the way to the bank."

Wesley didn't respond.

Jim Wechsler II pulled two one hundred dollar bills from a stack and handed them to Wesley.

"The rest will be in the Jackson First National waiting on Mr. Fugate. I'll make the deposit today."

"Thank you, Jim. I'll let him know."

"You didn't happen to do a title search of your own on that property, did you, Wesley?"

"Now why would I've done that, Jim? Like I said, I don't have twenty thousand dollars in cash to invest in land."

As Wesley left the room, he overhead a final question Sheriff Watkins asked.

"You think I should have done a complete title search, Jim?"

"I've already answered that question, Sheriff. You should have listened to me. Remember, you signed a waiver acknowledging my opinion."

Wesley couldn't help but smile. The smile quickly vanished when he remembered his statement to Tom Fugate: let a dead dog lie. He knew the fleas would be active over at the Troublesome. He decided then and there to have Tom move his family immediately to the North Fork where it would be safer.

CHAPTER SEVENTY

~

It was worse than Nancy expected: unwashed dishes stacked in the sink, newspapers cluttering the living room, curtains drawn tight and unopened bills littering her father's desk. Worst of all was the frail condition of her mother. Nancy realized immediately her dire emotional state.

"Why didn't you tell me, Aaron." She scrubbed and rinsed dishes.

Aaron, working alongside Nancy, placed another plate into the cabinet before he answered.

"I'm sorry, but I didn't realize it was this bad. I knew she'd become reclusive, but I've been so busy at the university…and my parents have been in Florida vacationing…"

"Sorry. That was unfair of me to accuse you. Mother's not your responsibility. She's mine."

"Still, I feel badly…"

"No, you and your family have been too kind to my family as it is. Mother's my responsibility. I must figure out a way to take care of her. If only I didn't have a few weeks of teaching left, my problem would be solved. I'd stay home and care for her."

"You could request a leave of absence. Didn't you say they're closing the school at the end of the school year anyway. Couldn't Mr. Deaton…is that his name…finish the school year?"

"Yes, Bill Deaton. You may be right. I could take a leave of absence. I'm sure Mr. Deaton would fill in until the end of the school year. But I feel so responsible for the students. Also, I promised Mr. Taggart I'd try and help Gary with his speech problem. You were right in your evaluation about his condition. He's talking some now."

"I'm sure the new school they'll be attending will be able to work with Gary. It'll have multiple advantages over the one room school. Mr. Taggart will do whatever is necessary to get him the proper care."

The mention of Mr. Taggart reminded Nancy of the unread note. She was hesitant to read the note while in the car with Aaron, for that seemed unfair to him. She had been too preoccupied since arriving home. She needed to read its contents; still, she feared to read its contents.

"Nancy?" her mother called from the bedroom.

"Yes, Mother."

"Is Aaron still here?"

"Yes, Mother."

"Would the two of you come here, please? I need to speak with you."

They entered the room and stood at her bedside. Nancy fluffed and rearranged the pillows that propped her mother up in bed.

"Thank you, dear. I'm so glad you're home."

"It's nice to be home, Mother. I'm going to get you well. Aaron and I were just talking about how I could stay home instead of returning to finish out the school year."

"I couldn't ask...."

"I've already decided, Mother. I'm not leaving you."

"Thank you, Nancy. You're so kind to me. I don't think I can make it without you being home."

"What did you need to speak to us about, Mother?"

"It will wait, dear. I'm so very tired. I think I'll rest a little while longer before I get up."

CHAPTER SEVENTY-ONE

～

A livid Sheriff Watkins stormed into the law office of Jim Wechsler.

"I can't believe I let Wesley Taggart hoodwink me so," he yelled as he fell into the chair beside Jim's desk.

"What's the matter?"

"Mineral rights were bought up fifty years ago. Them dumb Fugates sold 'em for about enough money to pay the taxes."

"How'd you find out?"

"Some dressed up city slickers stopped by the office a few minutes ago and asked for protection while they do some surveying of their mineral rights on the Troublesome. Tom Fugate's land was included. I want my money back, Jim."

Jim slowly rose from his chair, walked across the room and closed the office door the sheriff had left ajar.

"Can't give it back, Sheriff. It's a done deal."

"Whatcha mean you can't give it back? I bought that property for the coal...and maybe some silver, too. It ain't worth a fraction of what I paid for it without them mineral rights. It's your fault for lettin' this happen."

"Sheriff Watkins, you signed a waiver, even though I warned you the property might not have clear title. I'm not going to rub it in, but I did try and warn you."

"How was I supposed to know they sold mineral rights but kept the right to live there? Who would've thought big companies even knew minerals existed in that troublesome place. Can't even get there except by horseback. You gotta get my money back, Jim."

"I'm sorry, Sheriff. I really am, but I deposited the money in an account Wesley Taggart set up for Tom Fugate. I can't touch it once I deposited it."

"I should've killed that..." his words trailed off in a mumble.

"What's that, Sheriff?"

"Just blowing off steam, Jim. Just blowing off steam."

CHAPTER SEVENTY-TWO

~

"Glad you stopped in, Wesley. Needin' to talk to you," Bill Deaton said as Wesley stepped inside the store.

"What about?"

"Received a telegram from Jackson…school board president." He paused.

"And?"

"Miss York has asked for a leave of absence."

"Did she give a reason? Is she okay?"

"I assume Miss York is okay, for in her request she stated she needs to look after her ailing mother. I've been asked to fill in until the school year ends. I figured you would want to know. Sorry, Wesley, that Miss York isn't coming back. I know how attached your family has gotten to her."

"Any news about the next school year?"

"They're closing our school. Consolidation. Children will cross the swinging bridge, assuming we can get it fixed by then, and they'll catch a bus on the other side of the river. They'll bus the children to the old Quicksand school."

"I'm sorry to hear that."

"Me, too. Times sure are changing."

"Any mail for me?"

"Yes. Looks like an official letter. You expecting something important?"

"I've applied for a small business loan. It may be the answer from the lender. I'm hoping to expand operations at the salt mine. The flood opened up a huge vein of salt, but to be competitive, I need some modern equipment."

Mr. Deaton handed Wesley the letter.

The return address identified the state government agency in Frankfort to which Wesley had applied for the loan. He tore open the envelope and scanned the contents of the letter. His eyes lingered on the second paragraph: Your loan request has been denied...

CHAPTER SEVENTY-THREE

~

Nancy read the note for the fourth time:

Dear Miss York,

By the time you find this note, many miles, responsibilities and a culture that is worlds apart will have separated us. First, I must apologize for the manner in which I delivered the note. It seems the coward's way, but I have not been able to say to you in person what I have wanted and needed to say. So, I chose the coward's way.

As people come and people go, each holds a special place. Some may think people are replaced as they depart, but that never happens. Special people are never forgotten and never replaced. We must go on without them, but we can never dismiss them from our hearts. Though years soften the pain of our loss, dear ones are never replaced. Such is the case with my wife. I cannot let her out of my heart; she will always be a part of my life.

At the same time, you have become a very special person to me, and likewise, to my children, especially Joyce and Gary. Though it seems strange to say this, for I still love my wife dearly, I have become very fond of you. Though I cannot find it in my heart to speak of forgetting and replacing, for those words may apply to pets but not people, I have come to realize you have just as dear a place in my heart.

242

To even ask of you to consider being a part of such an awkward position may seem very selfish on my part, but I've determined I must share with you how I feel. I can no longer deny my feelings for you, and with or without you in my present life, you'll always hold a special place in my heart.

I'm asking nothing of you. I'm simply being honest with you about my feelings. I wanted you to know before you made your decision about returning.

Respectfully,
Wesley

Nancy pressed the letter to her bosom. Has the school board responded regarding my request for a leave of absence? Does Wesley know? If so, he thinks I have rejected him. How can I leave Mother?

CHAPTER SEVENTY-FOUR

~

Hiram Callahan, brandishing a firearm, burst through the doorway into the Fugate's new residence at Copeland. Thomas lunged for his rifle, too late, for Callahan slammed him into the wall and came down hard against his skull with the butt of his pistol. Emma cradled her baby and fought back screams. Their two older children hunkered in the corner with a neighboring child.

Thomas lay on the floor groaning.

"Shut up and listen, Fugate," Hiram commanded.

Blood flowed from Thomas' right temple.

"I know you got a lot of money fer the sale of your property. I want it. I'm gonna take one of these here boys of yours with me as assurance, and I'm gonna keep'em till you get me the money. You understand?"

"I can't do that, Hiram. I gotta have that money to pay fer this house and take care of my family. All I got in the house is two hundred dollars. You can have that…"

"I'll take the two hundred, but I hear you got nigh to twenty thousand in the bank at Jackson. I want that, too. You get it fer me or else you won't see your boy alive again."

"Give'em the money, Tom, please. We'll get it fer you, Hiram, just don't harm my children." Emma hugged her baby to her bosom.

"Better listen to 'er, Tom."

"You ain't gonna kill my children, Hiram," Thomas replied through gritted teeth, clenched to dull the pain. "You're just drunk and you ain't that mean as to kill an innocent little child. You got two children of your own, and you can't do that. Let's just forget you ever come in here like this…"

"I said I'd kill your boy, and I will lest you get me that money, Tom Fugate."

"He...will...Mr. Fugate..."one of the children stuttered, "cause he... killed... my... Momma."

"What's he talkin' 'bout, Fugate."

"That's Wesley Taggart's boy, Hiram," Thomas said.

Hiram stared at Gary.

"You...killed...my...momma..."

Hiram's features softened. "I didn't kill your momma, boy."

"Yes...you...did..."

"No," Hiram waved the gun in the air. "I did not kill your momma. You don't understand, son, I loved..." His words trailed off, and he held the gun loosely by his side.

"Please, Hiram, don't make things worse than they already are fer you and your family," Emma begged. "Somebody's put you up to this...don't do something else that you'll regret the rest of your life."

"I didn't kill nobody," Hiram screamed. "It was a dumb thing I did...I was drunk...slapped the rump of the black...but I didn't kill Nancy Taggart...I loved that woman..." He abruptly turned and fled the house.

Emma started crying, then sobbing hysterically. The boys stood stiff and silent. Tom crawled to them, pulling them into his arms.

"It's alright boys. It's alright. He's gone. It's okay, Momma... you need to stop crying...you'll frighten the boys."

"Can't...stop...crying...Thomas," Emma said between sobs.

"That was a brave thing you just did, Gary Taggart, standing up to Hiram Callahan like that. Mighty brave. I'll take you home now...need to tell your daddy what happened. He'll want to know."

CHAPTER SEVENTY-FIVE

~

Wesley tried to ignore Nanny Sue's indignant actions. She continued to fulfill her duties, such as washing the dishes, but always with an edge: banging, sloshing and slamming. And silent. She had little to say to him since Nancy York had left and nothing to say since the notice that Nancy wouldn't be returning to teach.

"Something on your mind, Nanny Sue," Wesley asked.

"Nope."

"You're quite silent."

"That's because I have nothing to say."

"Nothing to say or not wanting to say to me what you're actually thinking?"

"Don't go puttin' words in my mouth, Wesley Taggart."

"You're upset I'm not pressing charges against Hiram Callahan?"

"Course not. Sheriff Watkins is probably the one who hired him. I can just see the sheriff arrestin' the man he hired to do his dirty work."

"I know something is bothering you, Nanny Sue. If I've done something…"

"You let that girl go without lettin' her know you cared about her. I know she cares about you, but you're just too prideful to let your true feelings show. Now she's not coming back. Can't say I blame 'er. You should've let her know you cared about her, Wesley."

"So that's it?"

"She cares about you, Wesley, but you didn't give her a chance."

"Yes, I care about Nancy York, but she deserves better. I have so little to offer. Life is hard here. I have five children to care for. My business is struggling for lack of improvement capital, and my loan application was denied."

"She would love you for who you are, not what you have or don't have. You should've given her a chance to accept or reject your affections."

"It wouldn't have been fair to let her know my true feelings. She would've felt obligated to me...to us. She deserves to have her own family, not to assume my family and my responsibilities. She's made her decision to remain in Cincinnati and care for her ailing mother, and I believe it's the right decision. I must accept it. We must accept it, Nanny Sue. Me, you and the children. Miss York's not coming back."

CHAPTER SEVENTY-SIX

~

Doris York recognized her plans to get Aaron and Nancy dating wouldn't work, though she'd hoped with all her heart. Aaron was such a wonderful young man, and she knew he loved Nancy, but she knew Nancy didn't love him. She liked him, but she didn't love him. She would never marry a man she didn't love, for she was too principled. Doris had come to realize it wasn't fair to keep plotting their future: unfair to Aaron and unfair to Nancy. How could she undo what she'd done? Nancy was home, but her heart was elsewhere. Aaron would survive his broken heart, for duty didn't bind him. Nancy was bound to her duty; she wouldn't abandon her mother.

"Nancy, dear, you've hardly eaten anything."

"I'm not hungry, Mother."

"Is Aaron coming by today?"

"I'm not sure."

"Have you heard from Mr. Taggart?"

"No."

"No letters."

"Nothing."

Silence filled the room; Nancy didn't pursue the direction of the conversation. Doris toyed with her napkin.

"What was it like, Nancy?"

"What do you mean?"

"The mountains. The people. Teaching in the one-room schoolhouse."

Nancy seemed surprised by her mother's question. She hesitated, as if staring into time and space.

"Beautiful but harsh. The people are simple yet complex. Challenging. Teaching at the school was always demanding, never two days alike. Most of the children live in poverty so your heart is always being ripped from your bosom as you become aware of needs but don't have the resources to help."

"I should have taken more of an interest in your career, dear."

"No, Mother, please don't think that. You and Daddy were more than supportive. I will always appreciate the opportunity to have been a small help to that community. Being there taught me so many lessons I'll never forget."

Silence again drifted into the room, broken only as Nancy absentmindedly leafed through a magazine that lay beside her plate.

"And the Taggart family? What was it like, you being an only child, living in a house full of children?" Doris again directed the conversation.

Nancy closed the magazine, picked up her fork, rolled some peas around her plate and mixed them with some potatoes which she scooped up and chewed slowly, as if in thought.

"They're sweet children, very pleasant to live with. Nanny Sue is so devoted to them."

"Who's Nanny Sue?

"She's Mrs. Taggart's aunt, sister to her mother."

"You miss them, don't you, dear?"

Nancy didn't answer.

"It doesn't hurt my feelings that you became so attached to them."

"Yes, I miss them very much."

"I'm sure they miss you, also. Perhaps we should visit them."

Nancy remained silent, again staring at her plate.

"Would you like for us to visit them? We could retrace the steps of your first trip, take the train."

Nancy looked searchingly into her mother's eyes.

"You serious, Mother?"

"Yes."

"Are you up to the trip?"

"I think I am. It might do me good. I've hardly left the house since your dad…" Doris began to cry.

Nancy reached across the table and held her mother's hand.

"Yes, Mother, the trip might be good for you."

"It might be good for both of us, dear."

CHAPTER SEVENTY-SEVEN

~

Wesley painstakingly pulled the weeds that blanketed the slightly mounded graves of his wife and Granny Brewer. He placed a plastic wreath of roses near the gravestone of each and then lingered with his head bowed.

He'd visited her gravesite daily the first few weeks of Nancy Sue's death. His visits tapered off over time; today was the first visit since they'd buried Granny Brewer in the fall.

Wesley rose from his kneeling position and brushed the dirt from the knees of his trousers and the toes of his black ankle boots. He whistled to the black that lazily grazed along the fencerow. The black trotted to him, seemingly eager to be off. He mounted the black, which immediately headed toward the single exit, but Wesley tugged gently on the reins, and the black pulled up, shaking his head as if in disagreement.

Wesley Taggart looked the stately part, sitting tall and straight in the saddle, his fedora tilted slightly to the right and pulled down on his forehead. He wore a tweed jacket to cut the chill of the early morning air. Nanny Sue saw to his ironing; his khakis sported a perfect crease, now with a stain around the knees.

Wesley stared contemplatively across the sweeping valley, a colossal arena that had witnessed a few hundred real-life dramas on this hillside. Each drama remained different, yet similar. The same tragedy repeated itself, simply stalking new victims.

Wesley mused over the tragedies he'd witnessed under this blue canopy of seeming serenity. Many of the deaths were from diseases now curable. Some were senseless deaths from fights. Most of the infant fatalities were from lack of proper child birthing care. The death of his wife defied logic.

The early morning sky created a canopy of blue, spanning the distance of the valley, beautiful and tranquil. Such a strange kind of blue! He thought of the blue skins and the bizarre phenomena of their disease. What is it like to be born blue in a world of pink people? What is it like to be shunned and called cursed from birth? What is it like to not understand why you're different and to hate being that way? If only there was a cure!

Blue? Who can understand what it's like to lose your spouse and have five small children needing you to be both father and mother? How many experience what it's like to be so lonely you wish to die, but living is necessary? I'm one, but I doubt I'm the only one. I hope I'm no longer angry toward God. He doesn't deserve my anger.

Blue? How foolish of me to become attached to a twenty-two-year-old woman and dare to think she could love a man seven years her senior? Especially when that same man sometimes seems rankled by her presence and cold at her every attempt to be helpful. How unfair of me to interfere with her youthful dreams and goals!

Yes, blue is the sky and smoky blue are these mountains of the Cumberland, but it's a troublesome blue, for the mystery to so many questions go unanswered. Though I've given up hope that some questions will ever be answered this side of heaven, it's a resignation to the inevitable, but not surrender of my will to live. I must go on living for the sake of the children. They need me more than ever; I must not fail them.

Wesley was finally fighting back against an elusive and sinister sculptor that had chipped away at his soul. He disdained the grotesque figure that was subtly appearing. He yearned for the simple faith he'd acquired while at the orphanage, a faith that had guided him for years. He was finding it less difficult to pray. He actually looked forward to the Memorial Day service.

Wesley goaded the black gently with his heels. Without hesitation, the black trotted toward the trail that led down the mountain.

CHAPTER SEVENTY-EIGHT

~

Preparation for the Memorial Day service had begun weeks in advance. Bobby Lawson cut the brush and repaired the log benches. He gathered up the weathered, plastic wreaths from last Memorial Day and lit a bonfire that sent black smoke billowing into the sky. Come Memorial Day, the appreciative would slip him a few dollars by way of a subtle handshake. He would nod his appreciation and stuff the money into his pocket. Grateful. It would help with groceries for a large family.

Memorial Sunday ushered in beautiful weather. Throughout the morning, a stream of people marched across the newly repaired swinging bridge spanning the North Fork at Copeland and walked down the railroad tracks, calling out to various friends of years gone by. They turned into the Nobles' yard where they rested a spell and exchanged pleasantries with the Noble family. They continued the final leg of the pilgrimage through the wide-open, straw-strewn center of the Noble barn and climbed the steep hill behind the barn where a meandering path, covered with a bed of dried pine needles from the towering evergreens, led them to a clearing at the top of the hill. A sagging wooden gate guarded the entrance to the cemetery.

Folks arrived from as far away as Flint, Michigan, and as close as Sulfur Gap. Most families carried a plastic bouquet attached to a Styrofoam cross with a metal tripod. Nearly everyone dressed up for the occasion. The ladies wore white heels that imprinted the yellow clay, leaving a distinctive trail. Some wore straw hats, with grosgrain ribbons. The aged men donned white shirts with open collars. A few wore ties. Handkerchiefs dangled from the hip pockets of their britches. Some of the locals wore overalls, clean and neatly pressed. Young boys in white shirts, some with clip ties that hung crooked around their collars, pressed hard to impress the girls, who, dressed in new gingham dresses adorned with lots of buttons and bows, giggled with delight. The local young ladies wore mail-order taffeta garments with matching crinolines underneath. The younger men had their neatly pressed white shirts tucked inside their creased dungarees. They stylishly profiled skinny ties, white socks and greased hair slicked back in a ducktail.

Cameras clicked as families and friends captured memories.

Friends, who time and circumstances had distanced, stood in huddled groups catching up on the past year's news of jobs, cars, deaths, marriages and births.

Multiple stories were etched on the headstones of the deceased: Gone But Not Forgotten; Here Lies My Sunshine; Killed In Action, WWI.

Beulah Mae Combs stood at the grave of her infant. Tears dripped onto a hand-chiseled tombstone, leaving stained evidence of her chronic grief. Her husband, Kelly, stood nearby, trying to muffle his usual hacking cough. He no longer shed tears.

Children played hide-n-seek among the markers and were reprimanded often for stepping on a grave. Birds leaped from limb to limb high in the treetops. A Hereford cow from the Noble farm approached cautiously, its bell clanging with each step.

The memorial service started at noon. The preachers sat on a crudely built riser just behind a makeshift pulpit, while everyone else sat on the log benches facing the pulpit. The funeral singers got the service underway with a few hymns. Their melancholic voices blended harmoniously and echoed across the serene valley, drifting heavenward upon the zephyrs of faith and sincerity. They sang of a better day, a brighter tomorrow, a faraway land of endless peace and freedom from pain and parting.

Words of comfort abounded from the speakers. The message was the same each year: life at best is too short; speak kindly to your family, friends and neighbors, for it might be your last words to them; let go of your grudges and bandage the wounds of others; mend the broken bridges and tear down the walls of division.

The array of silent stones also spoke a distinct message that lingered with the pilgrims as they descended the hill, each one contemplating their loss.

Wesley huddled with Joyce and Gary at the graveside of their mother and grandma. He wondered what emotions they felt, how much they understood, how much they'd forgotten or would forget about their mother. His thoughts raced a gamut of emotions: loneliness, pleasant memories, regrets and guilt. Guilt for wanting to be happy without her. Wesley knew there was something else; it was the absence of an emotion he'd previously felt. The intensity of the pain had let up, and the former anger was gone. Strangely, he was glad when Gary became fidgety; it was a good reason to leave and go home. He wondered if it was abnormal for not wanting to stay longer at her grave. He felt in his heart she wasn't there; indeed, she was with the Lord. Before it was mere words, spiritual jargon that he recited out of expectations, but now he believed it. She was in heaven. Peace flowed over his being. The words of an old hymn echoed sweetly in his mind: It is well, it is well, with my soul.

As they walked the center of the tracks toward home, Joyce held Wesley's hand while Gary ran a good distance ahead of them. When they turned the bend that revealed their house, Gary suddenly stopped, leaped into the air, and then started running toward their house.

"What's got into Gary," Joyce asked, "stepped on a hornet's nest?"

"I'm not sure."

Then Wesley saw them: three women sitting on the front porch, each rocking one of his children. Gary stopped at the front gate, turned and called out haltingly to Wesley and Joyce.

"It's…Miss…York…. Miss…York…has…come…back."

CHAPTER SEVENTY-NINE

~

Nancy hastened down the steps. Joyce and Gary threw themselves into her outstretched arms.

"I've missed you two."

"We've missed you, too, Miss York."

Wesley stopped a few feet from her.

Nancy slowly released her embrace of the children and looked toward him. For a moment, both of their rigid bodies seemed immobile. Awkward. Nancy wanted to speak but couldn't find the right words. Why is the greeting of total strangers easier than that of two people who secretly care for each other but are unsure of the other's affections?

Wesley tipped his hat.

"Miss York."

She nodded.

"Mr. Taggart."

"Nice to see you again. I've…the children and I have missed you."

"This is my mother, Doris. I hope we're not imposing but …" Why did I not say I missed him?

"Not at all, Miss York. I'm delighted to meet you, Mrs. York. I'm so sorry about the death of your husband. I know somewhat how difficult that is."

"Thank you. Yes, it has been very difficult, for me and for Nancy. And I'm sorry for your loss, Mr. Taggart. Nancy has shared with me about your wife's passing."

"How kind of you, Mrs. York. Oh, and these are my other two children, Joyce and Gary."

"I've heard so much about you two. Nancy is quite fond of you. What beautiful smiles!" She reached out and clasped the hands of the children. "I see why Nancy's so fond of you, now that I've met you. I'm pleased to finally get to visit with you."

"Dinner is almost ready," Nanny Sue said. "I need Joyce and Gary to go wash up. Doris, you can help me set the table and get the children ready."

They left Nancy and Wesley standing alone on the porch. The vacuum of their departure soon filled with additional awkwardness.

"Forgive me, Mr. Taggart, for coming back without letting you know. It was my mother's idea, a spur of the moment decision." Why not just tell him how very happy I am to be here that I can hardly contain my emotions.

"Your mother's idea?"

"Of course, I thought it was a wonderful idea to come for a visit, and I wanted to see the children, and you, but I should have asked..." Why can I not say what I really think? I've missed you every day since I left.

"The note I wrote...I assume you found it?"

"I found it the day I left. I've read it over and over...and I've wanted to respond...but mother needed me to care for her...I was torn, Mr. Taggart...between your expression of affection for me and my duty to her...but now she seems to be doing much better." She could never ask what she wanted to know. Do you still feel the way you expressed in the letter to me?

"My fondness for you, Nancy York, has only grown since you left, but..."

"But what?" Her heart sank. He's changed his mind. He's angry at me for leaving.

"Though I'm very fond of you, I've also realized how very selfish it was of me to pursue my affections for you. I've made it extremely awkward for you to complete your work at the local school. Even if you did reciprocate my feelings for you, I have little to offer you except the burden of helping raise my children. My business is struggling and..."

"It's not a burden to help raise children one loves, Mr. Taggart. Neither is it a one-way street. I believe your children love me. As for your business, you can modernize and make it better."

"I've considered that and gave it a try. My loan was denied."

"Money's not a problem. Daddy left me a sizable insurance policy. I can—"

"Absolutely not, Miss York. I cannot accept your charity… I refuse to allow our relationship to be built on pity."

"Then allow me to finish my offer, Mr. Taggart."

"What do you mean?"

"I want to partner…to buy stock in your business…become a lender…own a part of the Taggart Salt Mine."

Wesley stared at Nancy but didn't answer.

"Do I sense a bit of male pride, Mr. Taggart?"

Before he could answer, Nancy took his hand and held it to her cheek.

"My father was a fine man. His character has guided me these twenty-two years. Now he's gone, but he'll always be in my heart. You're still here. I think you're one of the finest men I've ever met, and I've fallen in love with you, Wesley Taggart. I don't believe I can stand to lose the two dearest people I know at the same time."

Wesley bowed his head and let it rest gently on the top of Nancy's head.

"What about your mother? Who will care for her? Can you stand to leave her alone?

"It's difficult, but mother's learning to let go. She's come to realize how much you all mean to me. That's why she insisted we come for a visit."

"Do you think she'd ever consider living in the Cumberlands?"

"Perhaps. Or else we can visit her in Cincinnati."

"So I'm not destined to spend the rest of my life alone, without happiness, and with only memories to sustain me?"

"No, Wesley, not if my presence can bring you happiness."

"That first day I saw you through the window of the passenger train, I'd spent the morning wondering if the pain in my heart would ever go away. Your coming into my life brought a ray of hope. Then, while I recuperated from being shot, I dreamed you married someone else, and my pain intensified. Tell me I'm not dreaming again, Nancy York."

"Please, never stop dreaming about me, Wesley, but dream only of us together."

Wesley didn't respond.

"Are those tears? Please, no tears. We've shed too many tears." She dabbed his cheeks with a kerchief. "How's the black?"

"Well."

"Did he miss me?"

"You'll have to ask him."

Hand-in-hand, they walked the path that led to the barn.

"The first time we walked this path together you hummed a tune. I never for sure knew what song you were humming," Nancy said. "Do you remember?"

"I remember well, *Love Me Tender*. In retrospect I can't believe I did that. I didn't mean to be presumptuous, but I was so happy that day."

"That day turned so tragic, Wesley."

"But God has smiled on me today."

"Smiled on us."

"Yes, us."

"I think I'm going to like having you as a partner, Nancy York. What title shall we give you at the mine? Chief inspector?"

"How about co-president?"

Wesley laughed. "I'll have to talk to the board of directors."

"Now that we're partners, I don't think we should withhold information from each other."

"Really?" Wesley held her at arm's length.

"Really! So, do you remember when we first met and you said 'I wasn't expecting—'"

"And you interrupted me by asking, 'Someone so young?'"

"And you said, 'No.' So, I asked, 'A female teacher?'"

"And I said, 'No,' again."

Nancy stared quizzically into his eyes. He smiled. "Well, Wesley Taggart, you never answered my question. What were you not expecting in this beginner, female school teacher?"

"Well, Miss York, co-president of Taggart Mining Company, what I started to say, before you rudely interrupted me that first day we met, was actually a compliment."

"Really? And what was that compliment?"

"I wasn't expecting someone so beautiful as you."